Gossamer in the Darkness

Also From Kristen Ashley

Jagged
Kaleidoscope
Bounty

Dream Man Series:
Mystery Man
Wild Man
Law Man
Motorcycle Man
Quiet Man

Dream Team Series:
Dream Maker
Dream Chaser
Dream Spinner
Dream Keeper

The Fantasyland Series:
Wildest Dreams
The Golden Dynasty
Fantastical
Broken Dove
Midnight Soul

The Honey Series:
The Deep End
The Farthest Edge
The Greatest Risk

The Magdalene Series:
The Will
Soaring
The Time in Between

Moonlight and Motor Oil Series:
The Hookup
The Slow Burn

Play It Safe
Three Wishes
Complicated
Loose Ends
Fast Lane

Gossamer in the Darkness

A Fantasyland Novella

By Kristen Ashley

1001 DARK NIGHTS
PRESS

Gossamer in the Darkness
A Fantasyland Novella
By Kristen Ashley

1001 Dark Nights

Published by 1001 Dark Nights Press, an imprint of Evil Eye Concepts, Incorporated

Sign up for the 1001 Dark Nights Newsletter
and be entered to win a Tiffany Key necklace.

There's a contest every month!

Go to www.1001DarkNights.com to subscribe.

As a bonus, all subscribers can download
FIVE FREE exclusive books!

Acknowledgments from the Author

Love, hugs and gratitude to...

Donna Perry, Jenn Watson, Kasi Alexander, Kim Guidroz, all my readers for taking so many journeys with me and asking for more.

And last but not least, Liz Berry, Jillian Stein and MJ Rose for making this gig all kinds of fun.

One Thousand and One Dark Nights

Once upon a time, in the future…

*I was a student fascinated with stories and learning.
I studied philosophy, poetry, history, the occult, and
the art and science of love and magic. I had a vast
library at my father's home and collected thousands
of volumes of fantastic tales.*

*I learned all about ancient races and bygone
times. About myths and legends and dreams of all
people through the millennium. And the more I read
the stronger my imagination grew until I discovered
that I was able to travel into the stories... to actually
become part of them.*

*I wish I could say that I listened to my teacher
and respected my gift, as I ought to have. If I had, I
would not be telling you this tale now.
But I was foolhardy and confused, showing off
with bravery.*

*One afternoon, curious about the myth of the
Arabian Nights, I traveled back to ancient Persia to
see for myself if it was true that every day Shahryar
(Persian: شهريار, "king") married a new virgin, and then
sent yesterday's wife to be beheaded. It was written
and I had read, that by the time he met Scheherazade,
the vizier's daughter, he'd killed one thousand
women.*

Something went wrong with my efforts. I arrived in the midst of the story and somehow exchanged places with Scheherazade — a phenomena that had never occurred before and that still to this day, I cannot explain.

Now I am trapped in that ancient past. I have taken on Scheherazade's life and the only way I can protect myself and stay alive is to do what she did to protect herself and stay alive.

Every night the King calls for me and listens as I spin tales. And when the evening ends and dawn breaks, I stop at a point that leaves him breathless and yearning for more. And so the King spares my life for one more day, so that he might hear the rest of my dark tale.

As soon as I finish a story... I begin a new one... like the one that you, dear reader, have before you now.

Foreword

There are two worlds.

The one we know.

And the one that has all the same people in it—our twins—but it's entirely different.

In this parallel universe, amongst many other places, there is the icy northern land of Lunwyn, the frilly clement land of Fleuridia, the forbidding southern lands of Korwahk, Keenhak and Maroo.

And the glittery enchanted land of Hawkvale.

In these places there are no airplanes or cell phones or sushi. There are no computers or cars or even electricity.

But there is magic.

As such, if there's a witch, one with great power, and any available motive, she can bring a twin from our world into the other.

Tales have been told in Lunwyn, Hawkvale, Fleuridia and Korwahk (as well as more told in the lands across the Green Sea).

This is a new tale from that other world.

A tale of magic.

A tale of love.

And a tale of very big hats.

Prologue

The Miracle

Edgar, the Count of Derryman

Hawkvale
Lancestor Sanatorium
Oxblood Region
The Parallel

"She's no better," he sniped irately, glaring at the pretty young woman with the masses of blonde, lustrous hair curled into herself on the bed.

She was studying him with terrified amber eyes.

"Please, my lord, modulate your voice," the doctor murmured.

Edgar Dawes, the seventh Count of Derryman, Lord of Posey Park Manor (and several other properties besides), located in the green, gentle, fertile valleys of the Oxblood region of north central Hawkvale, turned to the doctor.

"You said you could affect improvements," he reminded the man.

"She *is* improved," the doctor asserted.

Edgar flung a hand toward the silent, fearful woman rocking rhythmically on her bed, staring at him in terror.

"She doesn't appear improved to me, sir."

The man got closer and said quietly, "With respect, my lord, this is due to your demeanor. Maxine…" He paused a pause that held great weight and took that further as he emphasized, *"your daughter,* needs calm. She's far more content with the familiar." Another weighty pause. "And she hasn't seen you in over three years."

Edgar refused to respond to the rebuke.

Instead, he retorted, "The world is not calm, as you well know. At any moment, a witch can bring a curse on the land. A Beast of ancient times can resurface to the Earth and cause havoc. You know this because *these things have happened*. And they have *in our lifetimes*." His tone grew all-knowing and imperious, a tone he adopted in some incarnation to the point it was his standard. "Every life is in jeopardy at every moment."

"That's a pessimistic outlook," the physician muttered to himself.

"It is nevertheless true," Edgar sniffed. "And she must be able to handle that."

And she must.

She *must*.

Imminently.

Time was running out!

As such...

"I'll be taking her to another facility," Edgar announced. "We'll see if a different staff can cure her."

The doctor immediately grew alarmed.

"Sir, please, don't. Maxine responds to routine. A habitual schedule. Staff around her who she's grown accustomed to. Familiar surroundings. Her paintings. Her strolls along the river with her nurses. Her reading. We've made progress, and if you move her"—and again there was a censorious pause—"as you have, throughout her life, hoping for results she simply cannot attain, she will digress, and that progress will have to be regained."

Edgar gazed around the room at his daughter's "paintings." As he did, his eyes fell on the "books" that sat on the table beside her bed.

He returned his attention to her physician. "A five-year-old could paint a better bird and she reads *children's* books."

"Before she came here, she was twenty-three, and she didn't read at all," the man returned.

"I—"

The doctor squared his shoulders. "My lord, I'm sure I don't have to remind you, your daughter...your lovely, sweet daughter, sustained a significant head injury at the age of six."

Edgar drew in an affronted breath at being reminded of something he expended quite a bit of effort to forget.

The doctor persevered, "It was an injury of such magnitude, at the time, the physicians you called in, all *four* of them, told you not only that you were very lucky she was alive, but that it would take a miracle for her to live what is considered a 'normal' life. However, in all her notes, throughout her life, every physician who has had charge of her care has recorded that they've repeatedly shared with you that she could lead a happy life. However, only if she receives the proper care. She needs stability. She needs patience. She needs predictability. And she needs…"—the man held Edgar's gaze—"care and *love*."

Edgar stared at him, thinking, *No, what* I *need is a miracle.*

He lifted his nose. "I'll be researching other facilities and will inform you by missive if she will be moved and where."

"*She* has a name, milord. It's the one you gave her. It's Maxine," the doctor retorted coldly.

Edgar glared at him, turned on his foot, and with his cloak snapping out behind him, such was the velocity of his departure, he left the room.

And he did so not sparing another glance to his daughter.

* * * *

Derryman~

Forgive that I offer no polite preamble. However, I do not for this is the sixth such missive I have sent in as many months.

Therefore, I will not delay before I remind you of clause 12b of the betrothal contract we two hold between my son and your daughter.

To refresh your memory, clause 12b states that if the Marquess of Remington should attain the age of thirty-five without you offering Lady Maxine's hand in marriage, and that hand isn't legally bound to my son and heir in order that they can pursue the efforts of continuing my line, he is no longer bound to the contract. As such, he will be free to choose who he wishes to take to wife.

It is time my son takes a woman to wife.

We shall be celebrating Loren's 35th birthday six months hence.

I do hope we'll be celebrating a wedding sometime before.

I daresay I will hear from you very soon.

Yours in loyalty to Hawkvale,
~Ansley Copeland
12th Duke of Dalton

Edgar tossed the letter on his desk in frustration.

He then stared across the room at the portrait of his very beautiful but very dead wife.

"I once was a titan," he proclaimed.

This was not pride speaking.

He was.

He was known as The Dealmaker.

So renowned for his intuition of the markets, any investment, people from as high as Lunwyn and as low as Fleuridia sought his counsel.

So renowned, the great Duke of Dalton sought an alliance between their families.

The Duke of Dalton!

King Ludlum's top general—the man credited with saving Hawkvale from total ruination when Baldur of Middleland invaded its sunny dales. A man revered, almost as much as Ludlum was (and he would have been more, if such wasn't considered treason).

It was, of course, Ludlum's son (and now their king), who eventually wrested the lands Baldur managed to conquer from that despot.

However, it was known by all that if it wasn't for Dalton, the whole of Hawkvale would have fallen to Baldur.

And it was *that* Dalton who sought an alliance with the House of Derryman twenty-six years ago.

But even Edgar could not foresee that horrible accident (and it *was* an accident—any father would wish to teach his daughter how to ride a horse, it wasn't *his* fault she couldn't control the damned thing).

He focused again on the image of his wife.

She had hidden from him her weakness of character, a flaw that ran deep. In fact, in the end, she brayed of it so incessantly, it had to stop.

Of course, as she obviously took great pains to do this, he could never predict how she would react to the accident.

But that was done, and she was now gone, his daughter (mostly) out of sight and mind in order that he could get on with his life.

However, that life did take a turn for the better.

Clearly no one could foresee what would happen to the markets when a curse hit the land.

With the fantastical things that occurred, not even his stable of rats could assist him.

And then some time later, when he was finally digging himself out from under the variety of fiascos he, and the men he advised, found himself in, some Beast across the Green Sea rears up and panics the entire planet. Only for the result of the vanquishing of that creature to be trade routes opening that no one ever imagined would clear, and Firenz, Airenzian, Dellish and Marish goods flooding the market.

There were opportunities everywhere.

He couldn't stay on top of it, no matter how many rats he recruited.

Edgar, of course, had contingencies in place, and he may not have advised his clients to do the same (for if they held money back, he would have less of their money to invest in his schemes, and in turn would make less himself).

But any man knew to protect his estate. It wasn't Edgar's fault they listened to him when he advised *all in* (and perhaps sometimes his advice could better be described as coercion, but he didn't regard it that way).

Many of his clients had been ruined.

He was called The Dealmaker no longer.

Once, every door was open to him. He'd arrive, a cheer would rise, and a glass of the best whisky was placed in his hand. They'd be falling all over themselves to pat him on the back, sit close to his side and be warmed by his brilliant, unfailing light.

Now, he hadn't had a dinner invitation in two years. Balls that were often held in his honor happened without him even knowing they'd been scheduled. Conferences that he'd keynote he was blacklisted from attending.

He was rich. He had more than enough money, he'd never be poor.

But he was a pariah.

And you couldn't make *more* money unless people would accept your investments.

They wouldn't even accept his letters.

He *needed* this alliance with the House of Dalton.

He *needed* his name linked with someone of such impeccable pedigree and reputation as Lord Ansley Copeland.

The doors would open to the father of a duchess, the grandfather of a future duke.

From the moment Edgar completed the flourish on his signature on that betrothal contract, he knew that was the next step to greatness.

That would be his legacy.

His blood would run through the veins of all future Daltons.

His daughter would sleep beside the Marquess of Remington.

She'd stand at his side when his father passed, and he inherited the Duchy.

She would first be called marchioness.

She would then be called *duchess*.

The only greater title was princess.

The only greater title than that was *Queen*.

And her first son, and every first son after—*his* grandson, would be *Duke*.

But now, no.

Simply because a useless six-year-old girl could not sit a horse.

For the last two years, he'd had his rats out scavenging in every corner in every city in Hawkvale, Bellebryn, Fleuridia, even all the way up to the frosty northern shores of Lunwyn and across the Green Sea to the continent of Triton.

There was no witch.

There was no sorcerer.

There was no cure.

There was no miracle.

Maxine, with her mother's leonine hair and eyes, would be six years old…

Forever.

And Edgar would never regain his standing. He'd never enter a parlor to smiles and cheers.

He'd never leave this Earth, his legacy being his vast wealth.

And the incorporation of Derryman into a Duchy.

* * * *

"Milord, sir…sir…*sir!*"

Edgar snorted, turned, and blinked through the curtains of his bed where his servant, Carling, had leant through, holding a candle.

"What the demon?" Edgar groused.

"At the back door…one of your…"—Carling made a face—"*associates*. He says he has something urgent to tell you. I told him to come at a decent hour, but he said you wouldn't thank me to make you wait."

Edgar made to turn his back on the man and resume sleep, murmuring, "Repeat he should come at a decent hour."

"Sir, milord, he says it's about your…"

He didn't finish, and the manner in which he was speaking made Edgar return his attention to the retainer.

"My what?" he prompted.

"Your daughter," Carling whispered, blame in his eyes, judgment in his tone.

Insufferable man.

It was rather a shame he was so very good at his job.

Edgar was still for but a moment, thinking on this, before he pulled the candle from the man's hand. Wax dripped on his bedclothes, but he paid it no mind as he threw his legs over the side, shoving his feet in his slippers.

He shrugged on his dressing gown as he hurried, ignoring the fact that in the last few years, due to his life narrowing rather drastically, his bulk had become somewhat…ungainly.

He descended the stairs and took a trek he rarely took, into his servant's domain, the kitchens at the back of the house.

There, in the opened door, thankfully not having strode over the threshold (he made a note to remember to offer a rare (very rare) commendation to Carling on seeing to that, and then immediately forgot that note) stood the filthy, unkempt person of Buttersnatch, one of his best little rats.

He felt his dressing gown billowing out behind him as he barked, "This better be good to pull me from my bed."

"A word, master," Buttersnatch begged, although it wasn't a plea, that was simply how Buttersnatch always spoke.

The rodent glanced behind him to the servants' alley before he looked back at Edgar.

"In private."

Edgar examined Buttersnatch's expression.

He had not been The Dealmaker solely due to his brilliant understanding of all things financial.

He'd been The Dealmaker because he could read people.

Mostly (he would admit only to himself), it was because of his rats.

What he read was that Buttersnatch had, at long last, succeeded.

Edgar felt his heart jump.

There was hope!

Likely, knowing this particular pest, it was a witch.

He didn't care what it was.

Just as long as it meant success.

Therefore, Edgar did not hesitate to step into the dark, moonlit, unoccupied alley and firmly close the door behind him.

He led Buttersnatch, whose rags rustled about him as he moved, well away from the door.

Only then, holding the light of his candle up so he could clearly see the man's face, did he command, "Speak to me."

"There is a witch…"

Of course there was.

"…she is powerful."

Of course she was.

"She's been 'idin' her accumulation of magic for years."

As she would need to do.

King Noctorno made things very clear after the last debacle nearly brought low all of the Northlands. No witch gathered magicks of any magnitude without the government's permission.

"You'll be needin' to bring your diamonds, you will," Buttersnatch went on.

Edgar's eyes narrowed at that.

His diamonds?

He did, of course, have a healthy cache of Sjofn ice diamonds. Rare. Flawless. Coveted.

Most of the foundation of his wealth was in such things.

This was because they never lost value. No matter what foul play was at hand in this land or any other, an ice diamond, an Ulfr fur, a Korwahkian jewel remained rare, remained flawless, and remained coveted.

"And why would I do that?" Edgar asked dubiously.

"Because"—Buttersnatch smiled, exposing yellowed teeth that were dark and rotted in places—"there's another world, milord. A world she can access. And on that world, master, each and every one of us…"

His pause was long, his smile got broader, and then he finished.

"'As a twin."

Edgar recoiled.

Dear gods.

There it was.

A miracle.

Chapter One

Top Shelf

Loren Copeland
The Marquess of Remington

Hawkvale
The City of Lincstone
Heddelly Arch District
Avon Bordello
The Parallel

One Week Later

"I feel like *I* should pay *you*," the whore purred behind him.

"That can be arranged," he muttered, reaching for his breeches.

He felt her hand touch the bare skin of his back.

"Another go," she whispered. And then, far quieter, "For free."

Her hand went away as Loren stood, pulling up his trousers.

He didn't look at her as he buttoned them at the same time he moved to where he'd thrown his shirt.

"Another time," he replied.

He said this, but there would be no other time.

There were those, and she was one, where he made a call.

He'd made that call.

This time, he came.

Then he went.

And it went without saying, *especially* this time.

He finished with his trousers and reached for his shirt.

"I'm not…" She didn't continue.

He didn't much care what she wasn't, but she was lovely and naked and a much better view than the maroon flocked wallpaper.

Therefore, after he pulled on his shirt and in a slapdash manner tucked it in, he reached for his waistcoat, turned to her and lifted his brow.

"I didn't fake it," she said softly.

"I sense you know that wasn't my first time," he replied, buttoning the three brocade-covered buttons at his lower abdominals.

She smiled.

Very lovely.

Pity she was a Come-and-Go.

"Therefore, dear heart, I know that," he told her.

He then bent to snatch up his socks and boots.

He turned his back on her to sit by the side of the bed to tug them on.

"I won't tell Winnow."

Winnow was the madam of this very establishment.

Winnow held great beauty.

Winnow had the soul of a snake.

He didn't like her. He didn't trust her.

But it could not be denied, she had an eye for talent.

He looked down at his companion for the evening, reached out and cupped her graceful jaw.

"She, or one of her lackeys, watched every second of our coupling, lovely Mayda. You're as aware of this as I. I will get away with no favors, no bonuses, and assuredly, no giveaways. I will pay for tasting your lovely cunt. I will pay for penetrating your round ass. I will pay for having you on your back, your knees, and I will pay for watching you ride my cock. I will pay for the two climaxes *I* gave *you*. And I will pay top tier, for you are top shelf, aren't you, dear heart?"

"My lord—"

He put a finger to her lips. "I have a rule. When a woman takes me up her arse, and in her mouth, not in that order, in the same night, she's allowed to call me by my name."

Her eyes flared at this unusual benefaction.

He took his finger from her lips. "Now, you were saying?"

Her attention darted over his shoulder to one of the several paintings in which, Loren knew, the walls had eyes.

A warning.

One she likely never gave another client.

Loren sighed.

It never failed to surprise him.

Give a whore an orgasm, and they became aggravatingly clingy.

He turned from her and reached for his frock coat.

"Loren," she said his name so low he had to turn back to her to prove he'd heard it. "You should—"

She lost his attention when he felt how his coat bunched in his hand.

Or, more precisely, what shouldn't bunch, but did.

He looked at his coat, running it through his fists.

By the gods, he'd thought they'd let him through unscathed.

He hadn't even felt it.

However, what he felt in that moment was the bed move as Mayda shifted in it. He heard the velvet and silks of the covers sliding against each other as she pulled them to cover her, but he glanced about the floor just in case it had fallen out.

It had not.

"Loren, I—"

"Silence," he hissed.

"It wasn't my ide—"

He turned his head to her.

She quieted.

"Did you do it?" he asked.

She shook her head.

"Is it here?"

She bit her lip.

And shook her head again.

That was when he heard it.

A noise in the hall.

Abruptly standing, he pulled on the coat, then he sat yet again, swiftly. He lifted one boot to his other knee, reached to the inner base of the heel, and hit the miniscule catch with his thumbnail.

Winnow didn't allow weapons in her establishment.

He had his suspicions, these being why he was there at all, but now he knew it was for this very reason.

Loren didn't go anywhere without a weapon.

As the catch released, the hidden blade jumped out of his heel.

Mayda gasped.

"Speak one word, you're the first cut I make," Loren warned, not looking at her.

He hadn't the time.

He transferred his other boot to his opposite knee and repeated these actions.

The blades were broad in width, blunt in length, with razor-sharp edges that came to a point. At the end of the short shaft was not a handle but a narrow rod that went side to side.

With a twist and click, the blade was at crosses with the rod.

Loren curled his fists around the rods, the blades protruding through his fingers.

He did this with his hands in front of him, his back to the various views to the room.

And he curled his hands carefully into the sleeves of his coat as he walked to the door.

He heard a noise, a wordless call.

His advance on the exit was noted.

The order was made.

Therefore, he was not surprised when the door burst open and two of Winnow's large, lugubrious henchmen entered the room.

"Leaving without paying, *your grace?*" the one in the lead asked snidely.

"You return the wallet one of your staff lifted from my coat, I'd be happy to do so," Loren drawled.

"We don't operate that way at Avon," came the reply. "And we don't give pussy away for free."

This was tiresome.

It always was.

He was rich.

He was titled.

His father was richer.

And his title was better.

Loren was not at fault for the happenstance of his birth.

But what never failed to infuriate him was that he knew just looking at them that neither of these men had stood proud for Hawkvale.

Neither of these men hunted the dying, but irritatingly prolific, bands of Middlelandian true believers.

Neither of them found their fourteen-year-old scout with his throat slit and a strip of his scalp taken as a prize.

Neither of them witnessed their best friend take an arrow through the throat.

Neither of them held his friend's mother in their arms as she wept when he returned her son's possessions.

He didn't expect pussy for free, not as a veteran who put his life on the line to keep their country safe, not as the son of a veteran who did the same, or the latest in a line of many men who did just that.

He didn't expect pussy for free because of his title or his connections, either.

He didn't expect anything for free.

He paid and he paid well.

Though one could say he liked games.

But only those he wished to play.

So Loren had no patience at all for this shite.

In five seconds, both men were on the floor, their blood flowing freely into the silk rugs.

They would never again take their feet.

Mayda whimpered.

Loren stepped over them and into the hall.

In the end, he was vaguely disappointed it wasn't much of a challenge.

Patrons and workers alike were shrieking and falling over themselves, as well as slipping on blood and bodies, in order to get out while Loren held Winnow against the wall of her office with his forearm.

"Where is it?" he asked mildly.

Her green gaze flicked to her desk.

He transferred one bloody blade to the other hand, still held at the ready, took her by the side of the neck and pulled her to the desk.

"Fetch it," he ordered.

With trembling hands, she took the keys that dangled from the ribbon that served as a belt, bent to the bottom drawer, and Loren stayed vigilant and alert as he watched her open the drawer.

She came out with naught but his wallet.

But he saw what else was inside.

He took the wallet from her and slammed the drawer shut with the toe of his boot.

"I hope my message has been made clear," he began. "It will be ill-advised that you ever do this again."

He then moved his hand to the back of her skull and slammed her forehead down on the desk.

She slithered, unconscious, to the floor.

Through the now quiet and deserted space, Loren sauntered up to Mayda's room.

Standing at the foot of her bed, where she was pressed to the headboard, covers to her mouth, weeping silently, he asked, "It's fifteen normal, twenty up the arse, five for the suckling, five for eating, no?"

She stared at him in horror for a moment before she slowly nodded her head.

Loren rifled through the paper notes King Noctorno had instituted several years ago, one of his many brilliant ideas.

Carrying coin was burdensome.

This was far better.

He tossed three twenty-pound notes on her bed, then regarded the dead men on her floor.

As such, he pulled out another two bills, both hundreds, and threw those down too.

"Thank you for a memorable evening," he said.

And then he walked away.

* * * *

The Next Morning

"Loren, I simply cannot believe I have to tell you again, *you are not at liberty to kill people willy-nilly*," his father admonished.

"They'd stolen my wallet."

"Yes, that happens at Avon Bordello. Everyone knows that," Ansley Copeland returned. "As such, you have two choices. Don't go to Avon Bordello. Or *don't go to Avon Bordello.*"

"I sense, Father, that they will not be stealing another man's wallet in order to extort a higher charge for their services as they detain him and expose him to his wife, his children, his employers, his commanding officer, or simply detaining him from his life until he agrees to pay for his own release. All of this on the weak excuse they provide to the constabulary that he intended to partake of their services for free, when he had no such intention at all."

"It's my understanding the constabulary was as aware as everyone else about this situation and working to sort it," Ansley retorted.

Briefly, Loren thought about what he knew the constables would find in Winnow's desk.

He then replied, "I've saved them that trouble."

Ansley blew out a breath.

Loren was seated at the front of his father's desk, hunched down, legs stretched in front of him, booted ankles crossed, elbows to the arms, fingers steepled before him.

His father was behind the desk, scowling at his son.

"Winnow Dupont is furious," Ansley noted.

"Winnow Dupont is an unscrupulous crook," Loren said quietly. "And sometime this morning, if she hasn't been already, Winnow Dupont will be detained by the authorities and asked to explain some of the activities she gets up to in Avon."

The regard his father was treating his son to changed.

"Did you...go there in order to...handle this?" Ansley asked.

Loren started studying his fingernails.

Ansley waited.

When the silence stretched, Loren broke it.

"The constabulary sometimes dawdles," he murmured his answer.

Ansley's voice was rising. "That's because they must act within the letter of the law!"

Loren straightened in his chair and leveled his attention on his sire.

"Is it not the letter of the law that a man has the right to defend his own person?"

"Yes, however—"

"And is it not the letter of the law that a man has the right to defend his property, in this case, my purse?"

"Son—"

"They connived to steal from me, detain me, and I can assure you, Father, that the men who confronted me at the door to the lovely creature's rooms were not there to politely ask me to sit down over a smooth whisky with Winnow and sort these matters. They intended me harm. I defended myself. A possession of mine was stolen from me. I retrieved it. That is the end of the matter. I've already talked to the inspector. They've put a line under it. It's done."

"You killed five men and dealt cuts that I'm told will visibly scar two others for life."

"Then they shan't forget the lesson they learned last night, shall they?"

"You had a friend detained by her, didn't you?" his father demanded to know.

"Farrell made a stupid mistake, visiting his favorite to say good-bye before his wedding. He is now without a fiancée, a woman, incidentally, he loved deeply. Though what he's gained is an angry father who is demanding he and his family cover the costs of the deposits set for a wedding that did not happen. Unfortunately, Farrell feels it is only proper he do so. Profoundly unfortunately, his lost fiancée had extravagant tastes."

Ansley's gaze turned to the ceiling.

"Are we done?" Loren asked.

Ansley's gaze returned to his son.

And when he spoke, he did it softly.

"You cannot right every wrong, my beloved boy."

On that, Loren stood.

And his only reply was, "How soon we forget."

"Learn from a father's mistakes."

"*That* is your mistake, old man," Loren replied good-naturedly. "Thinking they were mistakes."

After delivering that, even though his father opened his mouth to say more, Loren turned and walked away.

* * * *

Ansley Copeland
The Duke of Dalton

He was still at his desk when his post was brought to him that afternoon.

And he was surprised to see the Derryman seal on the back of one of the letters.

He broke it, unfolded the paper, and read,

> *My dear Dalton~*
> *It is with joy that I share that my beautiful, darling daughter, Maxine, has finally finished her studies, returned from Fleuridia, and is now amenable to meeting her affianced in order to begin preparations to be wed.*

Would you like us to come to you at Dalwin? Or would you be our guests at Posey Park? Or we could meet in the middle as we both have houses in Newton.

Please advise.

We so look forward to this alliance of Derryman and Dalton.

It will be a jubilant day for us both!

Yours in humble service to Hawkvale~

Edgar Dawes

7th Count of Derryman

Ansley stared at the note, aghast.

Maxine Dawes, albeit lovely, and very sweet, and a young woman he had enjoyed spending several visits with at Lancester Sanatorium, was in absolutely no condition to marry his son, and she never would be.

He had, of course, set about discovering why Derryman persistently avoided all communications and attempts to bring the betrothal contract to fruition.

What he had found was that Derryman had been lying to him for twenty years.

His daughter had taken a tumble from a horse when she was but six years of age, she'd hit her head, and she hadn't been the same since.

Or, rather, she was the same.

In behavior, she was still six.

However, her age was twenty-six.

This might also answer the question on everyone's lips, when Maxine was supposedly sent to Fleuridia to attend boarding school, and shortly thereafter, Derryman's wife took her own life in a ghastly manner that still was spoken of with shock.

He had hoped Derryman would beg off himself, however the man needed to do that to save face.

But this…

Ansley sat back in his chair.

He'd had a lengthy, and confidential, discussion with her doctor. He was told she would never recover. It was an impossibility.

Unless they found some miracle.

He couldn't even begin to imagine what Derryman's play was.

But he would find out.

And then they would finish this, and Loren would be free.

Further, Ansley would be free to put his foot down.

His son was to find a woman, settle down, make her heavy with child (repeatedly) and stop galivanting about Hawkvale (and farther afield), bedding women, partaking in games of chance, larking about…with heavy, terrifying doses of his activities of the night before.

Playing a vigilante.

The House of Dalton was at stake.

And every Duke in his line made several vows when he accepted that title, all of which were crucial.

But the continuation of the line was the most important of all.

Even more important than their vow of loyalty to the king.

On this thought, Ansley sat forward and took out a crisp piece of his stationery.

And he wrote his reply.

Chapter Two

Maxine Dawes
Community Manager

Hawkvale
The Road to Pinkwick House
Marbleborne Region
The Parallel

Two Weeks Later

Turkey baster.
    If she wanted a kid, she should have used that damned turkey baster.
    These were my thoughts as the carriage…
    Yeah, that's what I said…
    The carriage…
    Slowly made its way down the road, bipping and bopping, swaying and bouncing, and serious to God, with all that movement, it was a wonder I didn't hurl all over my gown.
    Yeah, that's what I said.
    My gown.
    Women wore gowns in this world.
    And *corsets.*
    One thing I knew for certain, the kind you *had* to wear was nowhere near as comfortable as the kind you bought to give a thrill to your guy.
    I looked at "my dad."

He was a lot heavier in this world.

This might be because he was a lot richer. Or it could be because he was a lot lazier (because when he wasn't all up in my face, teaching me things about this world, he pretty much did nothing but sit around and plot, or maybe it was sulk). Or it could be God's punishment because he was a gigantically bigger dick than my real dad was.

And considering my dad was a colossal asshole, that was serious.

But I had a plan.

Play his game. Pretend I was doing his bidding (and FYI: his bidding was that I was supposed to let some royal guy marry me, have sex with me, make me pregnant, and once I had a son, I could have my mom back and go home, leaving said son behind—uh-huh, *that* was his bidding).

My plan was, while I went about doing this unconscionably awful stuff (or going through the motions), I'd figure out where Mom was. Once I did that, I'd get her, and that troubled woman who looked exactly like me, who was now with her.

After that there would be the small matter of finding a witch to send us from this Disney Movie from Hell back to the real world.

And when we were home, I'd need to sell a kidney and about a million pints of plasma in order to afford the therapy it was going to take to see Mom through the aftermath of this nightmare. Not to mention the ongoing care that chick was going to need. Because I knew another thing for certain, she seemed docile and sweet (albeit freaked way the heck out), but she was messed up and she needed someone looking after her. And for certain this guy, who was her father, wasn't doing a bang-up job of it.

However, that someone looking after her should maybe have twelve degrees that taught them how to do that adequately, and thus should *not* be my mom behind bars in a fucking *dungeon* somewhere in this Disney Movie from Hell.

I looked out the window at the countryside rolling past, hating it was so gorgeous.

But it was.

The colors were ridiculously vibrant. The flora and fauna plentiful. The air even seemed like it had glitter floating through it, and it smelled amazing. Fresh and clean. Wherever we were right then, you could smell the grass or the flowers. But when you got near a river, you could smell the water (yeah, *the water*, I wasn't kidding, and it smelled fantastic).

My favorite? When you rode through a village and you got a whiff of bread baking or meat roasting.

I was Belle drifting through town (though, countryside, and not doing this dancing and reading and bopping in a carriage).

Except my "dad" was Gaston grown up and a hu of a villain than he was in the movie.

Years ago, Mom and I had sat at her kitchen table, as we were wont to do, drinking wine, as we were also wont to do, bent over laughing so hard (again, as was our wont) after she said she should have forgone the whole dad thing and just gotten some guy's sperm and a turkey baster.

We then went on to make up all sorts of ways we would respect and honor said turkey baster, with shrines and offerings, giving it a birthday and presenting it with a cake (the baster, we decided, liked angel food, which, obvs, was an excuse for us to make angel food cake).

Sadly, I was not conceived with a turkey baster.

Suffice it to say, Dad had broken Mom's heart (repeatedly).

Mine (repeatedly).

And the last time he did that was three weeks ago when he sold us to his doppelganger from a parallel universe, me to stand in the stead of his daughter and act as brood mare to some dukeling, and Mom to be imprisoned so I'd do what I was told.

Oh yeah, right.

I forgot a part of my plan.

Once we got home, find my father, kick him in the gonads and spit in his face.

Only that man could discover there was a parallel universe (I mean, *really*?). Trust me, I could go the rest of my life not knowing this place existed and *never, ever* coming here. I didn't care how many flowers there were and how cute it was to see a plethora of cotton-tail bunnies scampering through the trees. And it was cute, believe me.

Not only did Dad discover it, but he found some way to get himself something from it (in this instance, if what had been scattered on his coffee table along with beer cans and overflowing ashtrays was the telltale sign, it was a bag of emeralds).

Hanging me and Mom out to dry in the process.

"You know the consequences if you should do anything foolish," Dad's voice came from not-Dad-but-still-Dad's stupid mouth.

I looked to him to see he was staring out the opposite window.

I looked out that window.

Oh boy.

That must be Pinkwick House, the country seat of the House of Dalton. One of, apparently, a bunch of properties these rich, royal dudes owned.

The big one?

Dalwin Castle, which was supposedly amazing and perched on a cliff.

But that might be for later, say, should I and my fiancé decide to be married there.

For now, things of note about Pinkwick House.

One, it was pink. A mellow, precious, perfect pink that was ludicrously appealing.

Two, it was large. It was not a house. Unless you referred to Downton Abbey as a house, which you did not. Because it was a huge-ass abbey turned into a house where rich people lived.

Three, it was so perfect, the air liked it better than other places in this world, because the air glittered a ton more there.

Four, there was a creek up the hill at the side of it that broke off into four tributary streams that rushed in front of and behind the house, the water twinkling diamond-like in the bright sun, making the picture-perfect scene even *more* perfect.

Five, there were flowers freaking *everywhere*. Profuse pink and white wisteria graced the arch above the front door and fell from the eaves of the house. Lush green ivy snaked up the walls. Huge urns filled with purple and blue blooms dotted all over the place.

Six, there were fountains flowing into baths on either side of the front door. The front area was an elegantly curved drive, the lawn around it manicured. But beyond that to the sides, and you could even see to the back, was a riot of meandering gardens you could get lost in for days.

Even the quaint stone outbuildings crawling with ivy and wisteria looked out of a fairy tale.

Straight up, on the cobblestone courtyard in front of what had to be stables, I'd lay money down Jaq and Gus were made into footmen there sometime in the last century.

It was gorgeous. It was exquisite.

I hated it.

"Did you hear me, Maxine?" Dad-not-Dad asked.

"I harbor a death wish for you. It is fervent. I have embraced it with all that is me. But sadly, this does not mean I can no longer hear your bleating. *Ow!*"

He kicked me in the shin.

Hard.

It hurt.

A lot.

I glared at him.

"You respect your father," he bit out.

"You're not my father," I returned.

He moved his feet like he was going to kick me again.

I shifted mine and snapped, "Fine. Right. You do know, I haven't forgotten my mother is in that hellhole taking care of *your daughter*."

He settled back and watched the pink house get closer. "Don't forget it. And don't forget our deal."

I wound a hand in a circle in front of me. Incidentally, it was a hand covered in a baby-blue kid leather glove with baby-blue-covered buttons on the inside at the wrist and intricate seam-work on the outside of the hand with delicate scalloping around the edges. They were lovely, and they felt like butter. I loathed them.

"Make him fall in love with me. Get him to knock me up. Produce a son. Get pat on the head. Be reunited with my mother and let out of this nightmare. Yeah, I didn't forget our deal."

He turned back to me. "We say *yes* in this world."

I didn't reply.

"Remember my teachings," he ordered. "I haven't spent hour after hour for three weeks molding you into a fine lady of Hawkvale, a woman fit to be called Countess of Derryman, *which you are*, for you to fall at this first hurdle."

You guessed it.

After that trip where he took me, blindfolded, to see where Mom and the other me were holed up, a whole lot of unfun Eliza Doolittle garbage had been going on for three weeks.

Which was apropos, considering a number of things, including my current outfit (baby blue, form fitting down to kickpleats that started at my knees, a smart, knife-edged bow at the back of said knees, a one-foot train trailing from it, a long-sleeved bolero jacket up top that buttoned over my breasts up to my neck, the dress under had short, cap sleeves and a square neckline that exposed cleavage, all of this made in silk wool—it was simple, but fabulous, however the large hat with enormous rosettes that sat at a tilt on my head was not simple, it was extraordinary, and I detested it...*all of it*).

I again didn't reply.

"You perform well," he stated, "your mother gets the reward."

"And your daughter," I prompted.

He rolled his eyes and scoffed, "She'll be fine. She doesn't even know where she is."

"She might have some issues," I said quietly. "But she's not stupid."

His gaze skewered me. "Speak not of what you know nothing about."

"I know that woman has no idea where she is, but she does know she's not home."

"She's home for the first time since she was six," he spat.

Six?

Did Maxine of this world get sick at six?

Maxine of this world.

God, my mom was having to take care of another me, one who was terrified, confused and not well.

But she looked exactly like me.

And Mom had to do this in a prison cell.

I noticed that he realized he'd said too much, his face closed down, and he reminded me coolly, "You handle this meeting with aplomb, they get mattresses and pillows, more blankets and an extra meal."

I gritted my teeth.

And then there was that.

I was informed they got breakfast "gruel" (whatever that was, but it didn't sound nice) and bread and broth for dinner. Plus water.

That was it.

And their blankets were scratchy wool, hopefully warm, but thin.

And their cots were just cots, no padding, nothing.

"You handle this *weekend* with aplomb, keep the betrothal intact, and we begin preparations for your wedding, they will be moved to a small cottage I own. There, they will stay until you finish your part of the deal. They will remain under guard, of course, but they will have more room, far more amenities and will be treated as my guests."

His daughter, treated as his guest.

He was repugnant. Totally a bigger dick than my dad.

The carriage made a turn and shuddered to a halt.

"Are we agreed?" he pressed.

"I'm here, aren't I?"

"You have no choice but to *be* here. Thus, I'll hear you say it," he demanded.

"You gotta let me do this my way," I returned.

His brows shot together in alarm. "Pardon?"

"I know you probably don't get this concept, but I love my mother more than my own life. And I have a heart, so I don't know your girl, I just know she needs to be somewhere not where she is now. If, for the next however long this takes, it's a cottage instead of a prison cell, with beds and good food and room to move, I'll take it. In other words, I'm not going to fuck this up."

He shot forward and snapped, "You're Lady Dawes, Countess of Derryman. You don't speak in that manner."

"Fuck you, *Dad*, and chill out. I got this."

And on that, before he could annoy me any further, and so I could get this show on the road and out of close proximity to him, I threw open the door, rose from my seat, put out my (cute, I had to admit, in a bright and happy steampunk kind of way) baby-blue, kitten-heeled, buttons-at-the-side boot and stepped on the step that the footman who was there had folded down.

I looked toward the pink house…

And nearly fell flat on my face.

The footman caught my hand and I somehow made it down the steps.

There was an attractive, tall, straight, still-broad-shouldered, white-haired, older man making his way to the carriage.

But behind him, leaning against a column by the front door, the drooping wisteria nearly mingling with his thick dark hair…

Holy *crap*.

Did they make men that beautiful?

Oh my God.

Pleasetellmethat'stheMarquessofwherever,
pleasetellmethat'stheMarquessofwherever, pleasetellme…

My mental chant was interrupted when my gloved hand was taken and I heard in a smooth, manly voice that had a thoroughly astonished tone, "Maxine, my goodness, my dear, you look…very well."

I tipped my gaze up at the older hot guy, and since I'd totally forgotten where I was, I just stared at him blankly.

His expression grew tender, his hand around mine tightened, and he said gently, and also sadly, "Oh, my dear."

Shit.

Right!

I had to do this.

Starting now.

"Your grace," I replied, kept hold of his hand, but fell into a curtsy, dropping my head and fortunately covering my face with my ginormous hat so I could have a second to think.

Okay, that guy at the house was probably his son.

Which meant that was my fiancé.

Well, kind of, but not really.

But that was the guy I was supposed to make fall in love with me.

Then I was supposed to have sex with him.

Lots and lots of it (I just added that part, but didn't you have to have lots of sex to get up the duff?).

Right, well…

Suddenly…

I could so totally do this.

(Not having the baby part, but I could kill time while I figured out where Mom and the other me were, rescue them and find some way to get us home, all while banging that…amazing…*man*—new item on my to-do list: figure out birth control in this world.)

His father's fingers squeezed mine, and I straightened, looking again to him.

"It's lovely to see you," I told him.

"It's…lovely…to see you…too," he pushed out weirdly, staring intently at me.

"Dalton, my good man!" Dad-not-Dad greeted jovially, pushing close to our sides. "Isn't she a vision? Just a vision."

I was only beginning to feel out my role, but I flubbed it right off the bat.

It was bound to happen.

And it happened right then.

I rolled my eyes.

The duke started.

I jerked and tried to pull my hand out of his, while I reminded myself to get it together.

I didn't succeed in pulling my hand out of his because he held fast.

I focused on him.

"You're well then, my lady?" he asked in a strangely searching manner.

"Peachy," I replied. "I'm out of that infernal carriage. I have company that is not my often quite irritating father."

Dad-not-Dad grunted, being the kind of man who could load that small sound with surprise, offense and disapproval.

Even so, I kept going.

"The sun is shining. This house is ridiculously perfect. I assume you have food, and intend to feed me, which I will welcome with heart and soul as I'm starved. And your son is remarkably ugly, but I fear I have no choice but to accept him."

The duke blinked at me.

I got concerned I'd taken it too far.

This was, of course, a whole parallel universe where there were no cell phones, cars, DoorDash or Ted Lasso.

I kicked butt at a meet the parents at home.

But I'd never met a duke, even in my world.

He busted out laughing.

Okay.

Shoo!

I hadn't lost my touch.

Still chuckling, he finally greeted Dad-not-Dad with a dismissive, "Derryman," then tucked my hand in the crook of his elbow as he started guiding me toward the house, stating, "We had such grave concerns, seeing as he turned out so unsightly. I must tell you how relieved I am you have a generous heart."

"So generous, the birds sing directly to me, and the mice are my friends," I replied flippantly.

His brows drew together, humor remaining on his face, when he returned in all seriousness, "Of course they are."

Um.

What?

He looked where he was guiding me and called, "Loren, son, are you going to come greet your future bride?"

Loren, by the by, had not moved a muscle. Not one of the many, seemingly magnificently defined, astoundingly attractive ones that made up his big, tall, broad-shouldered, lean-hipped, fabulous body.

He was still leaning against the column wearing light beige breeches (that left nothing to the imagination with those beefy thighs, or the delectable bulge between them), dark brown boots, a white shirt with billowy sleeves contained by a chocolate brocade, low-dipping vest (wrong, I needed to remember, they called them waistcoats).

No neckcloth, so I could see his tan, corded throat, and it made my mouth water.

I'd been in that world three weeks. It all seemed like a sick joke in the beginning (and still did), including the clothes.

But although I would perhaps commit murder to see this guy in jeans, I was suddenly getting the clothes.

He had his arms crossed on his wide chest, his boots crossed at the ankles, and his lazy brown eyes with their lush lashes trained on me.

We stopped at the foot of the four steps that led to the front door.

A sudden wind swept through, taking wisteria petals with it, and they floated with the glitter in the air between us.

I'd already fallen in lust, but being that close to him, for the first time thinking this was a different kind of Disney, the adult kind, but it wasn't from hell in the slightest, I fell a whole lot deeper.

Loren's eyes moved down my length and then up, without showing even a smidgeon of real interest, and it was then I became uncomfortably mindful of the fact that I was on display.

A ware.

He was a dukeling.

Royal.

And in this moment, he could take me.

Or pass.

"She'll do," he murmured.

My lips parted in shock.

They did this not only at his words.

They stayed this way when he turned and strolled into the house, disappearing in the shadows, not uttering another sound.

Chapter Three

Scarlett O'Hara

Maxine

Hawkvale
Pinkwick House
The Parallel

I stood, staring out the window at the gathering clouds, the same, figuratively, forming in my head.

Prior to his most recent betrayal, I hadn't seen my father in over a year. Mom hadn't seen him in a lot longer. Life was good. Healthy. She was dating that nice Keith. I had a decent job I liked that paid okay, and I loved our residents at the over-fifties community I managed.

We were steady.

Safe.

Why did we both run to him when he called (or, as it was, texted)?

Yes, he said it was urgent.

Yes, he said he was terribly ill.

But he was a conman with a charlatan's heart and a grifter's soul, and his gut instinct was always to fend best for himself even if doing so meant he lay devastation in his wake.

We'd learned that time and again.

When did you stop hoping your father would become a worthwhile human being?

The answer to that question for me, apparently, was...on his deathbed.

Except, he hadn't been on his deathbed.

He'd made another deal with another devil.

And anyway, why would someone text to say they were on their deathbed?

Then again, why did Ed Dawes do anything?

More importantly, why did I believe Ed Dawes when he did something?

Thunder rent the air and I jumped.

"That came on quickly," Dad-not-Dad mumbled from where he was seated in the duke's pretty yellow, cream and green sitting room, reading a paper behind me.

Loren had not shown his face again.

Ansley (he told me to call him Ansley, and not what Dad-not-Dad ordered me never to fail to call him: your grace, Lord Dalton, or Lord Copeland) had served us tea with scones and jam and cream (Lord, *heavenly*, I ate two, even if Dad-not-Dad stared daggers at me while I did, and the seams of my tight dress threatened to burst).

Ansley had then said he had a few things to see to, asked us if we would be all right on our own for half an hour, and when Dad-not-Dad fell all over himself to say yes (I kinda wanted to be shown to my room so I could unbutton a few buttons after tea), he left.

In that time, the storm had come in.

And I had found that standing made it easier for my dress to make room for the scones and cream.

"The carriages are still out there," I announced.

These would be plural, seeing as Dad-not-Dad's valet, and my lady's maid, Idina, had been in a carriage behind us.

Our trunks had been brought in.

But the horses, who had been dragging those carriages for three days, were still hooked to them in what was becoming a rather whipping wind.

"The grooms will be having their own tea," Dad-not-Dad muttered.

I turned to him. "The horses need tea too."

His head came up and his brows knitted. "Horses don't drink tea."

"No, but they've been doing a hell of a lot more work than you, me, or the groomsmen have the last three days. So they should be somewhere warm, sheltered, with water, oats and maybe a few apples or carrots."

I was talking out my ass, since I was a city girl and didn't know anything about horses, but people were always feeding them apples and carrots and oats in movies.

"They'll be seen to," Dad-not-Dad dismissed.

"A storm is coming, they should be seen to now."

"They'll be seen to when they're seen to, Maxine, it's not your issue."

"It is when I'm standing right here"—I swung an arm to the windows—"and I can see them."

"I can assure you, the grooms know the storm is coming, so if they're worried about the damned horses, they'll get the damned horses. They're horses! They can handle some rain."

"After dragging your *very* healthy behind over what has to be at least a hundred miles?" I retorted. "I mean, I don't wish to fat shame, *Dad*, but they've served us, now it's our turn."

His face turned purple.

A throat was cleared at the door.

Loren stood there, again leaning, now against the jamb.

Wonderful.

The papers rustled frantically as Dad-not-Dad hauled himself out of the fancy yellow settee.

"Loren, my boy, we didn't have a chance to greet each other earlier. It's lovely to see you again."

Loren studied Dad curiously, like he was a speck of dirt in this pristine, but very attractive, sitting room, and he had no clue how he managed to be missed by the maids.

In our very brief acquaintance, Loren had shown some dickish tendencies, but now I was thinking I might like the guy.

"I'm afraid the tea's cold," Dad-not-Dad went on gamely. "Shall we ring for some more?"

"I don't drink tea," Loren declared.

"Really? What do you drink?" Dad-not-Dad asked eagerly. "Obviously, my darling Maxine will need to know *all* your preferences."

I looked to the ceiling and mouthed, *Oh my God.*

"Maxine!" Dad snapped.

I righted my head and caught Loren now studying me, not like I was a speck of dirt, but like I was a fascinating specimen, and he didn't know what to make of me.

At least the fascinating part was good.

"Yes, of course, my lord, please, I beg of you, share *all your preferences*," I said to him, lifting a hand and placing it on my chest for added emphasis of how deeply I desired this knowledge.

Loren's eyes fell to my hand.

They stayed there.

He smirked.

Well, there's one.

I'd taken off my jacket.

I was baring cleavage.

And he was a tit man.

Thank goodness I had ample in that region.

More thunder, closer, and the darkening room lit with lightning.

I dropped my hand, turned back to the window and saw the rain come sluicing down.

This wasn't an afternoon thunderstorm.

This was a monsoon.

And the horses had their heads ducked, all eight of them on the two carriages, as the deluge pelted them. The wind was tearing at their manes and tails. And I could swear to God, I saw one of them shivering.

I whirled on Dad-not-Dad.

"Are you going to call a damned groom?" I demanded.

My not-father dropped all pretense, and his face twisted.

"Watch that mouth, lady," he snapped.

I dropped my chin into my neck, mouthed, *Fuck it*, then stormed toward the door.

Loren still lounged there.

He was lit with another flash of lightning as thunder rattled the house, and he was hot even with spooky lighting. He was also now watching me with open interest, but I didn't take the time to enjoy it or do anything about it.

I swept past him.

"Maxine! Where are you going?" Dad-not Dad shouted.

I didn't answer.

But I wasn't going to ramble around a humongous house looking for the grooms when the horses were fifty yards away from my person and I knew where the goddamn stables were.

I had no clue how to drive a carriage, but if Scarlett O'Hara could drive one, by God, I could too.

I stomped out into the rain, and immediately regretted my decision, not only considering my updo was instantly ruined and it had taken Idina a million years to curl and arrange my hair that morning before we left the inn where we'd spent the night last night (I would never take electricity for granted again). But because a monsoon even in Disney Come to Life was no joke.

However, I was rolling, and there was no going back now.

"Maxine!" I heard yelled over the rain and wind.

And it wasn't Dad-not-Dad.

It was Loren.

I was going to look over my shoulder at him when, instead, I stopped dead because his fingers wrapped around my upper arm pulled me to a halt.

"Get in the house," he ordered.

I blinked up at him through the rain. "I'm taking care of the horses."

"Get in the house," he repeated.

I pulled at my arm. "The horses need to be taken to the stables."

He dipped his face right in mine, like, *an inch away*, and I didn't have a chance to process how sexy his lashes were when they were spiky with wet as he barked, "*Get in the godsdamned house!*"

Oh no he didn't.

I yanked my arm from his grip. "Don't tell me what to do!"

I then turned, and as fast as my tight skirt would allow me, I ran toward the carriage.

This was not fast, and I was probably moving like a geisha, so, unsurprisingly, he caught up with me.

When he did, what he didn't do was drag me to the house.

He picked me up.

Yes, me and my rather generous ass.

He then pretty much tossed me high into the driver's seat of the carriage.

My hip banged against it (no worries, the seat was padded), and I nearly fell to my knees on the floor.

I did not because Loren was up after me, his arm sliced around my stomach, he hauled me around and deposited my ass in the seat.

He then sat next to me, nabbed the reins, shouted, "Hee-yah!" while he flicked them, and the horses were so danged ready to *not* be in the freezing, driving rain, they bolted forward.

I nearly rolled ass over head off the back of the seat and had to grab on to Loren in order not to do that (important aside, his arm felt like it was made of steel).

Either the grooms were making their way to get the carriages or folks were battening down the hatches, because there were people doing things at the stables. When they saw us speeding to them, two of them rushed to the doors and opened them.

We raced in, and Loren pulled back the reins, yelling, "Whoa!"

The horses stopped, the carriage creaked ominously behind us, I nearly went head over ass forward this time, but I didn't because Loren grabbed hold of me, then he immediately stood.

He dragged me across the seat until I was sitting where he had been. He jumped lithely to the ground (and yikes, that was a shocker, the seat was pretty high up).

He then reached up, caught my waist in his hands and hauled me down to my feet.

At that point he commenced towing me through the stables, ordering, "You get that other carriage inside, you disappear. Am I heard?"

"Yes, milord," someone said.

I wasn't paying attention.

Because we weren't leaving the stables.

He was taking me to a room off where all the horses were (and proof positive this place was scary awesome: the stables didn't smell like stables—they smelled like fresh cut hay and summer rain, which someone needed to make into a candle).

We got to that room.

I lifted a hand to push back my sodden hair and saw there were a bunch of saddles lying on beams lining the walls (like, a *bunch*, as in, they could open a store). Pegs that held bridles and reins and such. A couple of benches with some scattered tools where it looked like they did work on the saddles. And a ratty armchair next to a little iron stove in the corner at the back, where one would rest after their weary work on saddles.

The stove was lit, and the room was cozy warm.

Okay then, maybe we were going to wait out the storm here.

Good idea.

Except Loren slammed the door *really* loudly, whirled me around to face him using my hand, and then shouted, "Have you lost your bloody *mind*?"

"I—"

"You're soaking, godsdamned wet," he declared.

He was too, and one could say that shirt plastered against his wide chest, even with the waistcoat in the way, was something.

Okay, deep breath and…

"That isn't lost on me, your grace," I replied.

"Women do not drive carriages," he proclaimed.

Ummmmmmmm…

"They do not stable them," he went on. "*Or* horses."

I sucked both my lips in.

"Servants deal with the conveyances," he kept going.

I held my breath in order to hold my tongue.

"And you do not"—he gave my hand he still held a slight jerk—"*ever* dash into a bloody storm."

"It's just some rain," I pointed out, though we both knew that was a tad bit of an understatement.

"You're a bloody *female*," he stated.

Okay, I needed to hold on to my patience.

I didn't hold on to my patience.

"I'm glad you noticed," I retorted sarcastically.

His expression changed and my immediate world changed with it.

He was furious, he wasn't hiding it, and he was this to such an extent, the heat of it felt like it was singeing my skin.

It was scary AF.

He let my hand go but advanced on me in a way I had no choice but to retreat.

"If this caper was to get my attention, it's both stupid and cruel," he said in a dangerous voice as he backed me toward the corner.

Cruel?

"I simply wanted to put the horses away," I told him something he knew.

"You came with two grooms, and we have at least that many. You wish the horses stalled, you pull the *fucking* cord to call a servant to tell them to tell the grooms to put the *fucking* horses away."

Wow.

He said the f-word.

Twice.

To me.

A lady (as far as he knew).

I knew they had that word in this world because Dad-not-Dad hated me saying it.

But I'd never heard anyone else say it (though, until very recently, I hadn't been around anyone but Dad-not-Dad).

And somehow, having that be the only time I heard it from someone other than me, it gave it much more gravitas.

I hit something, it was the armchair, so I was forced to stop.

Loren stopped toe-to-toe with me, so close, I could actually feel the hem of my skirt resting on his boots.

"I think you're being a bit dramatic," I whispered, sounding uncertain of my own words because his presence was overpowering, and it was that not only because he was a pretty big and definitely powerful guy.

"Do you?" he asked with an almost sneer. "Is that what you think?"

I wasn't a fan of the sneer.

"Actually, right now I think you need to step back."

"My mother was seeing to some villagers. She did that when people were ill and needed assistance, or were recovering and needed company. She was in a phaeton. The weather turned when she was on her way back. She got caught in the rain. She caught a chill. A week later, she was dead," he shared.

I blinked up at him.

"My sister had a puppy who fell into the creek. The one right out there." He jabbed a finger toward the window, but he didn't look that way, he kept his eyes locked to me. "She went in after it. It was late fall. Warm in the morning, chilly by the afternoon. But the creek was freezing. The puppy lived. She went down with a cough that turned into a wracking fever that eventually burned her little body away. She was eight."

"Oh my God."

His head twitched.

Damn.

Dad-not-Dad told me they had more than one god here.

"My…my *gods*," I covered.

"Am I being dramatic, Lady Maxine?" he asked.

"I didn't know about your mother and sister."

"Everybody knows about my mother and sister."

Although I knew how to wear a hat and how to address a duke, this very important fact about my husband-to-be had not been covered in my tutelage, thank you so much (not), Dad-not-Dad.

"I've been away in Fleuridia at school, your grace, until very recently. Father wanted me to stay down there, especially during the troubles, and I became enamored of my studies. He isn't much of a correspondent, and I didn't get a great deal of news from home. I'm sorry, but I really did not know," I told him.

"You've been away in Fleuridia," he stated.

And he did this *dubiously*.

Oh boy.

Why would he be dubious?

I mean, of course he should. I not only wasn't his fiancée, I wasn't even of his world, and I intended to play him and then disappear.

But why would he be?

"Yes, I extended my studies there." God, how to rattle this off without sounding like I was rattling it off? "Art history and—"

"It matters not whether you know art. What matters is if you have a fertile womb and know how to host a party."

Record scratch and repeat.

Oh no he…did…*not*.

But he did.

And he kept going.

"And you have the sense not to run out into the rain. And you know your place in a household, or perhaps more importantly, a servant's place. But you have enough of a hold on *your* place never to speak to me in the manner you address your sire."

"I would certainly not speak to you that way," I said softly.

"I should hope not," he replied.

"Unless you were acting like an utter ass, as you are now. On those occasions, I make no promises."

His eyes flared.

"Now, sir, step away from me."

"Considering we're set to spend the rest of our lives together, there are things we should discuss."

"And we shall do that," I retorted. "When I'm not sopping wet and…" I got up on my toes, "*insanely* angry at you."

His brows flew up.

"Angry at *me*?"

"Allow me to make one thing clear, your grace."

He didn't move away even if he gave a sense of settling in.

"And that would be?" he prompted.

"I have been living on my own, in charge of myself, for some time. I am more than likely not what you're accustomed to in this world."

"This world?"

Shit.

"Country. Hawkvale. *Whatever*," I snapped. "I am independent. I know my own mind. If I feel the need to speak it, I…um…*shall*. Now, allow me to assure you, I *kill* at hosting a party."

"Kill?"

"I murder a party, as in, I'm bloody good at throwing one."

"Excellent," he muttered, his gaze beginning to drift over my face.

"And I have a variety of things to say about servants, and the bourgeoisie, but I suggest we save those for another time as there is not only a variety, but also a great deal to be said."

"Mm," he hummed. Then asked, "Bourgeoisie?"

"That would be *you*," I stated.

"And you, dear heart," he retorted. "And I'll add, very Fleuridian of you."

I had figured out, in some of Dad-not-Dad's teaching, that in Fleuridia, the country south of Hawkvale where I was supposed to have spent the last twenty years of my life, they spoke French.

Though they didn't call it French, of course.

Sadly, I did not speak French, which I worried would eventually be awkward to explain.

But that wasn't for now.

"We're getting off topic," I warned.

"Are we?"

"I'm enumerating all the fabulous things you'll get when you get me, regardless of my fear that you won't think they're fabulous."

"Indeed. Fleuridia is known for producing headstrong females."

"Oh my God...*zzzzz*," I hissed. "Did you just use the word 'headstrong'?"

"Do not fear, Countess, I'm changing my mind about the manner in which I'll allow you to address me."

"A-allow?" I choked.

His eyes settled on my mouth. "Do you need me to stroke your back?"

My nipples suddenly perked up.

"Why on earth would I need that?"

His gaze came to my own. "You seem to be choking on your words."

I shifted out from in front of him, declaring, "I think we're done here."

He caught me with an arm around my belly and pulled me back.

I looked to where I stood but a moment before, then I looked down at the toes of his boots that were again amongst my skirts.

Then I looked up at him.

"Did you just deny my departure and do that physically?"

"I did, as I disagree. We are not done here."

"A warning, Lord Remington," I said low. "When I wish not to be somewhere, I do not allow a man to waylay me."

"Do you not?"

"It would seem we're destined to wed," I pointed out.

"It's lovely to know you understand the concept of a contract."

I allowed myself to smile.

His eyes raced to my mouth with that.

So he watched my lips say, "And it's lovely to know I haven't scared you off and you have more mettle than I first assumed."

His lips twitched, accepting my score.

And then I shared softly, "So I will be your wife, and I may give you daughters. I urge you, your grace, to consider for a moment how you would feel if another man prohibited me or them from going when we wished to go."

His gaze came to mine.

"Countess," he whispered, appearing contrite.

In other words, he got my point.

"Call me crazy, but I've enjoyed our *tête-à-tête*. However, it would mean a great deal to me if you would make an effort to learn when to back me into a corner, and when...*not*."

My heart skipped in my chest when he immediately stepped aside.

Okay, um...

Why was that the sexiest thing a man ever did around me?

Feeling weirdly nervous all of a sudden, I touched my wet hair and moved to the door, mumbling, "I must be off. I fear my toilette prior to dinner will take twice as much time."

I stopped after I opened the door and turned back to him.

Damn, he was good-looking.

Also, he liked ass too, since when I turned, his eyes were aimed at mine before they came up to my face.

"I'm very sorry about your mother and sister. I'm also sorry, with what happened to them, that what I did with the horses concerned you. I'll make a point not to do something like that again."

"I would be obliged, Countess."

I dipped my chin.

He watched me intently.

I slipped out the door.

During our discussion, the rain had gone.

Dodging puddles, I dashed to the house as quickly as my skirt would allow me, feeling unsettled.

Because before I got to Pinkwick House, Loren Copeland, Marquess of Remington was just a guy I had to play to buy time to get my mom safe and get the hell out of there.

Now he was a guy I might just like.

And that complicated things.

Greatly.

Chapter Four

Highest Bidder

Loren

"You're absolutely certain the woman you saw in the sanatorium was Lady Maxine Dawes?" Loren asked his father.

They were in Ansley's study. Drinks to be shared with Dawes and Maxine were to be served in the parlor in fifteen minutes. Thus, they were both in evening attire.

And his father and he were further discussing the bombshell Ansley had landed on him that afternoon, just prior to his brief, wet adventure with the Countess Derryman.

"She was the image of the woman who arrived this very afternoon," Ansley replied.

"And the doctors told you that the damage done when she was a child was unrecoverable?" Loren pressed.

"Yes, son," Ansley replied sharply, his deep voice pitching louder.

"Calm down," Loren said low.

"It feels like you're questioning my sanity."

"I'm not, but I believe you are."

Ansley blew out a breath, tore his hand through his hair and turned to stare out the window into the darkness.

"As we did not have time earlier today, now, can we speak for a moment about the fact you didn't tell *me* that my affianced had a debilitating brain injury?" Loren requested.

Ansley turned back to his son. "If you'd known you'd been released from the contract, what would you have done?"

"I've no idea. However, I think whatever that is should have been mine to decide."

Ansley let it sit a moment.

And then he said, "You are all I have left, Loren. It is, indeed, about our line. Mostly, it's about me wanting to precede at least one member of my immediate family to death."

Loren flinched.

His father did not let up.

"I am proud of your service to our kingdom, but I fear you've become addicted to that chase."

"What chase?"

"The one to danger."

Good gods.

Not this again.

"Father—"

Ansley lifted a hand and waved it in his son's direction. "Let's not argue. You say she was quick-witted in the stables?"

"Quick-witted" did not cover it.

"I've never met a woman with a sharper wit. It's quite the wonder I don't have cuts all over me."

Ansley watched his son closely.

Then he noted quietly, "She pleases you."

If the woman was half as clever in bed as she was out of it, she was to be the perfect wife.

He did not share that.

He stated, "She's lovely to look at and she has the spirit of a bull."

"That's an odd comparison."

"Bulls are stubborn. I'd pit her against any bull breathing, I don't care how sharp their horns. She'd best it by just not giving up."

His father smiled. "In other words, she pleases you."

"Her father is a toad."

Ansley's chest expanded with the big breath he took, and then he released it. "Even before he lost the stature he built for himself conniving and borderline thieving and making himself richer off the hides of his friends and acquaintances, Edgar Dawes was a man with whom you watched your back." A pause before he asked, "You heard them have words?"

"The exchange I witnessed was brief. But one thing was made clear during it. She can't stand him."

"Hmm," Ansley hummed.

"What are you thinking?"

"His wife killed herself, you know."

Loren nodded.

"After he sent Maxine away to boarding school."

Loren said nothing.

"No one quite understood it. He was respectable enough. His title holds power. He has great wealth. At the time, he was quite good-looking. He's gone rather to seed of late. But that's only recently. She had the life many women struggle quite valiantly for."

Loren remained silent, though he did it wondering what Maxine would think of that remark.

"No one sends their child away to school for twenty years without her coming home at least to visit," Ansley remarked. "While you were with her in the stables, and I'd rejoined him, Derryman told me she hadn't been back to Hawkvale since he sent her away. Not once. In two decades."

"Should I take a seat, or are you going to get to the point?" Loren ribbed.

His father's mouth quirked.

Then he said, "I think Maxine is a twin."

Loren had no idea what he expected his father to say.

But it wasn't that.

"A twin?" he asked.

"Perhaps she actually is Maxine, and the woman I visited with is her sister, who, for whatever reason, is registered at the hospital as Maxine. Perhaps it's the Maxine with us who is pretending to be her sister. Although your mother wanted you to have the proper schooling, and thus you went to a proper school, you were always home for the holidays. I, personally, would never dream of losing that time with you."

Loren said nothing, but he felt his face soften at the memories.

Because his father told no lies.

His early life had been marked with mourning, his mother dying when he was five, his sister dying when he was eleven.

But he'd learned to crave adventure because his father dropped everything and gave one to him every school holiday.

Ansley carried on, "I think one of the girls was hurt in a way that couldn't be fixed, and perhaps the wife was responsible. Edgar sent the other girl away. And the guilt ate at her until she couldn't take it anymore."

"And once she took her own life, then why would the daughter not return?" Loren queried.

Ansley shrugged. "Perhaps she's an unhappy reminder of the wife. I sadly forget the woman's name, but I do remember what she looked like, and her daughter certainly looks like her."

"Has word of twins ever been uttered about Edgar's offspring?"

"What other possible explanation could there be?" Ansley queried. "When I say she's the woman I sat with on several occasions, Loren, I do not jest. Except for the fact that Maxine was bright and sweet, what she was not was droll and quick-witted."

In that moment, considering the possibility of twins, a thought occurred to Loren.

A thought about something he held in strictest confidence at the behest of his friend, a friend who was also his king.

Something that was a state secret of such magnitude, he'd die before he breathed word of it.

However, upon thinking of it, he dismissed it.

It was too fantastical.

And from what he knew, it took grave magic to affect it.

That being producing such a "twin."

There wasn't a witch in all the Northlands *or* Southlands who held this much magic. Not anymore.

But even if there was, no one but a very select few knew of the existence of that other world. A world, it was his understanding, that was markedly different from his own. It would be a profound shock to anyone who made the switch, impossible to recover easily.

In fact, decades had passed, and Loren could still see how living in a different world affected his queen. She navigated it rather well. But he noted when things surprised her, or at other times he caught it when Tor was covering for her.

Lady Maxine was not like any woman he'd ever met.

But she didn't speak or act like Queen Cora.

She was definitely of his world.

Considering the impracticality of it, Loren set that thought aside and asked, "You made the betrothal arrangement with him at her birth. Obviously, at that time, he didn't speak of another child. And as far as we know, no one has heard word of this. Why would a father hide one of his daughters…ever?"

Ansley shook his head. "I have no answer to that. But I'm also not Edgar Dawes. He'd sell her to the highest bidder, something he did in terms of status, if it meant he'd get something out of it. Perhaps he saw what he wrought in the deal he struck to make his girl a duchess, and he held his other daughter back to see what she might bring. In the meantime, Maxine, or her sister, was irreparably injured, the woman with us was in Fleuridia, perhaps not desirous of return, and he delayed your wedding because he was machinating to convince her to fulfill her part of the contract or fill her sister's shoes."

"You do know that sounds preposterous," Loren noted, saying this even if he knew of another explanation, which was even more preposterous.

"I also know of no one, even the mightiest of witches, who can mend an injury like the one the woman at the sanitorium had. I've dispatched a man to ascertain she's still there. When she is, which she will be, as she surely isn't the woman with us, it will at least assuage my concerns that it's not *me* who's being preposterous."

"There's an explanation, Father, and might I suggest we simply ask them?"

"Absolutely not," Ansley replied stiffly. "Perhaps, if you start to build a relationship with her, and trust blooms. But until then, we must proceed understanding a Dawes is a Dawes, and we must treat them with the trust they've earned. That being *none*."

This was another query to which he wished a response, and he set about getting it.

"If you dislike Derryman so badly, why did you promise me to his daughter?" Loren asked.

His father, as ever, had a ready reply.

"Because it was my responsibility to you and your future to secure the most advantageous alliance I could. Because his wife was stunning, and he's rich as sin, and his daughter was, as far as I knew, his only child. Her dowry alone, added to our personal wealth, will make you the richest man in Hawkvale, Loren, outside Noctorno. And now, as they produced no other child, again, as far as we know, you'll inherit it all when Derryman dies. This means, eventually, you might even be wealthier than the king. His tactics to acquire that wealth might revolt me, but it does not negate said wealth."

One could say this was a good reason, as no one, including Loren, had issue with being rich. Therefore no one, including Loren, had issue with being *richer*.

However, his father wasn't finished.

"And you'll be the most titled noble in the land, as you not only hold mine, you hold your mother's, and your children will also hold your wife's. You will need for nothing. You will want for nothing. Nor will your children or your children's children, for generations. And you will hold power in the realm. You've already been asked to sit on Noctorno's council, but Noctorno doesn't see titles. The nature and fortitude of a man are what matters to him. But he's not the only one in his council chambers who will be playing the game. And for many of them, the title, and where it stands, is *all* that matters."

"So you thought about it, you didn't just sell *me* to the highest bidder," Loren joked.

Ansley tutted.

Loren smiled at his father.

Ansley grew serious. "I will find a way out of the contract, my boy, if she does not please you."

Call me crazy, but I've enjoyed our tête-à-tête. *However, it would mean a great deal to me if you would make an effort to learn when to back me into a corner, and when...not.*

Loren greatly relished the idea of being in a situation where she was happy for him to back her into a corner.

Or back her somewhere that had a far more comfortable destination.

"I'm intrigued," Loren admitted.

"And *that* pleases *me*, my son," Ansley replied. "And I am not referring to wealth or power when I state that."

Loren felt the softness again, this time around his heart, at his father's words.

He didn't share this.

"I think you need a drink," Loren prescribed.

Ansley moved to him, clapped him on the back and stayed close as they both walked to the door, his father saying, "I believe we both need one."

And he was, as through his life Loren knew his father often was (though he would rarely admit it), right.

Chapter Five

Caught a Chill

Maxine

"These worlds are known by very few, and there is a reason. A reason that must be guarded closely. Therefore, if you speak a single word...even that first *word...about these different worlds, I will settle a curse on you and your mother, a bitter curse so powerful, you'll rue the day the words left your lips."*

That was what the witch who transported us had said after Mom and I, bound and gagged by Dad and a couple of his buddies, melted from our world into the new one.

She'd been wizened and haggard and looked ready to drop.

But she scared the beejeezus out of me.

And she had the power to rip me from everything I knew and deposit me somewhere I didn't want to be.

Not to mention, it seemed Mom and I were pretty badly cursed already.

In other words, I knew to keep my mouth shut on that score.

Something I sensed was going to make it difficult to recruit help by being honest with people, telling them I wanted to get home, and just where that home was.

"I think you're ready, milady."

I came back into the room.

And it was a gorgeous room, with a huge bed with scrolled head and foot boards padded in buttoned pear-colored velvet, with creamy covers accented with a green floral design, ruched pillowcases and a forest-green velvet bolster. These colors and accents, along with the soft, dove gray flocked wallpaper on the walls, completed the room with its impossibly delicate, feminine furniture and fixtures.

I was seated at one of these impossible pieces, a dainty dressing table with bi-fold oval mirrors on the top. It was covered in pearlescent tubs and crystal bottles and vials. All mine, I knew, as one thing my dad-not-dad was not was a man who skimped when it came to presenting his product to its prospective buyers.

I'd learned this the last few weeks, considering, after I was given a brief, harrowing visit with Mom and Maxine of this world, the only people I was allowed to see were Dad-not-Dad, a dressmaker and her assistant, and a cosmetologist, who created powders, paints and scents personally for me.

Edgar had been at every one of these meetings, overseeing them, acting an ass and making certain I said nor did anything untoward. And even if the women openly, in manner if not verbally, shared they thought this odd (like they thought my clothes were odd, considering the fact, until the dressmaker made some for me, I wore my jeans and tee), that was how it happened.

Otherwise, I lived in his house with him, and he took great pains to make sure his servants, which I heard, but never saw, also never saw me.

Now, I had Idina, who I'd met the day before we left.

And I could not get a bead on her.

She was definitely shy, although very good at her job, if the new, and utterly gorgeous, soft, upswept hairstyle she gave me (along with all the others she'd done, as well as the subtle makeup) was anything to go by.

She also seemed reserved.

This was a problem.

I needed to make friends with the servants.

As far as I could tell, they were the only hope I had to hear things or get into places I could not, hopefully discovering where Mom was.

Also, helping me get to her.

And then helping me find a witch to get us home.

I wasn't sure how I was going to communicate this, because I thought it was probably imperative not to bring a curse on Mom and me prior to us getting the hell out of here.

But I'd have to find a way to do it.

I made another attempt at this by catching her eyes in the mirror and saying, "It's beautiful, Idina."

"I'm pleased you like it, milady."

I smiled at her. "I'm sorry I gave you more work by getting drenched."

She appeared a touch confused. "It would have had to have been redone for dinner regardless, milady. You can't wear a day style to dinner."

Of course it would. Edgar had told me, on most days, I'd have at least two changes of outfit, it could be three or more.

A morning gown, should I be staying at home, inside.

A traveling or strolling outfit, should I be going outside.

And evening attire, always, for, "We, in this world, have proper decorum, unlike what I saw briefly in your world," he'd said. "Therefore, we *always* dress for dinner."

And dinner was a fraught affair. I knew this with how many times he'd struck my fingers brutally with a thin rod after I went for the wrong wineglass or fork.

I'd been denying it (more like trying to ignore it), but the weight in the pit of my stomach that I'd been holding made itself known. I began to feel slightly nauseous and definitely like I was about to burst into tears.

All of this happened as I was reminded, if I didn't spring Mom and the other Maxine early, it was going to take me at least a year to get this done. I might have to have a kid in the meantime, and for sure, she or he'd have to come home with us.

This meant I'd be taking him from Loren.

Then there was Loren. And his dad, who seemed to be sweet. And Idina, who was shy and reserved, but I thought…

"Shall we get you dressed, Countess?" Idina queried.

I came back again and whispered, "I'm sorry, I have a lot on my mind."

"I'm sure," she whispered in return, holding my gaze in the mirror.

I drew in breath and said, "Let's get this done."

She tipped her head to the side and hesitantly asked, "He doesn't please you?"

At her question, the weight in my belly felt the slightest bit lighter.

Was she making an overture?

"He's very handsome," I told her.

"That he is," she agreed.

"He's also very overbearing."

She scrunched her mouth to the side. It was cute.

She stopped doing that to say, "They tend to be."

"Of course they do. However, perhaps I can break him of that."

She made a surprised pip of a laugh, and I grinned at her.

Then I said, "Bring on the iron maiden."

Her eyes got huge.

"My corset, Idina," I explained.

At that, she actually giggled.

That was cuter.

Cripes, now I was building a bond and making friends with a girl I was probably going to have to use.

Okay.

All right.

Gah!

This sucked.

All of it!

We moved to the dressing area.

She laced me into the contraption.

And it was (almost) worth it after she put a silk scarf over my head to protect my hair and be certain that my makeup didn't get on my dress, before she dropped a very heavy, but outrageously beautiful gown onto my body.

It was pale pink with an embarrassment of rosy-pink beading and sparkling crystals, mostly around the bodice and the empire waist, but also dripping in swoops down the skirt from the center between my breasts at the front and along my spine at the back. These were thick along the hem. And there was a rather long train.

It had cap sleeves made entirely of strings of the crystals.

It also had a set of rosy-pink gloves that fitted all the way up to my biceps.

Completing this ensemble, pink satin slippers that had pointed toes and the beading of the gown.

I stared at myself in the mirror.

I looked amazing.

It was exquisite.

I abhorred it.

"The finishing touches," Idina said quietly, and we moved back to the vanity.

While I sat before her, she slid a diamond-headed comb in the side of my hair. She then draped a necklace around my neck that sat at the base of my throat and was a simple row of diamonds, but there was nothing simple about the stones, their size (each had to be at least three carats), or their perfection. And finally, Idina fixed a matching bracelet over my glove at my left wrist.

She looked at me in the mirror. "You're ready."

"I'm perfect, and it's all because of you," I replied, the words feeling funny in my mouth, because they were true, but I was partially saying them to make her like me so I could ask her to do things that might get her into trouble.

She ducked her head shyly then murmured, "Which scent would you—?"

The door opened, and startled, we both looked that way to see Dad-not-Dad storming in.

"Ah, the lost art of the knock," I bemoaned wryly.

"Leave us," he ordered Idina.

She instantly made to exit.

I got up from the velvet seat, waited for the door to close on my maid, looked to Dad-not-Dad, and snapped, "You shouldn't speak—"

I didn't finish that because his arm went down and across his body, then flashed out, and he caught me on the cheekbone with a vicious backhand.

I reeled to the side, catching myself on the dressing table, the tubs and vials and bottles clattering dangerously, pain exploding through one side of my face into the other.

I started to turn back to him in shock, only to receive another, more brutal blow, one which took me down to sitting sideways on one thigh on the seat.

Stars filled my eyes, I blinked at them as my brain was forced to do nothing but experience the blinding pain, my hand drifting up to touch my burning skin.

"You audacious *trollop*," he clipped into my ear. "Behind closed doors in the stables, of all places, *without a chaperone*."

I was still blinking.

He caught my chin and wrenched my head around, something that also wrenched my neck, and I couldn't control my whimper.

"We will not do this *your way*, you cheap, inveterate *whore*. To continue your education, my fair daughter, a man of noble blood does not marry *a whore*. Lord Remington has had his fair share of whores, and likely will have more, but he won't take one *to wife*."

He let my chin go in order to wrap his meaty fingers around the lower part of my face, the pads digging into my wounded cheek, spiking pain into my eye.

And then he got in my face.

"You will behave like *the lady you are*. You will represent the House of Derryman with *chastity* and *decorum*. You will not cause scandal *to my House*. And you will treat your father *with respect*."

His fingers bit in deeper and his despicable face got closer.

"Remember, I can reward your mother, Maxine, or I can punish her. It's your choice. Choose wisely," he spat, literally, his words landing dots of spittle on my face.

He let me go so roughly, I flew back into the vanity, the edge of it digging into my spine, and I heard at least one lovely bottle crash to the floor.

"I'll have a tray sent up, a *spare* one. You carry *too much weight*. A man wishes to bed a graceful doe, not a charging *heifer*. And I will tell the duke and his son that you, sadly, will not be able to grace their table tonight, you've caught a chill."

You've caught a chill.

I felt his presence move away.

You've caught a chill.

Emeralds scattered over a coffee table.

Don't worry about me, baby, Mom, eyes wild, pretending to have it together, whispered through the bars at me, *Keep yourself safe.*

"She's had a tumble, bring her a cold compress, or a piece of meat," Edgar ordered someone.

"Of course, milord," Idina breathed apprehensively.

I will settle a curse on you and your mother, a bitter curse so powerful, you'll rue the day the words left your lips.

I reached out, curling my gloved fingers around the edge of the vanity, feeling the soft satin encasing my skin, as well as the harsh burn enflaming my cheekbone.

Woodenly, I turned to face myself in the mirror and reached for the top of a pile of crisp, ironed linens that sat in a sterling silver bed, what passed for tissues in this world.

I dabbed at small spots of spittle on my face.

My father was a liar and a cheat, but he'd not once hit me.

Mom either.

I'd never been struck in my entire life.

I set the linen down and reached for the powder puff, carefully righting Idina's artistry.

Do not fear, Countess, I'm changing my mind about the manner in which I'll allow you to address me.

I had to have sex with him.

I sensed I would enjoy this.

I also sensed, once I was gone, he'd know me as nothing but a woman who used him, then threw him away.

I had nothing. No money. I didn't even know where the hell I was. I didn't know how to drive a carriage. I'd been on a horse exactly once in my entire life, on a docile trail ride in a state park on a date with a boyfriend. I didn't even know the name of the city we left three days ago, much less how to find my way back there.

My mother was eating *gruel.*

"Countess, come to bed, let's get this on that cheek," Idina urged from my side.

I turned my head and stared at the large slab of red beef held on a coarse piece of paper in her hand.

It felt like I'd sat there mere moments, but while I did she'd been down to the kitchen and back up.

"I don't want meat on my face," I said tremulously.

"I'll get a compress then," she said hurriedly.

Caught a chill.

If Edgar said that to Loren and Ansley, they…would…*freak.*

I stood.

Idina reared back and gazed up at me.

"Are they still in the drawing room?" I asked.

"Madam, your face, the color is changing, it's swell—"

I wrapped my fingers around her upper arm. "Idina, honey, are they still having drinks in the drawing room?"

She nodded uncertainly. "I think so."

I turned.

The silk and beads and crystals turned with me and the train behind me designed to follow my lead elegantly did so.

I lifted my head, took a deep breath…

And walked from the room.

Chapter Six

Mistake

Maxine

As I hadn't had a tour of the house, I got lost trying to find the drawing room.

But considering there were a bevy of servants around, I startled one by coming on him as he was rushing to do something. He stared in shock at my cheek (which should have shared how bad it was, but I was so out of it, I didn't take this in) as I asked him to point me to the drawing room. He did as I asked.

It'd take me a minute to realize, in my daze, I was making a huge mistake.

In my defense, I had, as yet, not given myself time to process all that had happened to me, to Mom, seeing a me who was not me, but was ill, having a father who proved what I'd known all my life, but had struggled against, he was inherently vile, learning I had another father who was worse.

And so on...

I also had not been around Lord Remington or the Duke of Dalton very long. I didn't know what made their character (but spoiler, I was about to find out).

Last, I had never been struck.

The pain was subsiding, though it lingered and there was a tightness so I knew it was swelling. That said, I was in a state of shock that any human being, much less one who looked like my dad, would take his hands to me.

So, I had an excuse when I did what I should not and glided in my gorgeous gown into the drawing room.

Edgar was the first to see me.

He turned, paled immediately, only for big splashes of angry red to suffuse his cheeks, and he hurried my way.

"Daughter," he bit impatiently, even if he was trying to make it sound concerned, "You're to be abed. It's lovely, you wish to keep us company, but let's get you back to your chamber."

He was crowding me, pushing me backwards, hiding me from the others with his body, and I was still partially in a daze, not to mention a little freaked at seeing him.

I was backing up.

"It's my understanding," I heard Loren drawl, "that the countess doesn't like to be backed somewhere she doesn't wish to be."

His voice was coming around our sides.

I turned my head that way.

And stopped dead.

This was because, if I felt his anger singe my skin in the stables, his fury now was burning me alive.

"What's this?" he whispered sinisterly, his attention locked to my cheek.

His father came up to his side, got a look at me, and his face turned to stone.

Edgar took hold of my upper arm and started jostling me toward the door.

"I'll return after I see my Maxine to bed," he said, trying again to hide me with his frame.

"You'll take your hand off her, or mark me, Derryman, you'll find it difficult to use after I crush every bone in it," Loren threatened.

Edgar's eyes narrowed on me, and he hissed under his breath, "*Punished.*"

And *poof*, my daze cleared.

Shit, what had I done?

He turned to the men, holding me at his side, and in an ingratiating tone, lied, "Maxine took a bit of a tumble. I didn't want to say. It's embarrassing to her. She can be quite awkward."

"She didn't take a godsdamned tumble," Loren gritted.

Edgar made a frustrated noise.

I belatedly started freaking out.

"I think we can all agree she needs to be resting with a compress," Edgar rejoined.

"I think you need to step away from your daughter, Derryman," Ansley stated flatly.

His fingers on my arm tightened.

I winced.

"If you gentleme—" Edgar began.

He didn't finish because he, and I (he took me with him because he didn't let go), reeled back.

Though it was only he who was slammed against the wall with Loren's hand wrapped around his throat, and Loren in his face.

"Release your daughter, sir," he clipped.

Edgar let me go.

"Father," Loren prompted, not moving from Edgar.

I felt my elbow taken with gentle fingers and I was carefully pulled away.

"Was it spending time with me in the stables? Or how she spoke to you before then? Or both?" Loren demanded.

Edgar made low choking noises.

"Loren, my son, step back," Ansley called.

Loren didn't step back.

"Have you hurt her before?" he pushed.

"Loren," Ansley persisted.

"*Answer!*" Loren thundered.

"Loren! *Now!*" Ansley commanded.

I held my breath.

Loren didn't move.

Edgar kept choking.

Loren pushed off and stepped back.

After he did, instantly, he turned to me, and tenderly ordered, "Come here."

I had no idea why (that's a lie, I did, that tone in his lovely, rich voice was mesmerizing), but I went right there.

When I did, he took my hand, lifted it, tucked it against the side of his chest and led us several feet farther from Edgar.

"We shall call your valet, Derryman," Ansley announced. "You're leaving tonight."

No!

I tensed.

I felt his regard as Loren looked down at me.

"Your daughter will remain," Ansley finished.

Oh God. Oh shit. Oh no.

"I did. I d-did. I t-tumbled," I lied (poorly).

"Countess," Loren murmured.

I looked up at him, feeling my eyes were huge, and desperately kept at it. "I did. I'm clumsy that way."

Loren's intelligent brown gaze roamed my face.

He then lifted it to his father.

"He goes, she stays," he decreed.

Damn it, he knew I was lying.

"Lord Remington, may I speak to you?" I asked urgently.

"Good, Eaton, you're here," Ansley said, and I whipped my head around to see him addressing a man who had a slightly more important outfit than the other servants. "Find the Count's valet. He and his staff will be leaving this eve. His daughter and her maid will remain."

Eaton nodded smartly and left the room.

Ansley looked to Edgar and delivered the final blow.

"It will be up to your daughter and my son if they should make their own union, but Derryman, you and I, the House of Dalton and the House of Derryman, will have no such public alliance. Consider this the cut direct, sir, and please do me the favor of never corresponding with me in any way again."

My gaze swung to Edgar, who was staring death at me.

Fix this, he mouthed.

Frantically, I turned full body into Loren, pressing into him.

"Please, your grace, *I need to speak to you.*"

Loren looked down at me.

"*Please*," I begged. "Privately."

He glanced at his father, then back to me and nodded.

Okay.

All right.

A start.

He began to draw me from the room as I thought, *Now what did I do?*

I caught Edgar's eyes, he narrowed his at me warningly, and I started to breathe funny.

I didn't know what I was going to do, but I was going to have to come up with something.

Loren didn't take me to the yellow, cream and green sitting room. He took me to a room that could only be described as a kind of this-world family room. It had warm, deep colors and comfortable-looking furniture, but was still stately and refined.

He closed the door behind us.

And as it would seem was his way, he got there first.

"Countess, you're safe here. I can well imagine what your life has been like with that man, and I'm now realizing the answers to a number of questions, including why you remained in Fleuridia as long as you did. But there are laws against this type of behavior. This isn't your mother's times. We have a new king. And you have my promise, we will see what is to come between us, but my father and I both will be certain you are seen to in the manner to which you're accustomed."

"You can't make him leave," I blurted.

"My lady—"

I tugged my hand from his, wrapped both around the sides of his neck, pulled him down to me, got up on my toes, met him nose to nose, and whispered, "Loren, *you cannot make him leave.* We must mend this. *Now.*"

He stared into my eyes and said not a word.

"I can't explain it, just, I beg of you, *play nice.* Go back to that room, share with your father that I'm a klutz—"

"A klutz?"

"Clumsy. Awkward. Two left feet. *Whatever*...just—"

"I don't know what hold he has on you, my lady," he said gently. "But you shall understand freedom. He will be sent from here, but we will be calling the royal inspectors immediately to investigate this. He'll be jailed, he'll be fined, and he won't be able to get to you again."

Oh my God!

It was getting worse.

If Edgar was jailed, I'd never find Mom.

And even *worse*, he might do something to her beforehand, or if he wasn't around at least to pay whoever was giving her gruel, she'd starve to death.

And the same would befall Maxine.

"Lor...your grace, *don't.*" I squeezed his neck. "Honestly, it's not that I fear him, or I've known nothing but this so I expect it, or anything like that. I just...Dad and I have a weird—"

He lifted his hands to wrap his fingers around my wrists, and he carefully pried away my hold.

"You must know, seeing what we've seen, it's our duty to attend to you, sweeting," he said gently.

Shit, shit, *shit!*

Why did this guy have to be a good guy? Tall and strong and interesting and tender and principled.

Fuck!

"Stay here," he bid. "It'll all be resolved shortly. I'll come to get you, we'll have dinner. In the meantime, I'll send someone to pour you a sherry so you can calm yourself, and bring you a cold compress, to perhaps contain some of the swelling."

With that, he gave my wrists a squeeze then let go.

He started walking away.

Goddamn it.

There was nothing for it.

"He's holding my mother and sister captive until I marry you," I said to his back.

Loren froze, statue still, his back to me.

I sounded like a lunatic.

I had no choice.

"I know it sounds insane, because it is, because he's a huge di...I mean, uh, *cad*, but it's true. I didn't want to...didn't want to...come home. From Fleuridia. Because, obviously, he's awful. And my sister, she's...not right. She needs to be somewhere where they can look after her. And...and...and..."

I trailed off because he'd been turning, slowly, as I spoke, and now he was facing me with a carefully blank look on his face that was scaring the beads off me.

"I know I sound mad," I said quietly. "But it's true. And I was playing his game until I could discover where they were, rescue them, spirit them away, and then...um, I don't know. I was making it up as I went along. But then he hit me, and it hurt a lot..."

I got off that tangent fast when his mood started heating my skin again.

"And I was dazed and made a mistake and now we have to go in there and pretend it's all right and...uh...your grace?"

I called after him in the end because he'd turned on his shiny, black evening boot and was prowling out of the room.

Uh-oh.

"I think I just made mistake two, goddamn it," I snapped to myself.

And then, with no other choice, I gripped silk and crystals and beads in my fingers and flew after him.

Chapter Seven

We're Away

Maxine

I caught up with him because my skirt wasn't tight this time, and the situation meant I was okay with running, something I had to do because his legs were so long and they swiftly ate up ground with his stalking, thus I had no choice.

He entered the drawing room with me on his heels, announcing, "As mad as it is, you were right, Father. She has a twin."

Edgar's gaze sliced to me.

But they...

Already suspected?

Oh my *God.*

This was a *disaster.*

"And her mother didn't commit suicide," Loren continued, words that made me stop in my tracks. "She's still alive."

"Make one more move to that door, Derryman, I won't call Loren off this time," Ansley warned.

I looked back at Dad-not-Dad, who was now stopped in *his* tracks on his way to the door.

He appeared both flipped out and fit to be tied.

But...

My mom from this world *killed herself?*

"I don't know what he's been up to or why," Loren went on. "But the Maxine you met at the sanitorium is now being held captive, along with her mother, so this Maxine would be forced to return from Fleuridia and marry me."

"You met my daughter?" Edgar asked Ansley, sounding horrified, so horrified, in those three words, he gave it all away.

I knew this with the glance Ansley shot at him before he spoke. "You were delaying," the duke returned easily. "I'm not a man to be put off. I set some investigators on it. Found your daughter. Discovered the story of her horse accident and subsequent head injury. But we had a lovely few visits, as she is that. Although frozen in time at the age of six when she was hurt, she's most lovely."

Horse accident.

At six.

Head injury.

Okay, that explained a few things.

I wondered if Mom had figured that out yet.

"Is she Maxine?" Ansley asked Edgar, then nodded to me. "Or is this Maxine?"

Edgar pushed his nose in the air and stated, "You cannot hold me here. I'll be away in the now. And *you*," he sniped at me, "can be trapped here and live to your dying breath with your regret."

He then made a move to leave.

This didn't work out too well for him because, within about five seconds, his ass was in a chair and Loren was looming over it, glowering down at him.

I witnessed it, and except for seeing moves like that in movies, I'd never seen anything like it.

It…was…*awesome.*

"Do you wish to suffer the indignity of being tied to it?" he asked Dad-not-Dad in the kind of tone you'd ask someone if they wanted another glass of champagne.

Okay, not awesome.

Bad…freaking…*ass.*

"This isn't to be borne!" Edgar shouted in return.

"You will speak when spoken to," Ansley proclaimed and then said, "Ah, Eaton, again, so sorry, but we're having a busy night. First, a cold compress for the countess. Second, please detain all of the count's staff. If you must be creative in that endeavor, do so."

Eaton, who weirdly seemed no stranger to such an order, assumed a look of contented excitement.

"Not Idina. She isn't involved in this," I put in. "She was only hired right before our trip."

"Have a care with the maid," Ansley agreed. "And last…" He turned his head to his son. "Loren?"

"Maitland," Loren grunted.

An unusual but attractive smile spread on Ansley's lips before he said, "And send for Maitland, *urgently.*"

Who was Maitland?

Eaton took off.

"Ummmm…" I hummed.

"Now, dear, are you Maxine, or are you named something else?" Ansley inquired of me.

Okay, things were happening fast here, and I had to think fast as they happened.

But it didn't seem to sound crazy to them that I had a twin, though I was sensing they didn't know about the parallel world, but Ansley had even met her. Also, they weren't surprised Mom was around, though that was strange considering the mom of this world took her own life.

However, maybe…just maybe…

"Satrine," I declared, giving them the name Mom nearly gave me. "My name is Satrine. I'm Maxine's my twin sister." I turned to Ansley. "And we need to find Mother and Maxine. It's not nice, where he's holding them, and he took Maxie out of her hospital, and she needs to go back as soon as possible."

"Oh, my dear," Ansley murmured sadly. "You've been enduring such a trial."

I so totally had.

But there was no time to feel sorry for myself.

"I would like to go back to the city now, please."

Ansley tetched and stated, "Of course. In a day, or two, we shall return—"

"No, really, *now*. Just, um, if you could, please get someone to bring a carriage around and Idina and I—"

Ansley's brows flew together. "You don't mean to go back to Newton on your own."

Newton.

Newton was the name of that city.

Remember, Maxine, I mentally noted. *Pay attention, listen, learn, and you might be able to pull this off.*

"When I say their situation is dire, sir, I mean that gravely," I shared. "There's no time to waste."

Ansley looked to Loren.

Loren was watching us, but when he had our attention, he looked down to Edgar.

"Where are they?" he asked.

"Go," Edgar sniffed, "straight to hell."

Okay, they had the concept of hell here.

Or maybe just the curse word?

"You can offer the information, or you can give me my most fervent wish for this evening. That being to crush each bone, one by one, in the hand you took to Satrine. Your choice, sir. Provide it, please," Loren returned.

Totally...

Bad...

Ass.

Edgar sat there, glaring up at Loren, and then...*shit*...he smirked.

"I have contingencies in place, of course. Maxine, she's no use to me, the woman..." he made a spitting noise without spitting, which wasn't nice, and pissed me off, because "the woman" was my mom.

But he wasn't finished.

"It is only I, in person, who can release them. And if I, in person, do not do that or send regular communications with a certain code so they'll know they're from me, communications sharing how they are to be treated, it has been instructed they are to be eliminated."

Eliminated?

I released a loud, terrified gasp.

Edgar's head bobbled because Loren had a hold of him by his neckcloth, saying, "Well then, arsehole, we're taking a trip."

"Unhand me!" Edgar shouted.

And that was all Loren could take.

Crunch!

Fist to the face.

And Edgar was on his hands and knees on the floor.

Loren pulled him up to just his knees with his hand in Edgar's hair and...

Crunch!

Another fist to the face and Edgar was sprawling on his stomach on the floor.

"It seems..." Loren said through his teeth, staring down at Dad-not-Dad with repugnance, "your situation is escaping you. I advise, sir, take stock."

"Son," Ansley said mildly.

Loren didn't move or take his attention from the form he'd, no other way to put it, laid...*right the fuck...out.*

Bustling and snorting with fury, Edgar pushed up to his feet, scrambled out of reach of Loren, and turned fired eyes to me.

"They're dead!" he sniped. "And you've killed them."

"No!" I cried, starting to dash to him.

Loren caught me and pulled me to his body.

"I will be released *this instant*," Edgar demanded. He jabbed a finger at Loren. "You will marry *my daughter*." He turned and jabbed a finger at Ansley. "*You* will offer your respect and referral to the Count of Derryman. If you do not, within four days, they're both *dead*."

"Is he bluffing?" Ansley asked, still speaking calmly.

"I cannot tell," Loren answered, just as calm.

I pulled from Loren's hold, whirled on him, and channeling Violet Crawley, I snapped, "I don't give *a fig* if he is or not. Do what he says. We can figure it out after." And that was when I lost it, and shrieked, "*I want my mother back!*"

"Figure it out after?" Loren asked carefully.

"I don't know, get a divorce, an annulment, whatever," I replied.

His jaw tilted sharply to the side.

"You will have his child. My blood will be Dalton!" Edgar proclaimed. He finished on a bellow. "*It is my final legacy!*"

Oh my God!

This dude was totally crazy!

I twisted to him. "Can it, *Dad*."

"You insolent—"

"If you insult me again, I'll..."

"What?" he bit.

What indeed.

I had no power.

I had nothing.

I could do nothing.

To, or more importantly, *for* anybody.

I closed my eyes, dropped my head, and whispered, "God, I just want my mom and I wanna take her home."

I felt it before it happened.

Fire in the room.

Nope.

An inferno.

My head jerked up.

Ansley thundered, "*Loren!*"

I wrapped both my hands around my throat as I watched Loren drive Edgar to his knees, and then he picked up a heavy crystal *objet d'art*, forced Edgar's hand flat on a side table, and savagely brought the bottom of the crystal onto Edgar's hand.

I heard bones break and cringed.

Dad-not-Dad roared with pain.

"Are we riding to release your wife and daughter?" Loren asked.

"I'll personally have you brought in front of Noctorno," Edgar threatened, pomposity still firmly in place, but it was now edged in pain. "He will not stand for this treatment of a member of his aristocracy, no matter who you are."

"Please do. I'll enjoy watching you explain why you faked your wife's suicide, imprisoned her with your injured daughter, hid that I should have been released from our contract twenty years ago, hid your other daughter's existence for reasons that could only be considered nefarious, then forced her to carry out your social climbing, and took your hand to her. In Tor's short reign, he's been quite lenient with the abuses of power of his aristocracy. I'm sure he'll be heavily disappointed *in me.*"

Edgar was breathing through his teeth, which gave me the sense that Loren was using sarcasm to make his point.

Seemed King Noctorno was a pretty standup guy.

"Shall we head to Bellebryn now?" Loren asked.

Edgar slowly turned his head and looked up at Loren.

He then whispered, "You will pay."

A chill slithered down my spine.

"Choose. Bellebryn? Or Newton." He lifted the crystal thing an inch. "Or do you need more incentive to make your choice?"

"Newton," Dad-not-Dad spat.

A gasp was heard at the door.

A woman in a black dress with a white apron and a little white cap with a black ribbon threaded through it was at the door holding a wet cloth on a silver tray and staring in dismay at Loren and Edgar.

"Your compress, Satrine," Ansley said quietly, moving to the maid. He took the cloth, murmured, "Thank you, dear," and she rushed away.

He brought it to me.

"Your eye, my lady," he instructed. "And then, as charming as that dress is, I believe you'll need to return to your rooms and change into a traveling costume. It seems in short order, we're away."

I took the cloth and put it to my eye.

Wow, that felt good.

Okay, maybe one down?

Mom and Maxine safe.

And one to go.

Getting home.

I let out a huge breath.

And for the first time in three weeks…

I hoped.

Chapter Eight

Reunion

Maxine

"Milady, awaken. We're here."

I started awake and looked around the carriage.

It appeared it was mid-morning. There were sunny skies, but (don't ask me, it was a thing with this world), I felt the freshness to the day.

And outside the carriage windows, I saw across the wide sidewalk, the massive, four-story graystone (instead of brownstone) where I started this nightmare.

We were in Newton.

Allow me to catch you up on the things I'd learned.

First, there was a reason Idina was reserved (and I should have figured it out myself).

Dad had bullied her, threatened her and demanded she report everything about me to him in the minutest detail.

She was terrified of him, and she not only liked me, she'd been a lady's maid for a while (in fact, her last "lady" had passed away, and her grief was exacerbating her reserve), thus she explained, "As you know, the relationship is sacrosanct. You don't inform on your lady. Ever. I didn't want to do that to you, but I didn't know how to deny him."

So that explained that.

Next, when you only stop to attend the call of nature, have a quick cup of tea and a sandwich while the horses on your carriage were being switched out before you were on your way again, a three-day journey turned into a day-and-a-half one.

Onward from that, I'd ridden in the more opulent carriage in which I went to Pinkwick House, doing this with Idina. Ansley and Dad-not-Dad rode in the carriage behind, with two riders on horses flanking them, probably as extra manpower so Edgar wouldn't think to try anything.

This meant I couldn't pump Edgar, or Ansley for that matter, for information so I could continue to ride this wave that seemed to be breaking my way.

However, Idina wandered off, as it was clear servants didn't hang with their "betters" when other "betters" were around (though, once she'd shared what had gone down with her and Dad-not-Dad, we'd had some lovely conversations in the carriage, in between jostled bouts of trying to sleep, that was).

So, while I sipped tea and nibbled sandwiches, I spoke with Ansley.

Fortunately, he was figuring everything out (translation: fitting what he was learning to what he knew, even if most of it wasn't true, and I didn't enlighten him, which sucked, and felt like lying, because it was, and that wasn't fun due to the fact he was a super cool guy).

This being, after Maxine had been injured, for whatever dastardly ends Edgar had (Ansley hadn't figured that out yet), Mom and I had been banished to Fleuridia and Edgar had faked Mom's death.

Incidentally, she'd killed herself in her favorite gazebo by sitting in it and setting it afire. Now, either the woman was in such pain she wanted to make absolutely sure that pain ended (though, she did it in what had to be an excruciatingly painful way), or she didn't actually kill herself.

Truth be told, Edgar was such a dick, I had my suspicions that she didn't.

In fact, I was putting things together too, and I had the feeling the asshole killed her.

Ansley knew she didn't, because we were racing to rescue her.

However, he now surmised her charred body was *not* hers, and instead a cadaver, or some poor "street urchin" (his words) that Edgar used in place of his wife. Taking this further (to myself, in reality, my this-world mom was dead, and I didn't like to think of that), since they didn't have DNA or other such things they could test, it was easy for him to get away with something like that.

Considering I was banished in Fleuridia with my mother through all this, while Ansley ruminated on these things, I could play dumb.

Sadly, we didn't often stop to change horses, and when we were stopped, we weren't for long, so finding out my mom of this world burned to death in her favorite gazebo was unwanted, but informative news.

It was also all I got.

Last, this time, unlike last time, when I wasn't trying to sleep, or talking to Idina, I'd paid attention on the journey.

They didn't have signs that announced village names, but there were ways to find out (like the sign above Sydawell Mercantile, in what had to be Sydawell). I also saw bakers, butchers and blacksmiths (obviously) and shingles out for thatchers and dressmakers and coopers.

Most everything was clean and sparkly and had a bent to a mashup of Disney's Fantasyland and an exceptionally conceived renaissance festival.

It was fascinating and amazing to see.

But it looked like the good news was, I'd get one thing accomplished, having Mom back and Maxine safe wherever she needed to be.

However, now that I could focus on it, my worry was that the bigger hurdle would be getting us back home.

Which meant I had to ponder the concept we'd have to figure out how to be there for a while until I could find a way home.

I was no baker, butcher, or dressmaker, and neither was Mom.

But I was the one out free in this world, so I had to do some reconnaissance and at least know a little something about where we were stuck.

So I was thinking ahead, even if I couldn't quite plan ahead.

Loren, by the by, took off while the servants were loading the trunks on the carriages back at Pinkwick House.

He swung up on a big steed with a glossy, luxuriant brown coat and black shading along his nose and around his feet. He tipped his chin to me with a low, sexy, "Countess," then dug his heels in his mount and took off, long cape flying behind him and everything.

It was *hot*.

I hadn't seen him since.

Which was a bummer.

That was, it was a bummer until now.

Since he was currently striding across the sidewalk looking gorgeous wearing tan breeches, a navy-blue coat, a white shirt that was frothy at the chest (and he worked it), this underpinned by a black waistcoat and grounded in black boots.

No neckcloth.

I'll say it again.

Hot.

He came to my carriage door and opened it.

I was suddenly very aware that I still had the hairdo I had at dinner a day and a half ago.

Though with a "traveling costume" which was a lot like my last one, except the train was longer, it was a salmon color, and there was silk frogging on the jacket and around the skirt above where it kicked out wide in a graceful sweep.

He offered a hand, I took it, and he helped me down the steps.

When I got to my feet, I looked up at him.

"Hey," I whispered.

His head twitched, as did his lips, and he replied, also in a whisper, "Hey."

"Milady, I'm sorry to interrupt, but...your hat," Idina called.

I turned and saw nothing but, suspended in what seemed like mid-air out the carriage door, the massive salmon concoction that was mostly stiff netting edged in darker silk binding or ribbon that had a variety of frills and flips with some feathers sticking out.

I felt myself blush (blush! God!) as Loren reached out and took the hat (because this felt strangely like he was reaching out and touching my person), then he offered it to me.

I took it, put it on my head, and now Idina, clearly one to be thorough, was proffering an enormous, gilded hatpin.

Loren took that too, and again extended it to me.

My cheeks flamed as I took it.

Why was this embarrassing me?

Better question...

Why did it feel so intimate?

It took effort, but I focused entirely on pinning the hat to my head, because, if I didn't hit a hank of hair, that pin would hurt.

I managed that, then, as Ansley strolled our way from the carriage that came to a halt behind us, somewhat desperately, I noted, "I'm pleased we made such good time, but can we go immediately to where my mother is?"

At this point, I saw the carriage Ansley was in clip clopping away.

I glanced around.

No Edgar.

"Where's Father?" I asked.

"Being taken to jail," Ansley answered.

Not blushing anymore, I felt the blood drain from my face.

"What? Why? He must—"

"My lady," Loren said quietly, and I turned to him. "Your mother and sister were released hours ago when Maitland and I arrived here."

I stared.

"Your sister's doctor has been called and will arrive with haste," he continued. "We offered your mother a maid, a meal and a bath, but she won't let go of your sister and is refusing anything until she sees you. I have assured her you are well, and your arrival is imminent."

I grasped the froth of his shirt in my gloved hand. "Where is she?"

"She's inside."

"You brought her here? How was she? Is she okay?"

"Okay?"

"Healthy. Well. Strong."

"We didn't bring her here. She was already here. She was imprisoned in the cellars."

I stared again, though I spoke through it this time.

"But he…took me on a carriage ride, blindfolded, before he showed me where she was."

"I'm afraid, if he did that to you, it was a ruse," Loren murmured.

"She was…in the same house with me all along?" I said in a small voice.

Could that even be?

She was right there?

With me?

While I was Eliza Doolittling, she was suffering *in the basement?*

"I'm sorry," he said in a quiet tone.

It was then I noticed a man who was big and tall and strong, like Loren, and handsome, like Loren (though not as handsome as Loren), strolling out the front door to Dad-not-Dad's townhome.

And I wondered what in good hell I was doing standing on the sidewalk talking to Loren.

I bound-thighs ran to the steps, up them, past the new hot guy, and pushed into the house.

"Mom!" I shouted.

"Baby?" I heard from my left.

Edgar's sitting room.

I ran that way.

And there she was, dirty, disheveled, much thinner than I'd ever seen her, in a filthy, white nightgown from this world, Maxine in the same state, clinging to her side.

Right, Mom and I had scrimped and saved and made do and dug in when necessary, and dug ourselves out when that was necessary. I'd started working at fourteen to help. We weren't hard. But we were survivors. We were tough. We were strong. We endured.

But in that moment, I burst into tears.

I hobbled her way and threw my arms around her.

Maxine recoiled, but I grabbed her with us as Mom burst out crying too.

We clutched and we wailed, and I was pretty sure my hat poked her in the eye, and she didn't care.

I ripped away from her hold, but caught her face in my hands, laughed through my tears because she was right there, so close I could touch her, and I was *touching my momma*, and I cried, "Oh my God! I was *so worried*."

"Honey, I'm fine." She held Maxine close. "*We're* fine."

I turned to Maxine. "Maxie," I whispered. "Hi."

She studied me, biting her lip and sticking close to Mom.

"But...what happened to your eye?" Mom asked.

"I'm fine too," I told her.

"Girl," she warned.

I sighed. "I don't think I have to tell you, the dude's a dick."

Her eyes lit in a blaze of glory.

Okay, time to move past the bad, and get back to the good.

I took a step back and clapped my hands.

Maxine jumped.

Mom kept hold on Maxine and gave me a slow shake of her head.

Right, no sudden movements or noise.

Noted.

"Okay, baths. Or food first? And clothes," I declared in a forced calm voice.

Mom took me in fully this time. "Good Lord, girl, what are *you* wearing?"

Oh.

Wait.

Mom hadn't been around and about to get the lay of the land like I had.

No.

Wait.

I turned and saw Loren, Ansley, and new hot guy standing in the wide doorway, watching the reunion.

Right.

I had to do this, and fast.

I moved in, trying to take care not to freak Maxine, and put my mouth to Mom's ear.

"I'm Satrine," I whispered. "This is my twin sister, and your other daughter, Maxine. They don't know about the worlds. They think Edgar faked your suicide. You've been banished with me to Fleuridia for two decades. Edgar's going to jail now. We're living in a renaissance festival, or more like a Victorian festival, actually, it's kinda both, but a really good one. And I'll fill you in on the rest when we don't have an audience."

I swayed back, caught Mom's eyes, she was staring at me like I'd lost my mind, and then I announced loudly, "Of course, baths first."

"Are you okay?" she asked.

"I'm okay if you're okay," I answered. "And the rest, we'll sort out later."

She held my gaze.

Then, thank you God, she slowly nodded before she turned to Maxine and asked softly, "Would you like a bath, my beauty?"

"Yes, Momma," she answered timidly.

Momma?

Oh.

Of course.

She looked like her mother.

Because she kind of was.

God, this was so *effed up.*

"I don't want her out of my sight," Mom told me.

"I'll take care of everything, Countess," Idina said from behind me.

Mom's attention shot back to me, she dipped her chin and mouthed, *Countess?*

I mouthed back, *Go with it.*

Out loud I said, "Follow Idina. I'll get you some food and bring it up. Yes?"

Mom nodded.

I walked out of the room with them, to the staircase, where I gave them over to Idina, who walked them up the stairs.

I stood at the foot and watched until they were out of sight.

Quickly, I went back to the sitting room.

"When she's back to herself, I'll formally introduce you," I told Ansley.

"Of course," he replied on a slight bow.

I didn't know how "back to herself" I could make her, since she was three inches shorter than me and twenty-five pounds lighter (maybe now more like thirty-five, fucking Edgar) and clothing for rich people was made to order, and I had a shit-ton to fill her in on without anyone hearing, but I'd figure that out later.

"I'll go make us all some tea," I decided.

"The house servants are still here, my lady," Loren noted.

Get yourself together, girl.

"Right, right, then I'll call for some tea."

I went to the cord Edgar always pulled when he wanted something, and I pulled it.

I turned back to them.

"So the guy...uh, guy-er-guard who was watching them?"

"He's been neutralized," Loren said quickly.

"Neutralized?"

"He's lying in a pool of his own blood downstairs. We've called for the mortician. That'll be cleaned up in a jiffy," new hot guy said.

I wasn't sure what I did just then, but I knew my mouth was hanging open while I did it.

"Loren is a no muss, no fuss kind of chap," new hot guy shared while sauntering to an armchair and throwing himself in it sideways, one long, substantial leg tossed over an arm, the other stretched out on the floor.

Stiffly, my body, and eyes, shifted to follow his voice and his movements.

"Allow me to introduce you to my friend, Marlow Gladstone, the Baron of Maitland," Loren drawled.

"Errrrrrmm…" A girl in an outfit a lot like the one at Ansley's house, except the dress was gray, and the cap had no ribbon in it, was standing at the door.

She stared at me.

Yes, I'd been kept under wraps.

Food was served, but I was always out of sight when it happened, and the halls were cleared when I was in them.

Dad-not-Dad was taking no chances.

"Could you bring us some tea?" I asked. "And scones, jam, cream, that sort of thing," I added, since I was starving.

"Excellent, cream tea at ten in the morning. I like this one, Lore," Marlow Gladstone declared.

Fantastic.

They only did those teas at a certain hour.

Well, whatever.

I was the lady of the house, in a sense, at least for now, so I could do what I wanted, and we were having it at ten in the freaking morning.

"Yes, um...*milady?*" the maid asked after the fact if I was, indeed, her lady.

I nodded to her.

She scurried away.

The men were all regarding me.

"Father was stingy with who he allowed to see me," I explained, and at least that wasn't a lie.

"Ah," Ansley murmured, then took his own seat.

Loren decided to grace another doorjamb, which was a good call, he looked fab doing it.

Though, it was disconcerting that his eyes never left me as he was doing it.

Until his head turned abruptly right before...

"Excuse *me.*"

A man appeared in the doorway wearing the same exact outfit as the bad guy in the *Aristocats* and looking more than mildly miffed.

But he'd lost his officiousness as he stared in shock at me.

"Lady Maxine?" he breathed.

"No, Lady Satrine," I stated, like he should know better (fake it 'til you make it, girl). "And you are?"

"Wishing to know who *you* are," he retorted.

"Edgar Dawes's other daughter," I replied, like I was reminding him.

Total confusion, unsurprisingly. "His other—?"

"I answered. Your turn," I cut him off.

"Carling." He squared his shoulders. "I run this house."

"Then you'll see to it that my mother and sister have something suitable to wear after their baths, but more importantly, a hearty meal," I ordered.

His face paled. "Your mother..."

"Father faked her death. I'm sorry, I know this is a shock. But I must ask you to get over it and take care of them. Father imprisoned them downstairs and—"

He looked away and hissed to himself, "I knew there was someone down there. He's always got something going on down there."

That didn't sound good.

"Well, yes, you were right," I declared imperiously.

"And you, you were in her rooms," he went on.

"Yes again," I confirmed.

"We thought it was one of his mistresses," he shared.

Ick.

Moving on!

"It wasn't. It was his daughter. Me. Now, they've been poorly handled. We must see to them."

Something else swept his face.

Something awestruck.

Hopeful.

"Lady Corliss is...*here?*"

"Yes," I said softly. "And Maxine."

"She's with her Maxine," he whispered solemnly.

My stomach clutched.

Something was not right here, something tragic and awful.

Carling pulled me out of these thoughts as he snapped to attention to the point I heard the heels of his shiny shoes click together, and he stated, "They are of a late fashion, but we never disposed of the lady of this house's wardrobe. We will see it unearthed. We will see it freshened. And immediately, I shall call the modiste and tell her to attend the lady urgently. We will outfit the countess as she is—"

"Carling," I called.

"Yes, milady?"

"Just clothes and food for now, please?"

He nodded. "Right away, madam. *Tout de suite.*"

And then he bustled off.

Right, I made it through that.

And I needed a break before whatever came next.

I made my way to the settee, and fortunately my dress was so tight, there was no other way to collapse onto it except gracefully.

This, I did.

I pulled out the hatpin, threw it in a bowl that sat on the table in front of me, swept off the hat and sent it sailing.

I then slumped down, rested my head on the back of the couch, and said, with extreme feeling, to the ceiling, "Thank God that's over."

"If you don't want her, my man, I'm officially scratching my name on the top of her dance card."

Ah hell.

I forgot about my audience.

How did I do that?

I sat up and turned to Maitland, who was the one who spoke.

His eyes were on me, and he made a manly noise in his throat when I stopped lounging, and I had to admit, I felt that noise in a very private part of me.

"Brother," Loren growled.

That hit in *several* private parts.

Maitland tore his eyes from me and grinned unrepentantly in Loren's direction.

"I apologize, I forgot myself for a moment," I mumbled.

"Forget away," Maitland allowed.

"You're as close to me as blood, please help me not to spill any of yours by ceasing panting over my betrothed," Loren warned silkily.

His...

What?

I straightened further.

"So you've made your decision," Ansley remarked.

"There is no other decision to make," Loren replied.

"Seems sound to me," Maitland noted.

"I've no idea what this takes, a dress, flowers, the temple," Loren went on.

"We'll see it done in three weeks," Ansley declared.

Loren's gaze landed on me.

"Excellent," he murmured.

"What are you talking about?" I asked.

"Our wedding," Loren stated instantly. "Which will happen in three weeks. And I'd like to make a single request." Pause while I held my breath, and then, "No hat."

So *this* was what was next.

Shit.

Chapter Nine

Agreement

Loren

As suspected, she didn't make him wait.

She popped off the settee and minced her way to him, that beautiful arse swaying, her lion's eyes firing.

"May I have a word with you, your grace?" she demanded in the form of a request.

"You may call me Loren, Satrine, as you'll be my wife in mere weeks," he replied.

She stopped at his side, ignored what he said, and invited. "Father's study?"

She didn't wait for his answer, she continued into the hall.

Loren gave himself the pleasure of watching her arse moving for long moments before he cast his eyes through the room, catching Maitland smirking and his father beaming.

Then, he followed her.

She stood with her hand on the door and swung it closed when he cleared it.

He turned and opened his mouth.

She lifted a still-gloved hand, palm out his way.

"I get to go first this time."

He crossed his arms on his chest and murmured, "By all means."

She drew in a big breath that made her glorious chest rise.

She let it out saying softly, "I'm sure I don't have to explain to you how indebted I am for your assistance. Mother and Maxie are free and safe and we're all together again. And I honestly don't have the words to express what an honor it is that you would even consider continuing to care for me, and my family, by making that sacrifice. But allow me to assure you, Mother and I have been going it alone for some time. We're used to it. She has Maxie...er...*back*, and as long as we're together, we'll be fine."

"Even an enemy of the king does not lose hold on his possessions once he's convicted of breaking the laws of the land," Loren replied.

"I'm...sorry?" she asked.

"He will be tried. He will be convicted. He will serve a term in prison. And he will be fined, likely heftily. However, he won't be in prison for the rest of his life and will come out in possession of everything he had when he went in, save the fine that is to be paid. And while he's incarcerated, he has rights over those possessions."

"All right," she said quietly.

"That is, should he wish to turn his wife and daughters away with nothing, he could do that."

Her lovely, expressive face registered understanding before her mouth did with, "Oh boy."

"Indeed," he agreed.

She stood with that for a moment before squaring her shoulders and stating, "That's all right. Mom and I have been in worse pinches."

This was interesting news.

"You have?"

"Father didn't exactly keep us in the lap of luxury. He was miserly with our care. It didn't matter. I had her and she had me. We survived. We'll do it again."

Gods, she was something.

And, perhaps, this was an explanation as to why she persisted in attempting to do everything without pulling a bloody cord to call a servant.

"Satrine—"

"You're very kind, Lord Remington—"

"Loren."

"—but I'll take it from here."

No.

She wouldn't.

He had never in his life met a woman so poised and spirited, so in possession of a singular depth of feeling, with a sense of humor and open naturalness to her personality.

She was herself at all times.

One-of-a-kind.

And he would have her.

"You're contracted to me. You, personally, have no say in that matter."

She shook her head. "I'm not, Maxine is."

"Maxine is incapable of bearing the terms of the contract, the same cannot be said for you."

Her brows knitted in consternation. "But, it wasn't me who was promised to you."

"No, it was a daughter of the Count of Derryman, which you are."

Her face scrunched up in frustration.

Gods, he wanted to kiss her.

"I'll be reading this contract," she declared.

She'd be doing nothing of the sort since he was lying through his teeth.

He was also going to have her.

And nothing, not even she, was going to stand in his way.

"We barely know each other," she stated.

"My father met my mother a week before their wedding, was in her presence thrice, and he fell madly in love with her and still mourns her passing."

Her eyes widened. "Are you saying you're falling in love with me?"

In lust, that deed was done.

In love, they'd see.

"You're soft, yet strong."

"Sir," she said urgently as she began moving backwards.

That was because he was moving toward her.

"You're cunning and clever," he went on, moving wide to herd her from the door.

"Lord Remington."

"Loren."

"I—"

"You dress impeccably."

"I didn't pick my clothing."

"I don't care."

"Ummmm…" She drew that out until she hit a chair in front of her father's desk, corrected the wrong way, and presently, she was pinned against the desk with his body.

"I like looking at you," he murmured to her mouth, one of the many things on her he liked looking at.

"Your grace."

He lifted his gaze to hers and growled, "*Loren.*"

"Oh my," she whispered, her chest rising and falling rapidly, brushing against his own.

"You'll forgive my brazen language, I'm sure," he said. "But you've also got an arse I'm fairly certain was made for my hands."

"Wow," she breathed.

"Mm," he purred.

"My family is currently a mess," she reminded him.

"Nothing like stability to sort that," he retorted.

"I know nothing of Hawkvale. At all. I didn't grow up here."

"And that matters?"

"My sister—"

"Yes, let's talk about Maxine. If your father cuts you off, which I feel certain he will, who will pay for her care?"

"Shit," she let slip, an odd word, perhaps improperly used, but since, either way, in Hawkvale they had its equivalent, it was not one he didn't understand.

"Indeed," he replied.

"I'm not sure a strong marriage is formed on the foundation of a woman who needs care for a head injury."

"I've seen them formed on less."

"Where I come from, you marry for love."

"Fleuridia has these fanciful notions, but that doesn't mean they're unsound."

"Do you have a response for everything?"

"Do you have any real, solid reason not to wed me?"

That stymied her.

He grinned.

She watched his mouth form it.

Fuck, he needed to *kiss her.*

"Satrine."

Her eyes drifted up to his.

And then she destroyed him.

"I don't want you to feel beholden to me," she whispered. "What you're offering is more beautiful than words can describe. And I'm grateful for it. But years pass, and thoughts inevitably form. As do regrets. You're a fine man, so very lovely and protective. You deserve to marry for something as fine as you. Not a woman who needs your money and protection to take care of her family."

"You've just described every aristocratic marriage in the realm, save the king's, and that was arranged by a malevolent she-god in hopes of bringing a plague to the land."

"Wh-what?"

"The troubles."

"Oh, yes. Those."

He spanned her hip with his hand.

Held her eyes.

And whispered. "Marry me."

Her body melted partially into his.

"God, that was sweet and hot and romantic. You're like, *impossible* to refuse," she mumbled.

"Then don't refuse me."

She studied his throat.

"Satrine."

Her gaze shot to his.

"Make me one promise," she demanded.

"What is it?"

"You'll never hate me."

"Why would I do that?"

"Just...promise."

Loren was an excellent judge of character.

One might even say expert.

So he had utterly no qualms answering, "I promise."

"Right then, let's do it."

Bloody...*yes*.

"Sealed with a kiss," he murmured, lowering his head.

"Oh God, if you're as good of a kisser as I think you are, I'm about to *die*," she said, watching his mouth fall.

With that mouth against hers, he caught her eyes and warned, "Prepare, sweeting. But rest assured, when I'm done with you, I'll revive you."

She mewed a mew he felt in his cock and arched into him automatically.

He slanted his head and took her mouth.

She opened her lips, accepted his tongue, then sucked it in deeper.

Bloody hell.

He knew it.

Magnificent.

He wrapped his arms around her and pulled her up, deep into his body.

She wound her arms around his neck, holding fast, and opened herself further.

No surprise, she gave. She gave it all.

And all of it was her.

Sweet and tart and generous and warm and tangy and heady.

Before what was happening in his cock made him take it too far, he tore his lips from hers, used his hand at the base of her head to tip it back, and ran his nose over her chin and down her throat.

Her scent was as intoxicating as she was.

Yes, by damn, he'd made the right decision.

And she had too.

"I'm not feeling revived, Loren," she gasped to the ceiling.

He lifted his head, righted hers, and smiled down at her, her swollen lips and her sultry eyes, but ignored the discoloration under the left one.

"Floating?" he asked.

Her dazed eyes narrowed. "Gloating?"

"That happens when my fiancée presses so close when my mouth is on hers, it's like she's trying to absorb me."

"Warning, my lord, it doesn't matter how handsome you are, arrogant is not a good look."

Snatching her ever closer, he roared with laughter.

"Ugh, he's smug. The *worst*," she complained, pushing with no real strength at his shoulders.

"Feel revived?" he asked.

"I'm wearing a hat to our wedding."

She wouldn't.

She'd give him anything he wished.

That was who she was.

He knew it to his soul.

It was why he chose her.

So he could give that back.

"We'll be happy, Satrine," he promised.

A shadow passed over her face before she covered by quipping,

"Whatever you say, dukeling."

"You think that's a cut, but you could say practically anything, still pressing your body to mine, and I wouldn't care a whit."

She tried to pull away.

He kept her close.

"You said no backing you in a corner," he remarked. "You made no demands about a desk."

It was then, he triumphed.

Because her beautiful eyes grew huge.

And then…

For the first time since they met…

Holding her in his arms…

He got to watch as she dissolved into laughter.

Chapter Ten

One Day at a Time

Satrine

"You're going *to what?*"

"Mom, *chill out,*" I whispered.

She was pacing, wearing a satin and lace negligee set that was *everything.*

I was up on her bed, my legs curled under me, wearing much the same, but mine didn't have lace, and it was clear Edgar skimped on a few things, because Mom's bedclothes were *rad* and mine were just awesome.

Maxine was out like a light in Mom's bed due to the "draught" the doctor had given us to help her sleep.

Yes, the doctor had come and gone.

He did this with Mom flatly refusing to let Maxine go back to the hospital.

With Loren, Ansley, Maitland, the doctor and me all watching her, while she wore an outfit Carling unearthed from the rafters (or wherever) that was okay, but it wasn't like any of mine (mine were more Victorian Cinderella, hers was more *Dangerous Liaisons* vixen), she decreed, "She's mine now. I have her back. We'll arrange instruction so we can learn what we're doing. We'll hire a nurse who just knows what she's doing. We'll come to you for regular appointments so she continues to have the care she needs. What we're *not* going to do is let her go again."

Damn, Mom was *into* being Corliss of this world.

The doctor seemed thrilled by this and replied, "She's grieved for you greatly."

"Well, that's over," Mom returned.

"Being with her loved ones in a stable environment will do her wonders," the doctor continued.

"Marvelous!" Mom cried, twirling her hand in the air. "We're all agreed!"

She then stopped *just* short of raising her fist to the heavens and exclaiming, "We'll never go hungry again!" which meant she was a bit overdoing it, but, whatevs.

So, apparently, imprisonment in a dungeon for nearly a month with her daughter-not-daughter and meals of gruel and broth wasn't enough to break my mother.

I should have known.

Obviously, they'd had their baths, eaten, and gotten dressed. Then Mom settled Maxine in with some sketchbooks by a window, met Ansley, Loren, Maitland, and the doctor came and went.

Mom returned to Maxine.

I wanted to go with her and get to know my "sister," but Loren took me aside before I could do that.

"There's much to be done," he declared.

I was thinking wedding.

"I'm sure."

"We need to go to the constabulary and make our statements."

Oh, well then.

Not wedding.

"Father and I'll do it now. We'll take you and your mother tomorrow."

I nodded. "Right."

"We'll be needing to make other arrangements."

I should not push this, considering the fact I was going to find a witch as fast as I could and let Loren off the hook, but still.

I hoped this world had peonies.

"Carling had a chat with Father as you were demonstrating how much you enjoy my mouth."

I squinted my eyes. "It wasn't like you didn't have a bit of fun, mister."

"Oh, I did indeed," he whispered, a lazy, sexy look in his eyes.

My clitoris pulsed.

Yikes.

Mental note: he was better at the comeback than me.

"Hello, fancypants Marquess. Carling?"

There you go. He was way better with the comeback.

He grinned.

God, he was going to kill me.

Gorgeous, normally.

Knock-you-off-your-feet when he was happy.

The grin died and he said, "Not for now, but Carling shared some things that were concerning. Your mother's return will cause a sensation. Your existence will as well. But it's untoward me, or Father, or even Marlow stay with you."

"Bummer," I muttered.

"Pardon?" he asked.

"Um...nothing. It's French," I said hopefully.

"What?"

Oh shit!

"Fleuridian," I amended.

"It is?"

"Do you speak Fleuridian?"

"Fluently."

Ah hell.

"Let's stay on track, shall we?" I sidestepped and prompted, "You can't stay."

"Your mother would be an acceptable chaperone, but we have a townhome two blocks from here. There'd be no reason *why* we'd be staying, especially me, except one. You'll have enough interest coming your way, we don't need to provide reason for more."

Yet more proof they were prudish here.

Not fun.

"Right," I replied.

"There'll be guards at the front and back doors."

Wait.

"Why?"

"Your father didn't keep great company and regularly had unsavory visitors."

"Wonderful," I said to the ceiling.

"Satrine," he called.

God, I hated that he couldn't call me by my real name with that beautiful voice of his.

I looked back to him.

"This will be over soon."

"Okay."

"There's that word. What does it mean again?"

Man, I needed to keep my guard up.

And that, too, sucked.

"It's a language Mom and I made up. It means 'all right' or 'fine' or 'good.' At least it does this time."

There you go times two. I was getting good at lying on the fly (Lord help me).

His lips curled up. "Okay."

Yes, he was killing me.

I smiled at him.

He bent and kissed my forehead, which was outrageously adorable and sweet.

When he backed away, he bid, "Enjoy your reunion. I'll return for breakfast at nine."

"Righty ho."

He shot me a hot smirk, a fabulous wink, and then he took off.

I couldn't spend a lot of time with Maxine because she didn't need to be overstimulated while she was getting used to being out of basement prison and in this house with me and Mom. Mom was her constant, so Mom stuck with her.

Though, before he left, the doc assured me that with time, she'd warm to me. I just had to be patient.

As for me, I went about checking out the house, making sure Idina was good, and casing the joint for stuff we might be able to sell or just plain steal so we could have our own pocket money (and then some) should anything go south, or we found a witch for hire, and we'd need the cash to actually hire her. I scored by finding two books that taught French/Fleuridian in the library. I also dealt with the fact that the servants were practically dancing on air (there was a definite feel of "Ding Dong, The King is Dead, Long Live the Queen!").

Eventually, I shared dinner with Mom and Maxine (who was timid and quiet, but I was right, really sweet), then preparing for bed.

Which brought us to now.

And me telling Mom I was marrying Loren.

"Okay, babe," Mom said while pacing, "the man is gorgeous, like, whoa, *what?* gorgeous, but this is not a good idea."

"I know. That's why I have an alternate plan."

She stopped and gave me her look that said, *Spill.*

"We're going to steal a few of Dad-not-Dad's things we can sell, and otherwise purloin whatever we can so we have a stash so we're not destitute should he cut us off, which Loren tells me he can, and considering he's a massive douchebag, he will."

"Damn," Mom mumbled.

Good to know I wasn't dim. She hadn't thought of that either.

"Then we're going to find a witch."

"How are we going to do that?"

"I don't know. This world is cray-cray. They probably have storefronts. We'll just wander town. Ask around."

"What I mean is, how are we going to find one, explain what we need, and get home without that other witch's curse turning everything to shit because we told someone else we're from a parallel universe?"

Oh man.

I hadn't thought of that.

She put her hands on her hips, glanced at Maxine, then looked to me.

"Honey, I think we're stuck here."

Something happened inside me that felt suspiciously like my heart leaping in joy, but I not only didn't let on, I didn't even admit to the feeling.

"What about Keith?"

She looked away.

Yeah, she liked Keith. He was a good, solid guy. One of the first who treated her right.

Really right.

"Mom, we'll get home."

She turned back. "How?"

"I don't know. Two days ago, it seemed impossible to spring you. Now, you're sprung and wearing satin. We just can't give up."

"And complicating things by marrying a hunk? How will that help?"

"I didn't say it would *help*. I just said I was doing it. Or letting him think I am."

"Why?"

"Because he wants to marry me, and he crushed Edgar's hand for me after..." I pointed to my eye, "*this*."

Mom's face got hard.

"Good," she snapped. "But you know, he also showed up downstairs, doing this making *no sound*, even while breaking in a locked door. It just happened that I was staring at that door longingly, which I'd become prone to do, and I caught him coming in. He snuck up on that jerk who was watching us and, *zzzzzziiiip*, slit his throat."

Holy cow.

Eek!

"Didn't blink," she stated. "Not even a flinch. The guy dropped. He nabbed his keys. His buddy tossed a blanket over him so Maxine, who was thankfully sleeping, wouldn't see. And then he came to the bars, opened the door, and said, 'How do you do, my lady? I'm Loren Copeland, Marquess of Remington, and your daughter sent me to fetch you.'"

"Cold," I muttered on a shiver, though it was also totally hot, and I had feelings of pride (and instantly denied them) and wonder (and instantly denied those too) and maybe titillation (because that was badass, and I didn't deny that part).

"Ice." She shook her head. "Now, our guard was always eyeing Maxine. Coming in too close. Touching her. Freaking her out. It was a matter of time, especially with that Edgar and you gone, which meant Edgar wasn't coming down checking on us regularly, before he took liberties. And he wasn't real gentle with me. Still."

Mom grew alert, her eyes locking on me.

Then she whispered a warning, "Maxie…"

"*Satrine*," I hissed. "And this is all effed up. That guy was gonna rape Maxine and he was rough with you?"

"He's very dead now. Your fiancé slashed his throat."

I was oh-so-totally okay with that.

Which was nuts.

I caught myself from falling back and hitting Maxine, and instead fell forward and moaned, "God, we're in crazytown."

Again, her gaze slid to Maxine. "She hit her head falling off a horse as a little girl?"

My momma had fallen in love.

That wasn't surprising either.

"Yes," I confirmed softly, gave her a second with that, and then pressed on. "Mom, we have to go to the constabulary. We have to get our story straight. Fleuridia. Where we lived. *How* we lived. How Dad-not-Dad brought us back. Who knows what he's going to do and say?"

She came and sat in front of me on the bed. "Not much he can say, baby. You look exactly like her. And I look exactly like a portrait in his study. If no one knows of our world, then what other explanation can he have?"

I'd noticed that painting, after Loren kissed me stupid, when we were on the way out.

At least we had that going for us.

"We have to have it down," I pushed. "Twenty years of it. Or an outline we can stick to. And you're going to have to have a crash course in living in his world and doing it like a lady. And sorry to say, that part is going to have to start tonight too. Loren's going to be here at nine for breakfast."

"You like him."

"He saved you."

"No, you like him."

"He's hot.

"*No*, you *like* him."

Gods damn it!

"Yeah," I whispered. "I like him."

She assumed an expression I never saw on her. A mix of sad and worried and happy and hopeful.

I totally got that expression.

Living it.

"You're right, as ever, my brilliant daughter," she said softly. "We have no choice. We go at this one day at a time."

Yes.

That was it.

That was always it, what we always did.

I grabbed her hand and held on.

And repeated, "Yeah, Mom. One day at a time."

Mom then struck her claim (again).

"You, me and, well…Maxine."

I held fast and repeated firmly.

"You, me and our Maxine."

Chapter Eleven

The Countess of Derryman

Satrine

A few things of note for the start of our next day in this world.

The first, when I was in middle school, I used to panic about big reports or projects I had to do. I never really knew why. It was just a block.

Whenever this would happen, Mom would dig in with me. Stick by my side all the way.

I was an A-B student, mostly Bs (admittedly, a few Cs). I didn't love school, but Mom impressed on me how important it was to be educated for a variety of reasons, including future employment, cultivating an open mind and nurturing what she thought was essential: a lifelong joy of learning.

Plus, I was good at it.

Every report or project I did with Mom, though, got an A.

By the time I hit high school, I was over that block, and all on my own made honor roll every semester from freshman to senior year.

In other words, wearing negligee sets, in a parallel universe, pulling an all-nighter in Dad-not-Dad's library, Mom and I dug into our latest big project to face not only what was to come at the constabulary, but what was to come for us in that world.

In order to kick its ass.

And, maybe a bit bleary-eyed, we met the day ready to do just that.

The second, I should have let Carling call the modiste.

The outfit Mom had to wear to the constabulary had huge skirts, including an overskirt, heavy embroidery and poofy sleeves. It was nowhere near as awesome as mine, and peering out the window of the carriage, it didn't look anything like what we saw the ladies strolling the pavements were wearing.

And everyone knew, when you had to inhabit a role, you had to have the proper costume.

I was, by the by, in all violet this time. Not a traveling outfit (in other words, no little jacket), but an outdoor one. Long fitted sleeves, high collar that tickled the skin under my jaw, silk covered in lace from chin to toe, with some thick grosgrain ribbons stitched over at the sides of my knees where the thick gathering of skirts flounced out.

The train was ridiculous.

And I picked this dress because the hat that went with it was the biggest I had. Violet with hints of black in a massive bow, a bunch of trailing ostrich feathers and massive rosettes (yes, all of that).

The instant I put it on before we left the house, Loren busted out laughing.

Which was precisely why I made that choice.

Now, however, Mom and I were sitting at a table in a room at the constabulary, dainty china teacups in saucers filled with tea in front of us, and we looked like we were waiting to be called in to two different auditions for two separate period dramas.

Mental note: first thing when I got home, tell Carling to send for the modiste ASAP. Mom needed to be kitted out for this world. And we needed to take advantage of Dad-not-Dad's money while we had access to it.

That meant, although the hospital was returning Maxine's personal things that day, she was getting a ton more dresses (and slippers and whatever).

And I was augmenting my own wardrobe.

He brought us to this world, he'd pay for us to exist in it.

One way or another.

For the now, I had to concentrate.

Because we weren't in there alone with the inspector.

We had witnesses.

The marquess and duke were standing at our backs like sentries.

The inspector, wearing his stuffy black uniform with chest panel buttoned across the front with brass buttons, sat opposite us.

He had a pewter fountain pen in hand, held over a sheaf of papers contained in a battered leather folder, and had gazed for long seconds at the bruise under my eye before he said, "Shall we begin?"

Mom and I had a plan.

We'd researched it as thoroughly as we could and blocked it all out.

I knew this world better, so I was going to take the lead.

But Mom was a mom.

Her daughter(s)'s health, welfare and safety were on the line.

Thus, instantaneously, she thwarted said plan and took over.

"Yes, indeed. My other daughter is home without me. Both daughters have recently, and *throughout their lives*, endured trials and tribulations at the hands of *their father*. So allow me to share the fullness of grievances I have against *my husband*, and do that swiftly, so I can take my one darling daughter, and return with her to my other darling girl, as they *both* need me."

She was gearing up to another "We'll never be hungry again!" moment, I could feel it.

"Momma—" I tried to cut in.

She turned to me, reached out, curled her gloved fingers around mine, locked eyes with me, and shook my hand.

"Darling, please."

Oh shit.

Back she went to the inspector, but she didn't release my hand.

"Beware, sir. My husband is a consummate actor. I know this, as he was acting with every breath when he *won me*."

"Milady," the inspector murmured in a way it seemed he was going to say more, Mom just didn't give him the chance.

"It was not simply when I gave him twins, but before, *well before*, when the mask slipped. But mark my words, it all fell apart when I gave him my girls. I, to this day, *do not* understand it. My daughters were not the first twins born in this universe, or any other."

I pressed my lips together at the "any other" thing.

"But he had an uncommon, *unhealthy* aversion to them. He considered them an aberration. It was mad. He sent Satrine away after I first nursed her. I couldn't believe it. I was *undone*. I begged and pleaded, but he'd hear none of it. Once she was gone, he wouldn't even admit to Satrine existing. She'd vanished from his life, and he considered that vanished from this earth. But for me, it was the worst moment of my existence." She drew in a delicate breath. "Sadly, I would have others."

"Countess," the inspector tried to get in there again.

He totally failed.

"Bereft of one child, I showered attention on the other. Only for her to suffer an accident that no mother, no parent, except my husband, could abide. But she was my baby. My other child lost to me, I didn't even know where my Satrine *was*. I grieved for her every day and loved her sister all the more for her loss. I had every intention, I assure you, sir, *every intention* to love and care for my Maxine, regardless of her state, for as long as I was breathing. To my *deep* misfortune, this option was cruelly wrested from me."

I gave her hand a *tone it down* squeeze.

She did not tone it down.

"Off I was packed to Fleuridia. And off Maxine was packed to cold, desolate hospitals where others, *not her mother*, cared for her. Make no mistake, they did this well, and I am grateful to them. But I am *her mother*, and it should have been me. The *only* consolation I had was that he sent my Satrine with me. I *finally* had my other daughter back."

I heard Loren and Ansley shifting behind me, I gave her another squeeze, but Lady Corliss was on a roll and there was no stopping her now.

"I'd no earthly clue, until recently, that he'd staged my death. Though, at long last, that does explain his behaviors. I would spend the next twenty years worried about Maxine, but with my Satrine. We did not have much. He kept us in a secluded cottage, well away from any populace, and disallowed us to have contact with anyone but each other. Now, I know this was because he did not wish for anyone to see me. And, perhaps, Satrine."

Holy wow.

We hadn't come up with that.

It was a stroke of brilliance!

"He had someone watching us, and if we should try to reach out to another, or attempt escape, something I gathered my daughter with me to do, we'd be punished by being brought back and having something we needed dearly taken away. Satrine getting new clothing when she was growing, our allotted flour for the month so we had no bread, no oil for our lamps so we had no light, fuel for our fires, that sort of thing."

She sniffed, like the next memory overwhelmed her.

"We had a kind husband and wife who provided us provisions. They did not hide they felt most sorry for our plight. They spoke the language of the Vale, and we could often convince them to sit for some tea, a quick game of tuble or enjoy an afternoon dram."

Dram?

"But they were sent to us by him, and those were the only interactions for which we did not earn a harsh rebuke." Her voice changed like she was uttering an afterthought. "And we did make friends with a few lonely roamers."

She came back to herself, thankfully didn't wander down the "lonely roamers" path, and her tone turned downcast.

"And regrettably, Edgar felt it was his duty to visit on a rare occasion. However, it had been veritable *years* since we'd seen him. We suspected that perhaps our confinement was over. He had forgotten us, and we could make moves to be free. We'd begun devising plans to sally forth and find our way on our own, without his meagre support. However, with his usual dastardly timing, he arrived some months past and demanded Satrine stand in Maxine's stead for her betrothal. Obviously"—she lifted her nose—"we declined." She then turned to Loren and murmured, "No offense, your grace."

"None taken, my lady," Loren murmured back.

I returned to pressing my lips together.

Mom returned to the inspector.

"I hope you don't need me to share in detail the indignities we suffered as Edgar made clear he did not accept our declination, and all that came after. I will just say, right here and now, regardless of the trauma, it was worth every moment to *finally* have *both my girls*. Do what you must to him. We're together. So we have everything we need."

She sat back, eyes still set on the inspector, and I fought the need to jump to my feet and shout "Brava!"

The unknown-until-now twin thing, check.

The mom-fake-death thing, (kinda) check.

Dad-not-Dad being a total asshole, check.

Us not knowing how to speak Fleuridian, check.

Us possibly not behaving like your average ladies, check.

Playing the weak, defenseless female card without any real weakness, check.

I shouldn't have worried.

Mom always had it going on.

I didn't get those As for nothing, that's all I was saying.

The inspector opened his mouth to speak.

And the door flew open, slamming against the wall.

We all jumped, and I felt the heat of Loren's body suddenly at my back.

But Carling swooped in, followed by two men in rough clothing, one well-built and rather good-looking, one slender and tall, with a kind face.

They were followed by a red-faced, angry constable.

"We will be heard!" Carling declared.

"Carling, what on earth?" Mom asked, and hopefully it was only me who heard the nervousness threading her tone.

Carling took a step forward, bowed to her, straightened, and said, "My lady, allow me."

"I sense you two know each other," the inspector noted.

"Indeed!" Carling cried. "I am Rutherford Carling! *Eighth* generation houseman, with the running of the Derryman House!"

"My guess is, you have something to say," the inspector drawled.

"I will allow no quarter to offend my lady with further grief and tragedy," Carling proclaimed.

Whoa.

Carling had some pluck.

"Will you not?" the inspector asked.

"No," Carling snapped. "I will not."

And the man was not backing down.

He turned to Mom and his face gentled.

"I'm sorry, but it must be said," he decreed softly.

"I'm afraid it must," Mom muttered.

Carling looked at me.

"My lady," he whispered.

"Carling," I whispered back, having no clue what he was about to say.

He shifted his attention to the inspector.

"What you see on my younger lady's face is not the first mark my employer made on one of the females who *should* have had his loving devotion and care."

Mom's fingers tightened around mine.

This was not good.

The real Lady Corliss...

And maybe even Maxine?

I stared at Carling, who was fit to be tied, and I knew.

I dropped my head.

Loren's hand curled over my shoulder.

"But I can assure you, it is with horror that I share it was the *least* of his transgressions," Carling continued.

What?

I lifted my head.

"No, I'm not speaking about the fact he was an unkind employer, and often more than unkind, rather cruel, especially to the females in his employ, who are my charges, but I was powerless to help them."

"Oh my gods," I breathed.

"No," Carling carried on. "I'm not speaking about the fact he gave no references, so one couldn't leave his employ even if they wanted to, for they'd never find another position, and they were forced to stay tied to him, like indentured servants."

At that, Mom and I both gasped.

"No, I'm talking about the fact that Beacher here"—he turned to the handsome fellow—"*and* Hagley"—he turned the other way and jerked his chin to the slim fellow—"*both* consummate grooms *and* consummate horsemen, warned his lordship *not* to put his little daughter *on* that large and unpredictable of a horse—"

Oh...my...*gods*!

Mom shot out of her seat.

Everyone looked to her.

I rose, getting close, holding on tight, staring at her ashen, distraught face.

"Mom."

"Carling, don't," she whispered to Carling.

"I'm sorry, milady, it has to be known," he replied.

"It does," the inspector said gently.

Carling hurried on, jumping forward in the story, thank God.

"She blamed him, as she would. Who wouldn't?" Carling asked a question with an answer everyone knew, so no one answered it. "He was beside himself with fury at what he considered her audacity. He *never* did anything wrong. He *never* took responsibility for mistakes he might make. To be honest, for twenty years, simply to stop his wife from demanding he return her daughter as well as stand up for what he had done and perhaps feel *a hint* of remorse for his actions, I thought he'd murdered her in that gazebo."

"Bloody hell," I breathed.

Carling sniffed the air and regarded Mom.

"I knew you didn't take your own life. You loved that gazebo, for one. You took Lady Maxine there to nurse her. If you felt it necessary to leave this world, you'd never have done it there. Not *ever*."

Okay, good news, Carling pretty much corroborated our story, in a sense.

Bad news, it seemed us being there meant maybe we'd just accidentally falsely exonerated Edgar for murder.

"I need to get back to Maxine," Mom murmured.

"Momma," I whispered.

She looked to me. "I'm fine."

She wasn't.

The dad of this world hurt the me of this world, a me who was now her daughter as sure as I was.

I didn't blame her, and I wasn't surprised. If I were her, I'd probably feel the same way.

But this further complicated things.

By a lot.

Now it was a definite that I had to get *all three* of us back to our universe, and how would Maxine handle that?

"If you have what you need, inspector, I'd like to escort the countess home," Ansley said.

"I feel we do indeed, from Countess Derryman. Though, I'll need a few words with Lady Dawes before she goes."

"I'll stay with Satrine, Father. Take Lady Corliss," Loren said.

"I'll send the carriage back," Ansley replied, then to Mom. "My lady?"

She took his offered elbow, whispering, "My gratitude, your grace."

Loren stood at my side as I watched them walk to the door.

But Mom stopped there.

And I stared as Carling stiffened with stunned surprise when Mom curled her fingers around both his arms, then went in to kiss his cheek.

"You are a good man, Rutherford Carling," she said quietly.

His face stained red and he shifted awkwardly, pleased and uncomfortable with the sentiment.

"Beacher, Hagley, thank you," she went on.

"Mum," Beacher said.

"Milady," Hagley mumbled.

She nodded to them, nodded to Ansley, and with her head held high, the Seventh Countess of Derryman strode through the door.

And they were away.

Chapter Twelve

Turn around the City

Loren

"Dear heart," he called.

She was beside him in the carriage, her ludicrous hat on the seat opposite them, her head turned, eyes aimed out the window.

Her mood…unknown.

"Satrine," he whispered when she didn't respond.

"I didn't know he…hurt her," she told the window. "Either…*her*."

Loren clenched his teeth at the thought and aimed his gaze out his own window.

He turned back when she lashed out, "Gods, I want him *dead*." Her attention came to him. "Is that terrible? Does that make me like him?"

"No, sweeting. You're angry. You heard some very ugly things today, and it hasn't been long after you endured other very ugly things."

"You know, we were always okay *without him*. It didn't matter we had to scrimp and save and make do. But the minute he showed his face, oh *noooooooo*." She dragged that last out. "It all went to hell in a handbasket."

Hell in a handbasket?

This language she created with her mother in their seclusion was, unsurprisingly, as amusing and clever as she and her mother were.

"Every incarnation of him is evil," she spat. *"Pure evil."*

"Satrine—"

"He hurt my sister and beat my mother!" she shouted.

Loren watched the bluster wilt, her face started to collapse, she tried to turn away, but instead found herself pulled into his arms.

Her body bucked as she attempted to hold back a sob.

"If you release it," he murmured his advice, "you'll feel better."

"She's beautiful."

"Your mother?"

"Yes, but also Maxine."

He smiled. "Of course, darling, she looks exactly like you."

She pulled away and locked eyes with him.

"She will never meet a handsome man, be backed into a desk and kissed stupid."

As lovely as her words were (even the "kissed stupid" part, as they were strange, but obviously a compliment), they nevertheless swept the smile clean from his face.

"She will never dance at a ball, and she'll never drive a carriage and she'll never, I don't know…there's so much she'll never do, because of him, I can't even say it all."

"Satrine—"

"I know exactly what happened. He decided what she could do…*at six*…and she was going to do it, no matter the consequences."

Loren grew quiet not only because there was no reply to be made, she was correct, and she was correct to be horrified by it, but also because she needed to get this out.

"Do you know how much it hurts when someone hits you in the face?" she asked.

He felt his mouth tighten, for he did, but it infuriated him that she did as well.

"It hurts, Loren, *a lot*. And I can take it. But he did that to *my mom*."

"He can't harm any of you again."

She sat facing front and crossed her arms on her chest, declaring, "I'm going buy so many gods damn gowns and hats and ribbons and slippers and boots and…and…*whatever the hell else I can think of*…so if he cuts us off, we'll have outfits for years we haven't even worn. I don't care if we're living in a shack."

"However, you won't be living in a shack," he reminded her. "You'll be living in a townhome or a country manor or a chateau or a castle, depending on where we are in the Northlands."

She looked to him. "I didn't forget, honey. But don't cut into my drama."

Honey.

Mm.

He liked that.

And she was now jesting.

It was a tossup, but he might like that better.

"How many properties do you own?" she asked.

"Many," he answered.

"Ballpark me."

"Sorry?"

"Give me a hint."

He again deliberated briefly on the odd language she and her mother devised after years of having only each other for company before he did a mental count.

He then said, "Six. Sorry, no. Eight."

She stared.

He grinned.

"Well, one could say *that's* a step up from a three-room cottage miles outside of Aisles," she quipped.

He kept grinning, because for the first time in his entire life, the vastness of his wealth and privilege had meaning.

"One can indeed say that, my dearest."

She turned more fully to him.

"So, here's the thing, my handsome, noble fiancé, I'm done with all of that. It's now your turn."

He was confused.

"Pardon? My turn?"

"My drama. Good-bye. It is officially no longer all about me. It's time to get to know *you*."

Loren felt his neck get tight.

"So, we have a few minutes before we're back home, tell me something I have to know about Loren Copeland, the handsome Marquess of Remington," she pressed.

"Right now, as is my state almost constantly when I'm around you, I wish to kiss you."

Her sweet tongue came out to wet her lower lip, he turned more fully to her as well, but she said, "Not that. Something else."

Right.

Something else.

How about the fact you've asked, and I feel unable to answer, which makes me wonder if my father is correct, and I have some addiction to danger, living for years eradicating King Baldur's final followers in the way my then prince, now king, instructed me to do, which is not for a gentlewoman's ears.

As such, much of what I did after is also not for your ears, as I was either seeking adventure, balls-deep in woman, righting wrongs in often brutal ways or participating in fights that either simply came about because of the company I was keeping, or I caused. I have vast experience both hitting men in the face or getting hit in my own. Thus, I know precisely how that feels to give and to receive, as you witnessed me doing the same to your father, and then some.

At the end of it all, the last twelve years I used might for right, creating death and destruction, and now…there's you and I have no bloody clue what to do with you.

"Loren?"

"Often, my father would take me out of school for the holidays a day, or two, or even a week early, because he would have some great adventure planned for the two of us, and we would need to give it the proper time. Traveling to Bellebryn so I could pilot a galleon around the bay. Going to Paisall to attend their tournament, which is the best in all the lands. Even sailing to Lunwyn to ski, or down to Benies, simply because Fleuridian warmed chocolate is delicious, even better than you can find in Lunwyn, though that is hotly contested between my father and me."

"Which side are you on?" she asked softly.

"Benies. Father took me there solely so I could compare. It vexes him that I came to what he erroneously considers the wrong conclusion. Though, what I did not share with him was that I liked Benies on the whole better than anywhere else at the time, because I was fifteen years of age. And thus, I was thinking with only one part of my anatomy, and Beniesienne women have no issue exposing a grand expanse of décolletage."

She smiled a small smile at him.

He took her hand, drew her nearer, and watched his gloved fingers fiddle with her own.

"We are all we had. Father made it so we made the most of it."

"I know something about that," she whispered.

Good gods.

She did.

He lifted his gaze to her.

"You can kiss me now, my lord," she said.

Thank the gods.

He did.

He was drowning in her by the time the carriage stopped, and as he lifted his head, he saw she was the same.

She was desirable always.

Dazed by the desire he wrought on her, it was nearly impossible to resist.

"I think we should tell our driver to take a turn around the city," she suggested.

"I think I do not wish to have you for the first time on a bench seat in a carriage with the curtains closed so it will not only be uncomfortable, but it will also be hard to see you," he returned.

She frowned.

He touched his mouth to hers.

Her footman opened the door.

She was out, forgetting her hat, so it was he who carried it inside.

She was grinning at him, turned to look over her shoulder as she walked through the vestibule, hands lifted to the sides of her head and twirling, all while she teased, "I envision feathers and bows and streams and *streams* of tule flowing from my wedding hat."

As a reply, Loren tossed the one he carried into the sitting room.

She laughed.

"Satrine, baby! Is that you?" her mother's voice came from down the hall, and it struck Loren, never in his life had he heard a lady shout.

There was something… *particular* about that.

These women—both of them—were glorious and graceful, and yet artless.

It was astonishingly refreshing.

"Yes, Mom," she called back.

"Come here, will you?"

She reached out a hand to Loren, he took it, and they walked to where the voice came from.

Her father's study.

They stopped just inside, in unison, because they both, at the same time, were hit with all they were seeing.

Loren's father stood at her back, just to the side, while Corliss sat at the desk, neck deep in ledgers.

Maxine was curled into a couch at one side of the room, watching the proceedings, a finger twisting in her hair, though not with nerves. Her mother was near, therefore she seemed quite content.

And what appeared to be the entire household staff (*sans* a groom and footman) stood at attention in a line across the other side of the room.

Corliss lifted her head when they entered and asked, "How did it go?"

"It went."

Loren reported more fully, and he did this to his father. "Multiple charges. Abduction. Abuse. Extortion. Coercion. The magistrate is ruminating on bail, but the inspector says, considering Tor's recent rulings on this kind of behavior for his nobles, it's doubtful he'll see light before his trial, and definitely not for some time after it."

"Marvelous," Ansley replied.

"Moving on!" Corliss declared, her gaze still on her daughter. She then stated, "Honey, did you know we're rich?"

"Mom—"

"Like, filthy, *stinking* rich. Ansley says so."

There seemed a curious warning note to Satrine's next, "Mom."

"So obviously, until he can get word to the bank to close his accounts to me, things need to be sorted. Ansley sent someone to check, and Edgar hasn't had a chance to do anything yet. We're still good. I'm withdrawing a chunk of change. Ansley says he has a safe and can keep the cash there for us. So no matter what, we'll have that."

Her hand still in his, Satrine took a step forward and tried yet again. "Mom."

But she'd lost Corliss's attention.

"Carling," she called.

Carling stepped forward and snapped his spine so straight, Loren felt a twinge in his own.

"Right here, my lady," he stated the obvious.

"His grace has gone over the books with me, and he shares you're woefully underpaid," Corliss announced.

There was a twittering among the staff, but at a hiss from Carling, they quieted.

"Milady," was all Carling said to Corliss.

"That will not do." She looked down at the ledgers, then back to Carling. "I'm giving you all a one-hundred-pound bonus for your loyalty."

No hiss was going to stop the twittering *that* caused.

"And the duke counsels me that you're all paid at least fifteen percent less than the going rate for your positions. Each of you will be brought to the upper grade for your salaries. And I'll be adding an extra ten percent to that."

There was shuffling, gasps, and a few muted cheers.

Loren watched his father's lips quirk.

"Carling, I bid you take your staff and discuss this with them, see if this is amenable," Corliss continued.

Carling sounded choked, as he would, since it was indubitably amenable, when he pushed out, "Will do, milady."

She swept an arm over the ledgers and stated, "You and I will go over these books and we'll see every member of my staff is compensated appropriately."

"That would be appreciated, milady."

"And please, allow two extra days paid leave per annum to each staff member, and an extra afternoon free every week as well. Ansley added the suggestion that we might be understaffed, which means you are all not only underpaid, but required to go above and beyond to see to the running of this house. Therefore, you and I will speak about whether we need to hire someone else to cover for those times when staff is at their leisure or add so you can adjust the workloads of your charges to more appropriate levels."

Carling coughed, sniffed, muttered, "My apologies," then in his normal voice said, "It will be done as you wish, madam."

She stood and smiled. "I'm delighted. Can you do that presently, but also, send for the modiste?"

"Right away, Countess Derryman," Carling said smartly.

"None of that, I'm Lady Corliss only, my daughters are Lady Maxine and Lady Satrine." Corliss pierced Carling with her gaze. "We are family here now, Carling. At long last."

There were some sniffles amongst the crowd and Carling's voice was thick when he said, "Indeed, Lady Corliss."

She drew breath in through her nose and addressed them all.

"Thank you for your time, and all of your hard work. Please, now, enjoy a cup of tea and have your discussions with Carling."

Loren pulled Satrine out of the way so they could file out.

The last to go was Carling, and he closed the door.

Satrine and he turned back to Corliss when she spoke.

"Ansley told me that the household will run as if Edgar were here, regardless if we are, also regardless of what might happen to him. It had to be done because it had to be done, but there was no time to waste. The books will be adjusted before I'm cast out, and the household will be managed as the books are set at that time, especially if Edgar has no idea

I've meddled. So all will be well with the staff."

"You rock, Mom," Satrine said strangely.

"I know, honey," Corliss replied.

They started giggling.

Maxine giggled with them.

Loren looked to his sire, who was gazing indulgently down at Corliss.

Yes.

He had no idea what to do with any of these women.

Women who had been held down, abused, neglected, exploited, and ended that taking pains to see to people they did not know and giggling.

And for the first time in a very long time, Loren had reservations about his own decision.

Because Satrine Dawes was grit and gumption, and he was blood and death.

And Loren was thinking she deserved better.

Chapter Thirteen

Future to Discuss

Satrine

I was in a new day dress, and so was Maxine.

I was curled into a corner of the settee with a cup of tea and a plate of biscuits (in other words cookies, delicious ones), reading a book.

The book I was reading was about the war between Lunwyn and Middleland that reunited both countries to Lunwyn.

It was a book I sought at a local bookstore (needless to say, to catch up on things, Mom and I had been doing a lot of reading) because Ansley had told me, in his role in the king's service, Loren had spent some time in former Middleland (now again Lunwyn). He'd been routing out conspirators who would not only see the restoration of Middleland, but also attempt to regain the territory they conquered years before from Hawkvale.

Maxine was sitting in front of the window at her easel, the plethora of paints Mom bought her scattered around, painting a picture of the pretty park that was across the street from the house.

My sister, by the way, was a really good painter. It looked impressionistic, what she did. I was no expert, but I'd seen things in museums which weren't half as pretty.

In front of me, scattered on the table, waiting for Mom's return, were a bevy of huge sheets of thick-stock paper on which were drawn a variety of flower arrangements we were to look through and settle on for my wedding.

I was ignoring them because I was engaged with what a dick King Baldur of Middleland was and wondering how on earth he could have any followers at all, much less ones who wished to restore him to the throne after he was deposed.

It was two weeks after Mom gave the staff huge-ass raises and Dad went down for a variety of this-world felonies.

News on that front, he hadn't been offered bail.

Even so, we had not, as yet (and I was concerned about what this might mean), been cut off from Dad's funds.

That said, it didn't matter anymore.

Mom told me later, when we were alone, that the withdrawal she made, "Ansley assures me is enough for us to buy our own townhome, staff it, and for me to live the life befitting the lady I am, doing this until I die. This as well as take care of Maxine until she goes. Though, he also assured me I shouldn't bother myself with that worry, as you and Loren would be around to do it."

In other words, we were set to carry on in this world for, apparently, ever, which was a load off my mind.

Because not only did witches not put out shingles, we'd discovered, after the whole Minerva-she-god-plague-on-the-land situation, practicing witchcraft wasn't verboten, but people were twitchy about it.

I mean, Idina nearly went into vapors when I casually tried to discuss how to find a witch.

I couldn't click my slipper heels together and ask to go home.

So, although Mom and I hadn't officially discussed it, it looked like we were there for the long haul.

Honestly?

I didn't really mind.

We'd had a couple of sit downs with her doctor to understand what Maxine needed and had hired a nurse who was a groovy chick, but we didn't much need her because Maxine was settled and content. And Mom and I made sure one of us was around at all times so she had stability, and although Maxie and I weren't giggling together, she'd definitely grown used to me (as demonstrated with how we were now).

Then there was the fact Mom was getting off on being Lady Corliss.

Also, the staff were in raptures at our "family" and they whistled while they worked (I am not kidding, though some hummed and others sang).

The curtains had been thrown open (literally and figuratively, Dad-not-Dad liked it dark) on the house. A ton of knickknacks and bric-a-brac (no matter how expensive, it was ostentatious and oppressive) had been cleared away. Mom had purchased some warm throws (autumn was around the corner) and bright toss pillows (Mom was doing a lot of shopping, then again, she'd never been loaded, neither had I, so there you go). She'd also moved around some furniture and had other pieces carted off to be reupholstered or auctioned because she didn't want them anymore. She'd even had two rooms repainted in lighter, brighter colors.

The place had totally been changed from dark, stifling evil den where the villain lurked to bright haven where the fairy princesses lived.

It rocked.

For my part, I hadn't seen Loren since we had dinner together (all of us, not just him and me alone), the night after it all went down at the constabulary.

We'd had a mini-makeout session prior to him leaving for the evening, and then he informed me he had "business to attend" and he'd be back in "no later than a fortnight."

Now, I was in a quandary.

Because I was thinking we were stuck there.

I was also thinking Mom was hunky dory with that because being a countess and rich as shit far from sucked, but also she adored Maxine.

As an aside, we'd managed to dodge the deluge of former friends and acquaintances sending letters or calling at the door in order to check out the Countess Come Alive, because she had the excellent excuse of sharing she was "finding her feet back home" and would "reenter society" during her beloved daughter, Satrine's wedding to the Marquess of Remington.

To do this, she had a new secretary, a widowed woman named Palma who worked part time while her adorable toddler daughter toddled around the study, and she wrote letters explaining this to everyone, and declining dozens upon dozens of invitations.

For now.

Yes.

As ever, we were taking each challenge as it came.

Maxine was, according to the doctors, blossoming under the care of her family.

We were set, money-wise.

I dug Loren a whole lot (though, I'd like to have the opportunity to get to know him better).

And due to his absence, the wedding had been put off for two months, so there was more time to do it up right, but also for me to find a way out, which didn't seem to be forthcoming.

But in the end, if we stayed, and I got hitched to my hot guy, our marriage would be based on a total lie.

He didn't even call me by my real name.

Obviously, I realized my mind had wandered from my book as I felt Maxine wander from the window.

She sat beside me, not close (we were getting there, but I figured the fact we looked alike freaked her).

She shuffled through the pictures, pulled one out and showed it to me.

Her pretty eyes (and our eyes were the same, but hers were still prettier) came to mine and she said quietly, "I think this one, Sattie."

Sattie.

She'd never called me that.

Yes, we were getting there.

I smiled at her and didn't make any sudden movements, just looked down at the picture.

Brides of this world didn't carry bouquets, by the by. They walked down the aisle *with* their intended, a garland of leaves and flowers wound from his elbow, over both hands, and up her elbow, connecting them.

It was pretty danged rad.

The one Maxie liked would not have been my choice, although it was lovely. It looked made of eucalyptus leaves, cream and pink sweetheart roses with some tiny pompom green things stuck in to give it fullness.

"I love it," I whispered.

Her lips curved.

"I love the picture you're painting more," I told her.

Her gaze drifted to the easel then back to me, and bashfully, she offered, "When I'm done, do you want it?"

"It would be my most prized possession in this world."

I said that, and I meant it.

Her eye warmed, her cheeks pinked, and seeing both was both a gift of the fates and a curse to hate Edgar Dawes, Seventh Count of Derryman even more.

Rushing footsteps came down the hall.

We both looked there and saw Carling sway to a halt right before we heard the front door swing open and Mom call out, "Look what the cat dragged in!"

She appeared, looking like the winner from the world's most flamboyant beauty pageant, carrying four humongous, individually-wrapped-in-paper bunches of spiky stems of different colored irises.

"Darling Carling," she greeted.

Carling blushed.

Mom grinned.

"Can you take these?" She handed off the flowers. "Please put them in water. I'll be down to stem and arrange them a bit later."

And there you had it.

Totes getting off on this Lady Corliss thing.

She then dramatically swept off her giganto hat, nearly hitting...

Loren.

"Oh my gods!" I cried, tossing my book aside.

I hopped off the couch, ran across the space, and threw myself at him.

I pulled his head down to mine and gave him all I had.

His arms closed around me, tight, he growled into my mouth, and obviously with all that yumminess, it instantly got heated.

I vaguely heard my mom tutting and muttering, "Kids."

I also heard a man clear his throat.

Loren tore his mouth away.

I pouted and panted.

He let me go but grabbed my hand and started dragging me down the hall.

"We'll be back," he said.

"Don't mind me," Maitland replied. "I'll be fine as my life just became all about studying this *extraordinary* painting of the park."

I looked over my shoulder to see Maitland wink at me.

And then Loren pulled me into the study.

He whipped me around.

I slammed into his body.

He slammed the door.

We went at it again.

My gods, I barely knew him.

But I missed him.

I was pressed back to the desk, and he was pressed to me when his mouth left mine and went to my ear.

"Fuck," he growled.

"Why'd you stop?" I bitched.

"Because I'm not having you first in a carriage, and I'm not having you first on a davenport in a study."

I grabbed his head and pulled it back to me.

We made out again.

He ended it…again.

"I feel it safe to confess I'm enamored of your greeting, dear heart, but we must talk."

"Okay," I replied, pulled his mouth to mine and kissed him again.

He groaned and pressed deeper into me.

And *harder*, if you get what I'm saying.

Yum!

He lifted his head, muttering, "Darling."

"Maxie picked our wedding flowers."

He pulled his head away further in a manner that made me surface from his consuming deliciousness.

"Maxie?" he queried.

"Yes. Pink and cream sweetheart ro—"

"Satrine, it's your wedding. Not hers."

"I—"

He shook his head. "I'm not being an ass. I've no doubt you wish to involve your sister. And we shall. But it's the only wedding you'll have so you should have what *you* wish."

"Oh my gods," I griped. "Stop being amazing when I'm mad at you for leaving me for two weeks *and* for stopping kissing me."

He grinned, dipped in, nipped my bottom lip, that was so hot, I experienced a mini-orgasm, then he pulled away.

"You're pulling away again," I complained.

"We have things to talk about."

"Is the world ending?"

He grinned again. "Not that I know."

I tried to draw him down to me, mumbling, "Then they can wait."

I cried out as I was lifted and my ass was planted on the edge of Dad-not-Dad's desk, but not for good reasons.

Loren left me there and moved to stand behind a chair.

I narrowed my eyes at his new position.

"I can't even," I stated.

"And you won't, until you learn to be good."

How could he be hot when he was being a wet blanket?

"Warning, Marquess of Gorgeousness, I'm very rarely good."

His expression changed, I was pretty sure I experienced a not-so-mini-orgasm, and then his expression gentled.

"We have a future to discuss, dearest."

He didn't know the half of it, and the thing that killed me was, he might not ever know it.

Because I was very probably stuck there, and I was totally down with marrying this awesome guy I barely knew.

But I could never, not ever, tell him anything about the real me.

Not only because he probably wouldn't believe me, but because I'd curse me and Mom if I did it.

"Well, I suppose I'm now listening," I grumbled.

"The business I had to attend to was that King Noctorno summoned me."

"No sh...fooling?"

"Sh-fooling?" he asked.

"I was going to curse," I admitted.

"You can be you with me, Satrine."

Yeah.

Right.

I could do that...

Satrine.

"Can we talk about a summons from *a king* and not my foul mouth?"

He nodded. "This is why I couldn't say what I was doing. When Tor calls, sometimes the matters he needs to discuss are confidential."

"Right," I whispered.

Badass, I thought.

"This time, it was about a couple of things, one of which was your father."

I felt my eyes widen. "Dad?"

Another nod from Loren. "Due to the nature, audaciousness and extent of his crimes, the magistrate sent a bird."

Update: they didn't have phones, or telegrams, they had birds. Like carrier pigeons, but instead they were ravens and they pretty much never failed in delivering their message, unless they were shot down during wartime and such.

Another update: I'd learned that in a book. I'd also learned it when the modiste, Madame Toussaint, asked Mom, "Would you like me to send a bird to Benies? You *need* their silk. It's from Firenze. It's *sublime*. It'll take perhaps six weeks to get here, that is, after the bird arrives with our order, so we'll say ten weeks, but it will be *very* worth it."

Further update: We sent a bird for the silk.

Last update (for now): The reason Ansley gave me that look when I talked about the birds singing to me and mice being my friends was because animals talked to you in this world. Birds. Cats. Mice. (I told you! This place was Disney in real life!) It happened to Mom and me with a stray cat at first. We were walking down the street with Maxie. We flipped out. This flipped Maxine out. Carling was escorting us to a patisserie. He flipped out when we all flipped out. It was a huge thing.

In the end, we had to pretend we were playing a game, and thank gods they bought it.

Wait, one more update: Mom adopted that cat, mostly because the cat asked to go home with us. His name was Mr. Popplewell (according to Mr. Popplewell). He was ginger with some white. He'd gained at least five pounds since we'd had him (and he was not svelte to start with) due to Mom stuffing him with chicken and fish. He slept with her. Doted on Maxine. And cuddled with me. Because, you guessed it, Maxine and I stuffed him with chicken and fish too.

"The magistrate sent a bird?" I prompted.

"Tor returned a bird and froze your father's access to his assets. You, your mother, any representatives you decide, can access what you wish. Your father can make no decisions about his estate until, perhaps, after his trial."

"Holy cow," I breathed.

Well, that explained why Dad-not-Dad hadn't taken any action.

Loren smiled. "Yes. It's unprecedented. But I can say, by the time I arrived to meet him, Tor was still decidedly displeased."

"I'd guess so," I remarked. "But what did you mean by 'perhaps' until after his trial?"

"Tor is traveling here to sit and hear his defense personally."

The king was coming to sit in judgment on Dad-not-Dad?

"Holy cow times a thousand. Really?" I asked.

More smiling and nodding from Loren.

"Will I meet him?"

"I'm afraid you'll have no choice. He and Cora will be expecting us for dinner after they arrive in Newton."

This just kept getting better!

"I get to meet the queen too?"

"Indeed."

This was awesome!

"Do you think he'll keep Father's access to his assets frozen while he's in jail?"

"The impression I get is that Tor is frustrated with his nobles behaving like they have the run of the country and can do anything they wish at any time to anyone, without any consequences. His father was a good man, a fine king, but he was a traditionalist. He tended to let the peers of his realm act as they always had, with veritable impunity. Tor is a far more modern sort of king."

Wow.

How cool.

Loren went on, "And he's felt he's done what he can to make his statement moderately, but there are those who aren't catching on, for instance, your father. So he's looking to set an example."

I could not for the life of me stop my smile.

Loren returned it.

"So what does that mean?" I asked.

"I've no idea, darling. But unless Tor's mood improves significantly before your father's trial, or Derryman finds some adequate defense, I'm afraid things aren't looking good for him."

"Good," I whispered.

"Indeed," he replied.

Except…

"Hang on, do you guys behead people or anything?" I asked.

"Not anymore," he answered.

"I *think* that's good."

He chuckled.

"Okay, that was *almost* worth you stopping kissing me."

His frame locked, weirdly, and his eyes bored into mine.

Then his lips stated, "You are extraordinary."

Aww.

"What a lovely thing to say," I replied.

"You mistake me, Lady Satrine Dawes soon-to-be Copeland. I have known many women, traveled near and far, and *you* are *extraordinary*."

Holy *fuck*.

My heart leapt, my eyes remained locked to his, and my situation became even more complicated.

Because I was falling for this guy.

Fast.

This was because this guy was amazing.

Incredibly.

"Stop being awesome," I warned, my nose stinging, my eyes getting blurry.

"I missed you," he said softly.

"You're being awesome," I warned.

He gave me a gentle smile.

I drew in a delicate breath.

"We have more to discuss, my darling," he shared.

"All right," I said hesitantly, because he was messing me up, in good ways, which was bad.

"Tor is aware of our betrothal and wedding plans. One of the reasons I sent word to Father to delay the wedding was that Tor wanted the Derryman business out of the way in time for all of us to get to Dalwin Castle. He and Cora will be attending the wedding."

"Yowza," I replied.

"He's also given me a choice, and I need to discuss it with you, for it affects you as well."

Intriguing.

"That being?" I asked.

"He's already offered me a seat on his council. He is not simply my king, I regard him as a friend, and he's made clear he feels the same for me."

"You are rocking my world, your grace."

He shook his head, mouth twitching, and carried on.

"I suspect he needs advisors around him he can trust. He does his business in Bellebryn, which would not be a difficult place to live. It's on the western coast, and it's beautiful there."

It seemed like it was beautiful everywhere, so I believed him.

"All right."

"As an alternate choice, he's also offered me an ambassadorship to anywhere of my choosing. Fleuridia, Lunwyn, even Korwahk or Airen or Wodell."

Dad-not-Dad had a globe in his office. Mom and I had studied it acutely.

So I knew where all of these places were (Lunwyn north, Fleuridia south, Korwahk *way* south, on another continent, and Airen and Wodell were on the continent of Triton due west across the Green Sea).

"They're both honors, am I right?" I inquired.

"Indeed." He nodded. "Grand ones."

"What do you want to do?" I queried.

"I have not been stuck in a secluded cottage in the Fleuridian countryside for twenty years. So rather, I'd prefer to know what *you* want to do."

Well…

Hell.

I, too, had not been stuck in a secluded cottage in the Fleuridian countryside.

In fact, just two months ago, Mom, Keith, my friend Holly and I had rented a boat and sped and tubed and sunned and swam while spending a happy day on Lake Pleasant.

"It'll be your work," I punted.

"It'll be your life," he rejoined.

"*Our* life," I corrected.

And that was when it happened.

It started with Loren saying this:

"Honestly, Satrine, I don't care what I bloody do. None of that has any real meaning. Politics have been played millennia before us and will be played for millennia after, without the people seeing any real change. So it doesn't matter. We could start in Wodell and make our way home. Hell, we could go to The Mystics and around the globe. Whatever you wish. But he'll want an answer when he makes Newton."

"At the joyous occasion of your return," I started cautiously, "I hesitate to get into anything heavy, honey. But that's a rather pessimistic viewpoint and I think maybe we should discuss why you have it."

"Can you refute it?" he challenged.

"My father's assets are currently frozen from his access because the new king gives a shit about right and wrong."

He shut up.

I gave him another example.

"I want to learn to drive that phaeton Father has, and you're going to teach me because I know in my heart that *you* know females can drive carriages, even if the men before you felt differently."

"Satrine—"

"Can we have time together, just you and me, please?"

He glanced around the study, making his point.

"Mom will want to spend time with you now that you're back. You're marrying her daughter. We need to get to know each other. And she needs to get to know you. Maxine needs to get used to you. And I don't know why Maitland is here, but I didn't even say hello. Now is not the time for me to provide you with ample proof that, in the long run, the world is good."

"Your father was a narcissist and a degenerate. Your whole life, you suffered for those personality flaws. And you sit before me and tell me the world is good?"

"I had my mom," I whispered.

"Six years into your life," he shot back. "And yes, let's get together, just you and I, and you can share about those years where you were banished, as a baby, and onward, for more than half a decade, from your mother's breast. You've spoken not a word about that time, and I sense I know exactly why you haven't."

He'd sense wrong since that would be difficult to discuss, since I wasn't banished.

Which was probably why I flinched.

He didn't miss it and bit off, "Precisely." Then he drew in a very deep breath and stated, far more gently, "That was reprehensible of me, darling. I should never have mentioned it. It is yours to share if you wish, or not, if that is as you wish."

I evaded by saying, "Can you and I have time, just you and me?"

"Of course, sweeting," he whispered.

"So you know where my mind is, I just got Maxine back too. I don't really want to be in The Mystics right now."

The Mystics, by the by, being due east.

"Of course."

"Can we start kissing again?"

He gave me a tender look and moved to me.

He cupped my jaw and declined, gallantly.

"I need to spend time with your mother and sister."

"Right."

"And Maitland is never good on his own for too long. He easily finds trouble."

"He's in my sitting room. There's no trouble to be found there."

"He could be painting the walls with Maxine by now."

I laughed softly.

"Don't mind me, my dearest," he said quietly. "I'm travel weary. I made haste in getting back to you. I'll be myself tomorrow."

He was totally lying.

Though, the "made haste" part was super sweet.

"Okay."

"Okay," he replied.

I smiled, and I was so worried, I didn't quite mean it.

Loren did the same.

But I feared he had a different reason for not meaning his.

Chapter Fourteen

Lady Corliss Knows All

Loren

"She has great tits, an exceptional ass, and I curry your wrath at not only sharing that, but also that I've dreamed of it frequently since I first saw it. I have been moved repeatedly to write sonnets to the glory of her hair, but fortunately for the world of verse, I've not had the time to start one. The instant she sees you she races into your arms and sticks her tongue down your throat. She is sheer perfection. And she's yours now, but in less than two months' time, she will officially be that until the day one or the other of you croak. So allow me to express the depth of my confusion that you're sitting here, looking like you wish to murder somebody."

Loren tossed back the whisky he was rounding in his glass and did not speak after Marlow stopped.

Lamentably, this meant Marlow started again.

"And my further confusion as to why the fuck you're not with her with your hand up her skirts."

He shifted only his eyes to his friend.

"I'll thank you to stop speaking about my future wife in that manner."

"And I'll thank you to stop acting like a brooding arsehole and tell me what's the matter with you," Marlow fired back. "You've been in Newton for five days. Racing to her townhome the moment you arrived in the city like Minerva herself was resurrected and chasing your heels. You spent what I *hope* was a pleasurable half an hour with her in a study. We lunched with her, her fetching mother, and her charming sister after that. Then you begged off an intimate dinner with her that evening to join Huxtable and Soucott in challenging some dishonorable gamesman whose magnets were making the dice jump in his favor, and the notes to jump out of Huxtable's wallet."

Loren scowled at his empty glass.

Marlow kept bleating.

"The next day, you had a picnic in the park, again in the company of her mother and sister, when the engagement has been officially announced. It's reached every paper, likely in three countries. The king is coming to the wedding, for fuck's sake. You are free to court her at liberty. You no longer need a chaperone. In fact, you can carry her to your townhome, take her to your bed, and not surface until your wedding, which, frankly, if I was in your shoes, is what I would be doing. But since that, I'm sure, highly enjoyable picnic, you've turned down her every invitation and haven't seen her once. However, you have time to sit in this magical establishment with me when I know you. You've no intent to take a whore. Though you might very well wish word to reach your betrothed's ears that you're sitting here, so she'll have reason to beg off of *you*."

A woman in knickers, a bust-less corset, which meant her breasts were exposed, garters, stockings and heeled mules strolled by, her eyebrows lifting.

In return, Loren tipped his head to his empty glass.

She nodded and looked to Marlow.

He shook his head.

She moved to the bar.

"I've sent gifts," Loren murmured.

"To the second wealthiest woman in the kingdom, behind Cora, the Gracious, our fucking queen?" Marlow scoffed.

Loren turned his attention again to his friend.

"Please do me the favor of fucking off."

"I was on the cliffs' edge, ready to jump, and you pulled me back."

Loren clenched his teeth and again regarded his whisky glass.

"Do you think I'm not going to return the favor when it's clear you're going about the business of fucking up your life?" Marlow pushed.

"She's too good for me."

"You are currently eighth in line to the bloody throne."

The woman came and set the whisky in front of him.

He didn't even glance at her when he handed her his empty glass.

"That doesn't matter to Satrine," he said, then raised the liquor to his lips and threw back a healthy dose.

"No. But *you* do."

Loren said nothing.

"We were in the bloody forest for two and a half bloody years without leave. We'd lost five men, half our number, and our scout, who was just a boy. No one knew of our activities, and if we were discovered, we'd vowed never to divulge. We were assassins being assassinated, one by one. I thought I'd never make it home on so many occasions, it almost became a mantra. You'd be lying if you said you didn't think the same. Not once did I consider I'd walk into a home and have a woman race into my arms. Or better, stand and watch that same thing happen to *you*."

Loren threw back more whisky.

"We had to keep going. If we didn't find them all, Tor could send no more after us. If Queen Aurora knew he'd sent a kill squad, relations with our greatest ally would have gone to shite. And regardless of the fact that Frey would likely have backed Tor's play, he wasn't their ruler. And *they've got dragons*. Tor made the tough choice. We had to succeed. Our people, and theirs, depended on it. We succeeded, Lore, and we came home. *Be home*. And *be happy*."

"I do believe, my brother, that you were at my side challenging that gamesman with his dancing dice," he noted.

"I don't have a beautiful woman selecting her wedding garland either."

He again turned to his friend.

"What happens when the darkness comes?"

Marlow's eyebrows shot up. "It's my understanding she was torn from her family for six years of her life, then lived doing without a single luxury, not to mention several necessities, for the next twenty. Is this a woman who cannot absorb the dark?"

"I cannot be an ambassador or sit amongst a council with members who have never in their lives picked up blade or bow in loyalty to this realm."

"Then tell Tor it's not for you. He won't mind."

"He needs me."

"Tor could rule the entire Northlands on his stubborn arrogance alone. Fortunately for we underlings, he has Cora to even him out." Marlow shifted closer and his voice lowered. "Tor doesn't need you, brother. He knows what you did. He knows what you gave. He wouldn't blink to release you from duty and continue to give you his love and esteem for who you are and what you've done."

Loren started twirling his whisky in his glass again.

Until Marlow suggested, "Take up the mantle your father dropped."

"Quiet," Loren whispered his warning.

"Tor wishes to continue those operations from Ludlum's reign, it was his idea to begin with. And I'm certain he'd be happy to recruit you. It's likely he hasn't suggested it because he knows he's already asked too much of you."

Loren narrowed his eyes on his brother. "I said, *quiet.*"

"You're already doing it, for the gods' sakes. You'd have a lot less hassle from the local constabularies if the king was at your back."

"Can you—?"

He felt it.

Stopped speaking.

Turned his head.

And saw them approaching.

"Delightful. And I thought tonight would be boring," Marlow drawled.

Loren's fingers closed securely around the glass.

They kept coming.

And in the mood he was in, he was more than ready for it.

* * * *

Satrine

I took a healthy sip of wine, and said to Mom, "So this is where we're at."

I set the wineglass down on the dining room table very close to the bowl of tuna Mr. Popplewell was hunkered over, snarfing down, and lifted my hands to grab fingers as I counted it down.

"No doubt, being no call, no show for over a month, my job is toast."

Mom lifted her glass and said, "Mine too."

"All my friends, your friends, our family, Keith, Aunt Mary, various acquaintances, perhaps the news media, definitely the police, have been alerted to our disappearances. They've freaked, spent countless resources trying to figure out what became of us, are terrified of what might have befallen us, and if we should get back, healthy and happy, we can't just say, 'Had a wild and wacky vacation in a parallel universe. Oh my *God!*

You should try it some time.' In fact, we have no excuse as to why we disappeared at all."

"Word, my girl," Mom agreed and sucked back a sip.

"Dad has likely cashed in those emeralds, used all that money on wine, women and poker, and is probably trying to figure out how to get us back so he can attempt to fleece us or sell us again."

"Asshole," Mom muttered, reaching to the bottle to pour us both more wine.

"Witches here have pretty much gone underground, so we can't find one. But even if we could, we couldn't tell her, or him…no gender discrimination here, folks, what we need them to do."

"Yup," Mom concurred.

"I'm engaged to be married to the most gorgeous man ever created, in *two universes*, though I barely know him. And now, for some reason, he's avoiding me."

"Gotta admit," Mom slurred. "Thas weird."

"We're gonna meet the king and queen. I'm going to have dinner with them, with my fiancé, who, it's worth a repeat, I barely know, and can't know him better if I never see his fucking gorgeous fucking annoying face. And they're coming to my wedding to said gorgeous, barely-known, insanely annoying man."

"I'm kinna excited about that, baby," Mom said.

I looked her in the eyes. "We're not going home, are we?"

She looked into mine, and she was drunk, but not drunk enough not to *really* mean what she said next.

"Your sister can't make the trip. She'd lose it in our world. And we can't leave her."

"Yeah," I agreed.

Mr. Popplewell got done snarfing, did some rolly-poly thing which meant he kicked his bowl down the table, before he landed on his side, his fat belly globbing out on the shining wood in front of him.

Mom watched this indulgently.

"Mmmrrrrm, thank you, Mmmmmmmuuuummy," Mr. Popplewell purred, then started licking his paw.

Mom turned back to me.

"You know me. I think things happens for a reason, honey. And it wasn't fun, and I hate the idea of what's happening at home, people we care about not knowing where we went, never knowing. I hate that. And I hate your father exponentially more than I already did because he's the cause of it. But I think we were meant to be here. I think we were meant to be here for Maxie, who until we got here, had no one. And I think *you* were meant to be here for Loren."

I blew breath between my lips and said, "Hardly."

She shook her head, took a sip, and with her other hand, reached out to scratch Mr. Popplewell behind his ears, making his loud purring go even louder.

She then replied, "I don't know. There's something about that guy."

"How can you tell? You never see him."

She focused soberly on me again and said, "I can tell because I'm your mother. I think you're the most wonderful being ever created. But you can still screw up. All of us can. We're human. But to him, you can't. He looks at you like you're going to say to him, 'Hang on a second. I gotta run and make sure the world is still spinning 'round. Be right back.'"

And there was that leaping heart again.

"He doesn't look at me like that."

"You came out of me. I fed you from my body. I cleaned your scraped knees. We cannot go here. So I'll say it fast. Hewantsinmylittlegirl'spants. *Bad.*"

"Mom!"

"But that's not it."

"If this was true, why is he not here?"

She shrugged. "You're asking *me* how a man's mind works?" She threw out her wineglass, nearly sloshing wine on the table and definitely putting Mr. Popplewell on alert. "My choice in men got us in this situation in the first place."

"You aren't responsible for us being here."

She avoided my eyes.

Mr. Popplewell settled back down.

"Mom, look at me."

She looked at me and stated, "We're gonna be okay. We've got money. We've got each other. And now we have Maxie. I like Satrine. She kicks ass and rocks a hat. And you gave yourself that name because I told you I was going to give it to you, but your dad wanted to call you Maxine, and that name far from sucked, so I went with it. But there are many people who are suffering because of your father's actions, and that suffering will never leave them. The question of us vanishing will never be answered for them. And I chose him. So I know I made a bad choice at age twenty-four of the wrong guy. I'm not the first, far from it. I won't be the last. Still, it's heavy, baby."

Yeah, totally heavy.

"I get that, Momma," I said gently.

"So I focus on you. And I focus on the fact that Maxine has had enough taken in her life, it's not a great tradeoff, those people who care about us never knowing what happened to us. But she gets us. And she's happy. Like I said, I think we were meant to be here. But the bottom line is, we're here. And as usual, we're doing what we do. Making the most of it. And I'm proud of us for that."

I was too.

"I love you, Mom."

"And I you, my girl."

"But you forgot to mention how much you're getting off on being Lady Corliss," I teased.

"Oh yeah, guuuuuuuurrrrl, I'm lovin' me some of that."

I started laughing.

When I stopped, even if she was smiling, her eyes were serious.

"He's scared. He'll come around."

"He doesn't strike me as a guy who gets scared."

"For some folks, the most terrifying thing of all is the possibility of finding love and happiness."

"I'm not sure he's that either."

"His mother died, honey, and his sister. Ansley told me they were both lost to him by the time he was eleven years old. You will be the next great, important woman in his life. If it was me, I'd find you *terrifying*."

Holy shit.

I hadn't thought of that.

"You are wise, my glorious momma."

"Lady Corliss knows all."

I started laughing again.

This time, Mom did it with me.

Chapter Fifteen

Shadows

Loren

"I think the score now, brother, is twelve to ten, sadly in your favor, but I'm gaining," Marlow noted.

Loren flinched as the physician pierced the skin of his side with a needle.

He then took in Marlow, his friend's eye already swelling so badly, it was nearly swollen shut, but the purpling had long since begun. Although he'd cursorily scrubbed his face, both of his nostrils were rimmed with dried blood. And a deep cut rent his upper lip.

Loren felt some heat at his jaw where he'd taken a glancing blow, but that was it.

Outside the gash at his side that came from a dagger.

Thus, Loren asked, "How is that tallied, my friend?"

Marlow also flinched as he crossed his arms on his chest, which he would do, as he'd taken some body blows (correction, that heat at Loren's jaw wasn't it, they'd both taken body blows, however, they weren't visible, so they didn't count).

Marlow did this saying, "I'm not on my back in my bed."

Loren sighed, as with that, he had no choice but to concede the point.

Marlow ceased ribbing when he stated low, "Winnow Dupont is going to be a problem."

Loren nodded once and agreed by stating the obvious, "Winnow Dupont is already a problem."

He was about to say more when his bedroom door opened.

Marlow twisted at the waist to peer behind him, making enough room for Loren to see his father strolling in, face set in granite.

Bloody hell.

Ansley stepped to the side.

And there was Satrine, the hood of a cloak over her head, its folds resting enchantingly on her shoulders, the rest of the cloak's black velvet a sheet all the way down to the floor.

He sat up abruptly, grimaced, and the physician hissed, "Remain still!"

Ansley and Satrine came to a halt at the end of his bed.

His fiancée's eyes were aimed at the doctor's work.

His father's eyes were aimed at him.

"Tell me you did not call her," Loren growled to his sire.

"After your return this eve, it occurred to me that your understanding of the fact your actions reverberate through the minds and emotions of the ones who love you was not quite being absorbed. Therefore, I've sought reinforcements."

He gritted his teeth, forced himself to stop doing that even as the needle again pierced his flesh, he felt the pull join the two slashed sides together, and he turned his attention to Satrine.

"Darling," he called.

She lifted her gaze from these ministrations to him.

"What happened?" she inquired.

He was about to say it was nothing, but he was thwarted again.

This time by Marlow.

"We were at a bordello, see."

He whipped his head to his brother and bit, "Marlow."

Marlow didn't even look at him.

"We were having a whisky. Little did we know that some weeks past, when Lore was spending some time at *another* bordello…"

He sat up further and clipped, "Marlow, *quiet*."

"Your grace, *remain still*," the physician snapped.

Marlow continued to ignore Loren.

"…he'd brought himself a little trouble. He did this with intent. He has a friend who also attended that same establishment, a favorite of his, and became embroiled in a game they like to play there, which is more fittingly referred to as blackmail."

"Brother, silence," Loren ordered, again to no avail.

"As such, this friend also lost the woman he loved and was imminently going to marry. Our man here"—Marlow tossed a hand to Loren—"felt something needed to be done about it, and this he did. They were not best pleased he intervened in their regular swindle, and this evening, the mastermind behind it sent some men to share her displeasure. Alas, the marquess has a terrible habit of leaving some jobs undone, especially when the villain is of our fairer sex, and we suffered for that oversight this night. Though, I will take this moment to point out, Lore suffered more than me."

Wordlessly, Satrine was regarding Marlow as he spoke, and she didn't stop when he ceased, therefore, Loren called her again.

"Satrine, my darling, please wait for me downstairs. Once the doctor has completed his work, I'll get decent and join you."

Now Satrine's eyes came to him as he spoke, and they didn't leave when he was finished.

She said nothing for long, weighty moments.

And then she turned her head side to side, and requested in a soft voice, "Gentleman, if I may speak with my fiancé alone."

"By all means," his father growled.

Marlow's face tightened in pain, but he beat back the wince as he gave her a short bow and said, "My lady."

Both men left, Marlow shutting the door behind them.

Loren looked back to Satrine to see she was already regarding him, or more to the point, his bared chest.

He opened his mouth but found his luck had not changed as he was foiled again.

"Allow me to get this straight," she continued in that soft voice, her attention lifting to his face. "You were at a bordello tonight."

"Dear heart—"

"And were set upon by rogues who you'd angered at *another* bordello you were at some weeks past."

"Satrine—"

"However, where you *weren't* tonight, or last night, or the one before, and the one before that, and so on, was anywhere near me."

The physician grunted a sympathetic, fraternal grunt.

Loren fell silent.

She said nothing.

He hissed in breath as the doctor poured alcohol on his now-stitched wound.

The man then stoppered the vial, set it aside and looked to Satrine.

"Milady, this request comes at an inopportune time, I'm aware. But it would be most helpful if you could aid me with the bandage."

Damn it all to hell.

She nodded, came forward, threw back the front folds of her cloak and lifted her hands to drop the hood from her hair.

Loren sat up as she assisted the physician in winding the bandage around his stomach and tying it off.

As usual, she smelled phenomenal.

She immediately retreated when this was done, the doctor packed up his bag, and bending over him, he whispered, "Good luck." He then straightened and said to Satrine, "If his grace rewins your favor, I ask you to be certain he rests, at least for a good week. Nothing strenuous. He must allow the healing to set in."

Loren found it alarming she didn't nod her agreement. She simply dipped her chin in acknowledgement.

The physician took his leave and Loren took his feet.

"I believe you heard him say you should rest," she noted.

He wasn't facing this on his back.

He also wasn't facing this with his chest bared. He knew the blows he took to his torso were already bruising, but even if he didn't, her gaze falling to those areas would have told him.

He swiftly walked to the wardrobe in his dressing room, seized a fresh shirt, and pulled it over his head while returning to her.

She hadn't moved from the spot he left her in.

He halted a few feet away.

Not knowing what to say, because he didn't know her very well, therefore, he didn't know how to read the strangely void expression on her face, he simply whispered, "Sweeting."

"Is it a lost hope this friend of yours was at his favored bordello only to sip a whisky?" she asked.

Loren did not answer.

"I see," she said, her voice again soft.

"It is not that he didn't bring misfortune onto himself. He did. It is that the greater wrong was what they were doing. He wasn't the only one they'd fleeced, Satrine."

"I'm pleased you understand that the architect of his own downfall was indeed your friend," she replied. "Now, I'd like to know if there were further nefarious shenanigans you were intent to see to at this establishment you were attending tonight."

He had no response to that either.

At least, no good one.

"I was spending time with a friend," he gritted.

He watched her swallow, something unbearably tragic moving through her expression, and then she said, "I'm not up on all things aristocracy, Loren, as you know. But one thing I do understand is that it's your duty to produce an heir."

This was not a good turn in the conversation.

He took a step toward her.

She took a hasty step back in a manner he stopped.

"I can't begin to imagine you don't know what a catch you are, sir," she said. "You can have any woman you want."

"I don't want any woman. I want you."

"You do?"

Shite.

With the way he'd been avoiding her, that was a pertinent question.

"Satrine, my dearest—"

"Were you with a woman?" she whispered.

"No, I was not. Nor was that my intent in being there this eve."

Her brows rose. "This eve?"

Fuck.

She was far too clever, and it was frustrating that it could be annoying when most of the time it was appealing.

"I cannot contend I have not partaken, my love, but that was before I met you. Not after. And not ever again," he promised.

"You seem to have missed it, your grace," she continued whispering, but her words were now aching. "I don't need you anymore."

The pain in his body, at his side, every blow he sustained that night was nothing compared to the pain those words sent searing through him.

"Even if Father could cut us off, we've succeeded in procuring all the funds we need to see to our futures. You are no longer marrying me to protect me, my family. But more importantly, I'm no longer marrying *you* for any of those reasons."

Loren stilled as his mind blanked.

Except for the understanding that she was marrying him for...

Him.

"The flowers have been decided," she shared. "My gown and Mother's gown *and* Maxine's gown are all currently being crafted. The menu has been set. We await Father's trial and then we're away to Dalwin. But we don't need to be."

He took another step to her, murmuring, "Satrine—"

Unable, it seemed, to utter many complete sentences that night, she retreated while interrupting him.

"I want you to have what you want."

"I already told you that's you."

"You deserve better."

"There is no better than you."

"You don't know this now, but that isn't true. And whatever is holding you back from me, I urge you to trust those instincts, and find the woman who's right for you."

Those words were alarming, but he had another problem that was taking precedence in the now.

She'd picked up her skirts and was actively leaving.

He followed.

He slammed the door she was opening, she whirled to him, and he kept his hand at the door by her head, his body blocking forward escape. His other hand he sifted into the folds of her cloak to curl his fingers at her waist and fully cage her in.

"Please step back," she said to his throat.

"My apologies, my lady, but in this moment, you've no choice but to be at my whim."

She lifted her gaze to his.

Amber swimming in desolation.

He caused that.

His gut wrenched.

As such, his next words, guttural and wretched, sounded torn from him.

"Don't let me go."

Her lips parted.

"My hold is slipping, Satrine, don't let me go."

"Your hold on what?"

"On anything that is good in this world."

He heard her pained gasp and felt her light touch at his abdomen.

"Loren."

"Darling, I don't seek your company because I don't want you consumed by the darkness."

"*Your* darkness?"

"Indeed."

"You aren't dark, honey."

"You will never know, because I will never tell you the shadows that live in me."

She lifted a hand to his jaw and moaned, "Baby."

He dropped his forehead to hers but did not lose his hold on her eyes.

And for the first time in his life, he begged.

"Don't let me go."

"You are good, Loren."

He shook his head, not breaking their contact.

"How can you not see how wonderful you are?" she asked.

"I would like to say that this is the reason why I want you. That you make me believe that, even if it isn't true. And perhaps, in part, it is. Mostly you, and your mother, and even Maxine remind me why I did the things I did. You also remind me strength can be both bold and gentle. You remind me that there are lights that do not dim. And I need that."

"Then you shall have it."

By the bloody gods.

He closed his eyes and dropped his forehead to her shoulder.

She wrapped both hands around the sides of his neck.

"I also hope part of it is that you want to ravish me…eventually," she jested.

He drew in breath and lifted his head to catch her eyes.

"Absolutely," he replied.

Her smile was tremulous, but it was there, and so was she.

She was also no longer trying to leave.

Which was the only reason Loren allowed himself to relax.

"Can you promise me not to dash about town, exacting justice with your flesh and blood, until, at least, that cut begins to heal?" she asked.

"I will make you that promise if you promise in return not to leave me."

"I'm not leaving you, baby," she whispered.

"I mean tonight. I mean now."

Her eyes got huge.

She misunderstood him.

"Make no mistake, dearest, I very much wish to couple with you, but that will not happen tonight, after I've had too much whisky, not to mention I gave and received a beating. Though I do want you by my side while I sleep."

"Won't people talk?"

He felt his brows draw together, for she had been sequestered for decades and thus did not know many of the ways of her world, but her mother was an adult when she'd been sent away, and she definitely knew.

Surely, she'd explained this to her daughter.

"Our pending alliance has been announced in the papers," he reminded her.

"Yes, Mom and I approved the wording when Ansley showed us what his secretary drafted."

Perhaps she and her mother had not discussed it, for it wasn't she who was promised to him, but Maxine. They might not have ever imagined Satrine would make an alliance.

And it was fair to say, much had been happening since.

Therefore, it was up to him to educate her.

"Propriety dictates I behave in a gentlemanly manner while courting you, but once our union has become official, that being announced and public, we are at liberty, and even encouraged, to explore what a life together will mean in all its manifestations."

Again with the big eyes and, "Wow."

He couldn't believe it with all that had happened that eve, but he felt his lips twitch.

"Yes…*wow*."

"Do you heal fast?" she asked.

There was his Satrine.

"I do."

She arched into him and replied on a grin, "Excellent."

And there was his save.

His savior.

His Satrine.

Chapter Sixteen

Loose Lips

Loren

At first, he felt Satrine moving.

And then came the pain carving into his side.

He opened his eyes and saw a dark that shared it was still the dead of night but felt Satrine fidgeting.

"Are you not comfortable, sweeting?" he murmured, his voice thick with sleep.

"Okay, honey, I get why you felt the need for barriers, but *you* try to sleep in a corset."

He roused at that.

"I need this dress off," she finished.

He had decreed they'd sleep in their clothes, an effort to fight temptation.

Therefore, he'd tugged off his boots and socks, she had slipped off her slippers.

And they were on top of the bedclothes with the duvet pulled over them that usually lay folded at the foot in case an evening was uncommonly cold.

He'd forgotten she was daily tortured with that item of apparel.

"Never understood why you women suffer that contraption," he remarked.

"I knew I was falling in love with you."

Startled, Loren was powerless to do anything but allow her words to flood through him, the light of them momentarily, but brilliantly, illuminating places that had long been dark.

He did this before he moved his hand to the top button at the back of her neck.

He released it from its loop, the next, and then, with practiced ease, he angled his fingers just so, in order to slide them down and release all the buttons in one go.

Nary a second after he accomplished this, she shivered against him and remarked, "Maybe we should keep our clothes on."

He grinned into the dark then pulled them both from under the duvet and onto their feet.

He heard the silk of her dress rush to puddle on to the floor. He then used her hips to turn her and found the ends of the satin laces at her back. He tugged them and loosened them, thankfully unable to see what he was doing. It was bad enough being able to feel it.

He stepped away to allow her to pull the corset over her head, which would leave her in nothing but her shift, and he turned his attention to the buttons on his breeches.

He pulled those down so that he was only in his undershorts, then reached beyond her to tug back all the covers.

With a hand at her hip, he guided her in and followed her.

With ease, he turned her into his arms, but this was because she was already heading there.

"Much better," she decreed.

His lips curved, he pulled her closer and tangled their legs.

Much better, yes.

And much more dangerous.

Nevertheless, his fingers found themselves wound into her soft hair.

She melted into him.

"How's your side?" she asked quietly.

"I'll live."

"The goal should be *not* to allow them to cut you," she teased.

"There were five of them, and only two of us. I can promise you, my lady, I did try."

"Okay, let's stop talking about that," she returned.

He gave her a squeeze and reassured, "They were rough. Hooligans. No training. We were never in any real danger. I delight you still want me regardless of the flaws I know you sense in my character, so I feel relatively secure in sharing, in situations like that, Marlow and I work well together."

"Did you two learn that when you were quashing dissidents in Lunwyn?"

Loren froze.

Entirely.

"Uh-oh," she whispered.

"Who told you that?" he all but barked.

"Honey—"

He shifted, cupped her jaw on both sides, tipped her face to his, even if he couldn't see her, and shared, "You are not in trouble. I'm not angry at you. But I'm angry. And I'm angry at whoever told you about that."

She made excuses instead of answering him.

"I think he might have done it so I would know you a bit better, and maybe, um…have a care should things happen like…erm, *tonight*."

Since Marlow was with him when they went to attend Tor, that only left his father, unless Middleton, Holton or Rycroft came to visit her, which, considering none of them were close, was unlikely.

Though they were possibly getting closer due to the announcement of his betrothal and the knowledge they could rightly assume they were all to attend his wedding, something not one of them would miss.

And Ansley undoubtedly did it for the reasons she stated.

But considering this knowledge threatened the realm's security, it still was the wrong thing to do.

"This is highly confidential information, Satrine, do you understand me?"

"Yes."

"We took pains not to leave any trace. Men died for that. What is done is done, it's been years, but what happened was not with the knowledge of the ruler of Lunwyn. She has since passed. A good queen. Even more clever than you, which means she's the only woman I've known who is such."

"Wow, thanks," she cut in softly.

"Darling, I'm pleased you grasped the compliment. However, I'm being deadly serious. Realms do not like other realms sending soldiers in and meddling with their citizens, ever, and perhaps especially not in secret."

"Yes, I can see that," she agreed.

"We share a border with Lunwyn. Good relations. Trade treaties that benefit both realms. Should trouble arise, and it always does, our militaries would fight side by side. King Viktor is young. Smart. Stable. His father is a born leader in more ways than anyone on this planet, and a very fine man. His mother is nearly a warrior herself, and almost as cunning as her mother was. But he's still young. Youth can mean impetuousness. He's just learning to trust us as his allies and—"

"Baby, baby, baby," she fussed, pushing up to touch her lips to his. "I *get it*. Loose lips sink ships. You're heard."

"Loose lips sink ships?" he asked, and before she could say anything, went on, "That's most ingenious."

"Well, stick around, buddy, I got a million of them."

He chuckled.

She cuddled closer to him and tucked her face into his chest.

When she did, he thought, this would be their nights. After he had her, they would tangle together to sleep.

In fact, this would be their lives.

They may have a babe squirming between them if it fretted in the dark. Dogs (who would eventually learn better and remain at the foot) when they got them.

But in that moment, with Satrine in his arms, Loren vowed that whatever his future brought, it would not take him away from Satrine and their bed in the nighttime.

He'd sleep by her side every night.

Until he died.

"That's where the dark started, isn't it?" she asked his chest, taking him from his thoughts.

He bent his neck and pressed his face into her hair.

There, he admitted, "Yes."

"Thank you for your service, honey."

He again went still as her words flooded through him.

Simple.

Meaningful.

More light in the dark before it faded away.

"You're welcome, my love."

* * * *

She shifted against him, and this time when Loren opened his eyes, he saw the dawn stealing around the drawn curtains.

He also smelled her.

Felt her.

Was still entirely tangled in her.

And realized his folly of asking her to stay.

As if sensing him awake, Satrine shifted again, stretched, and felt his morning readiness, he knew, for she stilled.

Then (he should have known), albeit gently…

She attacked.

He was on his back, she was draped down his good side, her mouth on his, her hand on his chest, her breasts pressing in.

He pulled his mouth from hers and warned, "Darling."

Hers was not a warning.

It was a plea.

"So you won't hurt yourself, you'll need to be creative. I know you're creative, baby. *Be creative.*"

He framed one side of her face with his hand, being both relieved and pleased from her behavior from the first kiss they shared that there was one aspect of life and living it that her mother did not hesitate to be open about. Satrine was not at all afraid of sex. And this was not a surprise to him. She and Corliss had a very close, honest, open relationship.

However, being secluded all her life, she was still a virgin.

"Satrine—"

Her hand strayed down his stomach.

He caught her wrist and chuckled. "My dearest, you know not what you toy with."

"I haven't *toyed* with anything yet."

He pulled her hand up his chest.

And then he got serious.

"If it is your wish, I will gladly bring you to release."

"It *is* my wish, and I will gladly return the favor."

He felt his eyes widen.

She used hers to roam his face, his neck, then she turned her attention to his chest.

"Gods, do you have any clue how beautiful you are?" she asked in an awed, breathy voice that scored from his throat straight to his cock.

All right.

Enough.

He took her to her back.

"Loren, your wound," she snapped.

"You wish it, my love, I'll give it to you," he promised.

Her gaze heated.

He lost that beauty when he took her mouth.

Then he took her neck, her chest...

Pushing up her shift, he spent quite some time on her breasts.

She was writhing under him, her fingers buried in his hair, so he knew she was ready for what was next.

He ran his lips down the lovely outward swell of her belly at the same time he pulled her knickers down her legs.

She kicked them off.

He spread her thighs.

And took her sex with his mouth.

She gasped a gasp he felt in his shaft, mewed a mew he felt drive up his arse, and after he threw her legs over his shoulders, she moaned a moan that made him bead.

She rocked against him, wanton, abandoned, her taste, sounds, smell, reaction, all of it was more than he'd imagined, more than he could have hoped. And with Satrine, he knew he could hope for a great deal.

And when she climaxed against his tongue, her heels digging into his flesh, her fingers clutching his hair, he nearly came himself.

He lapped until it left her, and only then pulled himself over her, holding his weight on a forearm in the bed, giving her his warmth, and nibbling at her neck as her breath steadied.

He shifted his mouth to her ear.

"Okay?"

"You're...that was...I can't even...you're, um..."

He lifted his head and grinned arrogantly at her.

"Talented?"

"I don't know. I've been robbed of the ability to think. I've never experienced anything like that."

He nipped her bottom lip, soothed it with his tongue, absorbed the tremor that caused, and promised, "There's more to come, and it's even better."

"Oh boy."

He nuzzled their noses, shifted to his back taking her with him and reached for the covers that had slid off them to pull over their bodies.

She was a heavy weight against him, and he lay, pleased with himself, understanding she was even still recovering.

It took some time before she asked, "Is it your turn?"

He started and tipped his chin down to look at her.

She was gazing up at him, and the heat was back in her eyes.

"You don't have—" he began.

"You're in a state," she pointed out.

He did not need to look at the covers to understand the veracity of her statement, he was living it.

"My condition will fade."

"Isn't there a better way to see to that condition?"

He began to gather her to pull her face to face with him so he could have her close as he explained how her offer was most wanted, though it was unnecessary, but she fought it, watching him closely.

"You won't deny me," she said, wonder in her voice.

He wouldn't. Anything she desired, if it was in his power to give, he'd never deny it.

But this…

"You mustn't feel you need to do this, my love. I'll be fine. I can wait."

"I don't want you to wait. I want something else for you. And you're going to give it to me."

"Satrine—"

She bent and touched her lips to his throat.

Her soft hair spread across his jaw, his chest, and he quieted.

Then she slid down and kissed his chest.

After that, mimicking the things he did to her, she explored, starting at his nipples, then down his stomach, tracing a path either side, top—and bottom—of his bandage.

And then, after she pulled away his shorts, he watched, his balls drawing up as did his knees, as she staked claim to his cock in her fist.

And with not a moment's hesitation, she swallowed him whole.

He felt the back of her throat and her lips touch her fingers.

Extraordinary.

"Fucking hell," he grunted.

She tipped her eyes to him, sucked, bobbed, and he was a man with experience. He was a man who knew control.

But this was his woman.

He was falling in love with her.

And it was the first time she'd sucked his cock.

So he did something he hadn't done since he was a young buck.

He broke.

Pulling away, coming to his knees, he gently took her hair in his hand, positioned her, she moaned her pleasure as she sensed what was coming, opened her mouth over his cockhead, and he commenced fucking her face.

"Bloody fucking hell," he groaned, watching her hungrily take him.

She grasped his thigh to hold on, sucking through his thrusts.

Loren reached out and yanked her shift up so he could see her arse sway as she absorbed the drives, feeling the rapture of her mouth and thinking about taking her cunt with that outstanding arse in his hands.

And he tried to pull out when the time was nigh.

But she took hold of his hips firmly in both hands, which made his orgasm, which was going to be huge, an orgasm that was earth-shattering.

He came and he came, and he *fucking came* in her mouth, thrusting through it, and she swallowed it all down greedily.

Every drop.

He wasn't nearly recovered when he pulled out, caught her under the arms, and dragged her up, growling, "Come here."

She had no choice.

She was there.

He fell to his back with her on him.

He felt the pain dig in at his side, the laces stitching into his flesh pulling, but he didn't give a fuck.

She did.

"Loren! Your injury."

"Look at me," he commanded in a tone, even Satrine didn't hesitate.

She gave him her eyes.

"You're bloody perfect," he proclaimed.

"Baby," she breathed, her gaze softening.

"Did you like that?" he asked.

"Yes," she answered.

"Perfect," he decreed.

That was when her body softened on top of him, and she said, "You are too."

He didn't respond, just lifted a hand to her face so he could glide his thumb across the lips that spoke those words.

Spoke them and believed them.

"That was a lot, er, um…was that a lot?"

He didn't know what she was asking, so he guessed.

"Of my seed?"

She nodded.

"It was a lot," he confirmed. "My climax was thorough."

"Okay, that's good."

"It's very good."

She smiled at him timidly.

Fuck, she was.

She was perfect.

And his.

All his.

His arms around her grew tighter.

"Were you all right taking that much?" he queried.

"It was hot," she answered. "You kept coming and it made me feel...."

"Powerful?" he finished for her.

She scrunched her nose in an adorable affirmative.

"It's been a while," he told her.

"Right, of course. Pent up, I'm sure."

"Indeed, of a sort, since I've been taking care of myself thinking of you every night and some mornings besides since the day I met you."

Her eyes widened.

He grinned at her. "The reality is so far better, it's rather astonishing."

"Awesome," she whispered.

"Obviously, it was watching me thrust into your face, alternating paying attention to your very beautiful arse."

"Hmm..."

"That said, it was mostly that you're flawless at sucking cock."

Her legs started shifting.

Which meant she responded to verbal stimuli.

He already knew she did the same to physical.

Loren smoothed a hand over her arse.

She trembled.

And there it was.

"I was otherwise engaged, my darling. I didn't get to watch," he said quietly.

"Oh my gods," she breathed, squirming on him even more.

The grin he gave her this time was different.

"Stay low but straddle my hips," he ordered.

"Loren, your side."

He shifted his hand around...and in.

Her eyes went half mast, her head tilted back, and her lips parted.

"Straddle my hips, my love, trust me, I'll be fine."

She straddled his hips, careful to keep her right knee from grazing his side.

Loren moved his fingers.

And this time, watched.

Chapter Seventeen

Sharing

Loren

She sat across from him at his breakfast table in the conservatory, the beams of the sun gilding her hair, her face aimed to the windows, watching the birds at their bath.

He was dressed, but she was wrapped in his dressing gown. It was too big for her. But it was all they had for the now as he refused to button her into a gown she'd worn just the day before. He'd sent word to Corliss to have her maid, her apparel and her toilette directed to his townhome so she could face the day fresh, preparing to do so there.

More importantly, this also meant he got to keep her longer.

"Stop watching me," she told the window. "It's ridiculously romantic. I'm melting in a puddle over here."

He grinned at his coffee cup, his attention remaining on her over the rim as he took a sip.

She turned in the midst of this, watched his actions, and her gaze heated yet again.

"You're a walking, talking, eating, drinking-coffee, sex-god hero from a romance novel," she groused.

"I love you think that, though I'm perplexed as to why this seems to put you in a foul mood," he noted, returning his cup to its saucer.

"I can't jump you over the table due to your injury, that's why," she explained.

He raised a brow. "Did I not prove my creativity this morning?"

"The bit where you were on your knees could have torn your

stitches."

The tone of her response communicated she was now being very serious.

"Again, darling, I'm fine," he said in the same tone.

"How worried should I be about this bordello woman you've angered?" she asked.

And there it was.

"You shouldn't worry at all."

"Loren—"

He went about picking up his fork in order to go about consuming his eggs, saying, "I'm now aware that she holds ill will with the intent to do something about it and will thus be prepared in the future."

"What actually happened?"

His head was slightly bent to his plate, and he kept it that way as he lifted his gaze to her.

"Oh boy," she said when she caught his eyes. "That bad?"

He took a bite of some eggs, chewed, swallowed, and answered, "We'll just say I made a statement, though, apparently, not a big enough one."

"Mom told me what you did to the baddie who was guarding her."

Loren grew motionless.

"It's okay, honey," she assured. "That guy was rough with Mom, and he was gearing up to...well..."

Loren kept her pegged with his eyes.

If they were sharing—and this had finally begun between them with depth and honesty, and as far as Loren was concerned, there was no stopping now—thus, she would too.

"Violate Maxine," she whispered. Then quickly, likely seeing and maybe even feeling his reaction to those words, she reminded him, "He's very dead. You yourself made him that way."

"I should have perhaps taken more time in that endeavor," he murmured, cutting into his sausage.

She released a surprised giggle, and he returned his attention to her.

She waved a hand in front of her face, shifted fully to her plate, reached for her coffee (a surprise she drank that with her breakfast, as he did, an unusual thing for a lady, they customarily drank tea), and said, "I know, I know. I shouldn't think it's funny that you murdered someone. But I can't call up any remorse for a man who would stand guard over captive women, not allowing them to bathe, eat properly, and, it needn't be said, all the rest."

"We share a similar sense of justice," he noted.

This time, Satrine pegged him with her eyes.

And she agreed, "We absolutely do."

When she gave him this, Loren made a decision, set his fork down and straightened in his chair.

"Winnow Dupont, the madam of the bordello running the extortion scheme, ruined lives. How frank would you like me to be?"

"As frank as you can," she invited.

He accepted her invitation.

"Farrell perhaps gave in to a moment of weakness, regardless, he behaved poorly. He had a favorite, and he assured me his intent in being there was to say good-bye to her prior to his nuptials."

He lifted his hand when she opened her mouth to interrupt.

Then he carried on.

"Agreed. He could have done that in a café. But he did not. And we both know why. He bears responsibility. But in that scenario, two hearts were broken by Dupont's greed, not simply one. And then there are others. Some who should not have been unfaithful to their wives. Some who simply have proclivities that are no one's business. She made them the business of people who were in the position to react and had the power to do something about it. Men lost wives, loves, but also employment, status, stature, not to mention quite a bit of money. I carry no judgment as to how a man finds his pleasure. Others, sadly, do. If he enjoys being tied up, or the company of another man, or a woman taking control, this means nothing to me. But men have slunk away in shame, and at least one took his own life, because it means something to others."

"Took his own life?"

Loren nodded.

Satrine let that settle before she angrily stabbed at her eggs, asking, "Are the police involved in taking down this scheme?"

He knew the word "police," he'd just never heard it used in that manner.

They had constabularies and constables. If reduced to slang it was bobby or copper.

The verb was to police, not the noun.

As this was more than likely another indication of how she used language unexpectedly due to the fact her circle had been egregiously small her entire life, he didn't remark on this.

"Yes. It's my understanding Dupont is currently awaiting her own trial. But even in jail, people can scheme and issue orders. With the money she earned, she can buy quite a bit of loyalty."

She swallowed her bite and asked, "Is it true what Marlow said? About you leaving this loose end because she's a woman?"

"Darling, I think you understand now when I say the others who confronted me that night were neutralized. So yes, I draw the line at doing that to a woman."

"That's sweet," she whispered.

He smiled at her.

"And totally short-sighted."

He frowned.

She speared more egg, and before putting it in her mouth, announced, "We have to defuse her."

His voice was dangerous when he asked, "We?"

She swallowed, opened her mouth, and...

"Jolly good!" Ansley decreed, strolling in.

They both turned in his direction and watched as Loren's father went direct to Satrine, bent and kissed the side of her head.

"Dear daughter, good morning," he bid. He turned to Loren. "Son. You look well this morning. Very well. Considering."

Before Loren could reply, Ansley turned and headed to the covered dishes on the sideboard.

"Your grace, I—" Satrine began, and Loren took in the pink tingeing her cheeks, and he knew it was about the dressing gown...and how that referenced Loren's earlier creativity.

Ansley scooped eggs and declared, "This is the best start to the day I've had in six months, maybe a year. Coming upon two people I love at my breakfast table."

Satrine's eyes came to him, her cheeks pinker, but Loren sensed they were now thus for a different reason.

She'd had a detestable father.

And now she had Ansley.

Loren settled contentedly in that knowledge as Ansley finished his plate and sat at the round table with them.

"That was a lovely thing to say," Satrine told him.

Ansley reached for the coffeepot, his regard on her.

"What is mine is my son's, and it's soon to be yours, and I enjoy sharing it."

Loren suspected, even if his father was regarding Satrine, that remark was, in part, aimed at Loren.

The next definitely was.

"So I hope Loren doesn't go about the realm buying his own properties where we already have them so you both can be *at home* in your *homes* and keep me company well into the future when we're near to each other."

"And that's even lovelier," she replied.

Ansley poured coffee. "I'm further pleased at your demonstration of patience and loyalty, my dear, but I hope a certain someone at this table learned his lesson last night."

Loren sighed, sat back, and reached for his own cup.

"I did my best," Satrine chirped, looking at him and winking.

"For fuck's sake," he muttered.

"Son, a lady is in our midst," Ansley admonished.

"Father, my intended not only enjoys my foul mouth, she has one of her own that I feel it's safe to say I enjoy far more."

Satrine choked on a bite of sausage.

"Good gods," Ansley groaned.

Now Loren was grinning.

It died when he pointed out, "Though, I didn't enjoy Satrine sharing with me how generous you were with the knowledge of my service."

"Loren." Now Satrine was admonishing,

And she was correct.

This was not for the breakfast table and should be between him and his father.

Or that was the case yesterday.

She was now theirs, so she'd have to learn to sit through this kind of thing, for his father and he did it often.

"Did your betrothed rush to your side last night?" Ansley asked.

Loren knew were this was going and elected not to reply.

"Is she sitting with us right now, gracing our table?" Ansley pressed on.

Loren spared his fiancée a glance and saw she was grinning into her coffee cup.

She knew where it was heading too.

"Would that you have children who think you're a fool well into adulthood," Ansley bid.

"I don't think you're a fool," Loren retorted. "I simply think you have a big mouth."

"You are recovered. You are yourself. Satrine is here," Ansley recounted the evidence. "There will be a day you will acknowledge I know what I'm doing. I simply hope that day comes when I'm still breathing."

"And I never contended you don't know what you're doing," Loren returned. "You're the wisest man I know, and you are that to me in a manner I know you always will be. This doesn't mean, from the time I was a child, you being thus wasn't supremely annoying."

When he finished, his father's face was warm, his mouth soft.

But it was Satrine who spoke.

"You two are incredibly cute."

Both Copeland men turned smiles to her then.

But they again died, and all of them tensed when they heard a woman's imperious, "Do not! Do…not. No. No. No. *I will no longer be denied!*"

And then a woman his father's age with a hat more enormous than any Satrine wore on her head, along with a severe traveling costume encasing her body, all in black, stopped, of a sort, in the doorway.

The "of a sort" bit was that she was batting Eaton with the handle of a black parasol.

Ansley stood and turned to her.

Loren and Satrine followed suit.

"Mary, stop that this instant," Ansley demanded.

She ceased assaulting Eaton and confronted Loren's father.

"Well, I never, Ansley Copeland!" she exclaimed. "I've been practically *buried* under your messages delivered by bird telling me, in your inimitable way, that way being polite to the point of painful, which is a skill you possess that has *always* been *impossible* for me to *fathom*. I digress! Messages telling me with the utmost courtesy to *mind my own business* when the world, it appears, is *topsy-turvy!*"

She was nearly shouting when she finished.

But no one was able to get a word in because she wasn't done.

"Who, twenty-six years ago, advised you to approach my nephew?" She jerked her parasol handle to indicate herself. "*Me.* And who received a bird with the news that contract would *not* come to fruition." She leaned forward. "*Not me.* The birds I received said something else entirely! Now, I demand to know who this *Satrine* is and what in the dickens is…is…" Her eyes went beyond Ansley, and she whispered, "By the gods."

"Aunt Mary?" Satrine asked hesitantly.

Mary Livingstone, Baroness of Longdon, dropped her parasol, opened the large bag hanging on her wrist, pulled out an almost equally large fan made of lace, flipped it open, fanned herself, all this while reeling dramatically and calling out, "By Brigid! By the Morigan! By Cerdwin! The glorious gods have wrought a miracle."

"Mary, calm yourself. This isn't Maxine," Ansley clipped. "It's Satrine. Maxine's twin."

Mary shot straight.

"Her what?"

"Edgar abhorred twins," Ansley told her. "He sent her away at birth. And he staged Corliss's death after he was responsible for harming Maxine. After that, he sent them both away. The story is long. Fraught. And I will share it with you later. Satrine has lived it. She doesn't need to go through it with everyone who learns it."

"Edgar abhorred twins?" she asked breathily.

Loren glanced at Satrine to see her deathly pale.

"By Caylek!" Mary spat, and Loren returned his attention to her. "He was a bad seed. I was but a child myself, but even so, I told his mother. I said, 'Smother that one, he's a bad seed.' Did she? *No.*"

"Oh my gods," Satrine whispered.

It was a poor choice of thing to do.

She acquired Mary's attention again.

As such, Mary stomped to her, lifted a hand high, as the woman was of diminutive stature, grasped Satrine's chin, and dragged it side to side.

"A great beauty. Like your mother. Your father was a looker too. Unfortunately, the rascal was born with the soul of a knave." She let Satrine go but didn't stop talking. "I am unsurprised he sent you away, although I'm sorry for it, for your sake. But you were saved having to be around *him*, and I daresay in the now, you take my meaning."

She didn't wait for Satrine to confirm this.

She whirled back to Ansley and finished.

"It probably wasn't abhorrence of twins. It was probably because he was tight-fisted with anything, unless it served his own pleasure. One child was drain enough on his vast fortune, but *two*? I cannot even *begin* to imagine what Corliss was thinking when she took him. Then again, he had the uncanny ability to charm the pants off a snake when he had a mind to."

"Wow, you haven't changed," Satrine remarked.

Mary stepped back smartly, staring at her suspiciously.

"How would you know? I've never met *you*," she snapped.

"Father told me all about you. I was supposed to pretend to be Maxine. He said I'd eventually meet you. He spent three weeks instructing me on everything I was supposed to know to be her," Satrine replied.

"Humph," Mary returned. "This is all tied up in why that cox-comb is currently gracing one of our handsome king's lowlier institutions, I gather?"

"Yes," Satrine confirmed.

Mary lost some of her spectacle and asked quietly, "Word is running amuck. I have acquaintances who've even seen her on the street. Your mother lives?"

Hesitantly, Satrine smiled and nodded.

"By Brigid," Mary whispered.

"Would you like to sit with us and have a cup of coffee?" Ansley offered.

"Huh! A lady doesn't drink coffee in the mornings. She drinks *tea*!"

Satrine's gaze flew to Loren, and she looked close to dissolving into laughter.

"You there!" she shouted at Eaton, who was five feet from her. "Bring me a pot of tea."

"Right away, milady." Eaton bowed and escaped.

Loren was reminded of a thought he'd had weeks before, and the fact he was incorrect.

He *had* heard a lady shout, for he'd been around Mary Livingstone.

"Look at you," Mary complained, regard fastened on Loren as she rounded the table. "You're ridiculous," she stated.

Satrine's back slammed straight.

Mary seated herself and said to Ansley, "Really, Ansley, a man that handsome? It cannot be borne. You should have done something." She sniffed. "A scar from a blade, or mayhap, acid."

Loren watched Satrine relax, a smile playing at her mouth as she sank back into her chair.

After both ladies were seated, the men joined them.

Now Mary was studying Satrine.

"It's uncanny," she said softly.

"Hmm…" Satrine hummed noncommittally.

"I visit your sister on the regular," Mary announced.

Satrine's expression gentled at this news.

"Or I did, until Edgar put a stop to it," Mary continued.

Satrine didn't gentle at that.

"She's home with us now, Aunt Mary," she said. "And flourishing."

"This, too, is unsurprising. Corliss doted on that girl. She was her very life."

Satrine pressed her lips together.

"Sweet child, she is. So very sweet," Mary muttered to herself, but did it gazing at Satrine. She turned that gaze to Ansley. "A miracle, my good man."

"Agreed," Ansley replied.

Satrine ducked her head, likely to hide as she controlled her tears.

Loren stretched his leg to rest his boot beside her foot.

When she felt it, she pressed that foot closer.

And then Loren resumed eating.

Chapter Eighteen

Choice

Satrine

Loren and I sat in the carriage, practically fused to each other's sides, and I was as enthralled as he in how he was fiddling with my fingers.

"I daresay…"

I blinked and my head came up to see Aunt Mary sitting across from us.

I was so into my guy, I totally forgot she was there.

Then again, my guy was *life*. All broody, needing-me, hot-AF-in-bed, romantic, dashing, with a healthy dose of kickass vigilante thrown in, who could blame me?

Mary had her own carriage but demanded to ride with us when Loren escorted me the short distance home, completely oblivious (or not?) to the fact that we might want some privacy while that happened considering I actually didn't need an escort at all.

Fortunately, this had given me the opportunity to run some interference. This interference took the form of me writing a heavily nuanced note to Mom about the fact Aunt Mary was in town and she was to stay with us, and then we sent her carriage ahead of us.

I just hoped Mom was preparing, and not freaking.

But considering how I felt when I first laid eyes on Dad's aunt, I had a feeling she was.

Aunt Mary, a woman who was born closer to Dad's age then my granddad's, so she was more like an aunt/sister to him. A woman who was totally OTT, but in a hilarious way. A woman who was sharp as a tack, and therefore had Dad's number (to the point she tried to warn Mom off in the beginning, alas, Mom was in love with a charming snake, so it didn't work).

A woman we got after the divorce because she loved us, we loved her, and we all shared something huge: We all kept hoping Dad would be a good guy when he just wasn't.

This world's Aunt Mary, one could say the drama was at fever pitch.

But she was a scream, and more, it seemed so far so good with Mom and me not getting found out.

"…you two owe me a debt of gratitude," she went on. "For obviously, you are *most* enamored with each other. And equally obviously, it is *me* who had the foresight, indeed, it could almost be described as beneficent *clairvoyance*, to arrange your marriage."

Loren did not make note that the woman had no idea I existed therefore she couldn't possibly have done that.

He said, "Lady Mary, rest assured, you have my undying gratitude."

Aww!

"As it should be," she snipped.

I swallowed back laughter.

Loren's fingers closed around mine and he tucked my hand close to his chest.

I looked up at his profile, his strong jaw, his long lashes, and my heart squeezed knowing Mom and me…

We were never, *ever* going home.

I was never leaving him.

I was in deep with him.

And he needed me.

So I was going nowhere.

Fortunately, from our discussion before it all went down last night, I knew Mom agreed with this.

So we were set.

We were here, and here we would stay.

And I couldn't say I didn't grieve our family, my friends, the concept that I'd never again drink a Diet Coke.

But the truth of it was, at this point, if I was given a choice, I would choose here.

Maxine.

Ansley.

And Loren.

As the ride was short, on this thought, it was over, I knew this as the carriage swayed to a halt.

And as was obviously her wont, Aunt Mary didn't delay in bringing the drama.

She released the catch on the door, kicked it open with her boot, and shouted to Edgecomb, one of our footmen, who was currently racing to the carriage, "You there! Stop dallying! See to these steps this instant!"

I couldn't swallow that giggle.

Loren gave my fingers a squeeze on his chuckle.

We were then treated to the highly enjoyable show of Aunt Mary trying to exit the carriage at the same time keep a hat on her head that was bigger than the door to said carriage.

She managed it.

Loren alighted before me so he could help me out as Edgecomb was escorting Aunt Mary to our front door, which was thrown open before she climbed the second step.

"Auntie Mary!" Maxine cried, darting down the steps.

I stopped dead.

I'd never seen her so animated.

They embraced.

I heard Aunt Mary mumble, "My beauteous beauty."

Maxine sprung back.

"You're here!"

"I am, my dearest," Mary confirmed.

"You met Sattie and Lorie?" she asked.

"Lorie?" Loren murmured.

I pressed tighter to his side, overwhelmed by this.

The doctor had said we needed to be patient. That Maxine would respond to stability, begin to sense she was loved and being looked after, and then she would blossom. That the more she was around the people with whom she'd be sharing her life, even if she wasn't directly interacting with them, the more comfortable she would be, and the more she would come out of her shell.

Loren hadn't been around that much, but he was around.

Thus, it seemed the doc knew what he was talking about.

"Yes, my darling girl," Mary responded.

"She's my *sister*!" Maxine exclaimed excitedly.

Oh shit.

I was going to cry.

Loren dropped my hand and wrapped his arm around me.

"Indeed, she is, my dear," Aunt Mary replied.

But her voice was weird.

This made me focus on her.

She was now gazing up the steps to where Mom was standing, Carling (as ever) hovering at her shoulder.

Oh shit times two.

I was about to hustle forward in an effort to continue running interference.

But Mom floated gracefully down the steps, took Mary by the arms, bent to touch cheek one, then cheek two, and kept hold of her as she pulled back.

"Mary," she whispered.

"I am...quite...overwhelmed." Aunt Mary's voice was husky.

And *again*, I was going to cry.

I turned into Loren and pushed close.

"Let's get you inside. There's much to share," Mom said.

Oh boy.

But Mary's hand darted up, she pressed her fingers to Mom's mouth, Mom's eyes crossed to look at them, I nearly let out a hysterical laugh, and Mary spoke.

"We shan't speak of it. *Ever*. It's *unspeakable*. It is good I've arrived, Corliss. I will be your shield. There isn't a member of the peerage who would cross me. The deeds have been done. The stories have been told to the proper authorities. They never need be uttered again. And that is behind us."

Okay, seriously.

Everything just...

Fell into place.

I mean, maybe Mom was right.

With the way things kept happening, it felt like we were supposed to be here.

Mary raised her parasol like a banner before her, hooking Mom's elbow with her own and forging forward so Mom had no choice but to forge with her.

"Now, *we look to the future!*" she proclaimed like she was releasing a battle cry. "And leave the wicked ways of the past behind!"

They disappeared inside.

Maxine came to us, and I wasn't proud of it, but my mouth was agape as she clasped Loren's other arm and made us forge ahead too.

"Auntie Mary's always a load of fun," she shared.

"We're learning that, poppet," Loren muttered.

Poppet?

Maxine gazed up at him with bright eyes.

Oh my God!

Wasn't he just *the best?*

We made it into the house just as Mary was nearly shouting, "By Brigid! The wonders you have wrought! And I'm barely but ten steps inside!" She whirled on us. "Maxine. Come here, child. You and your mother are going to take me on a tour of these delightful changes you've made. I don't want to miss a thing."

Maxine let Loren go and dashed to Mary.

"Carling, send someone to follow with pen and paper," Mary demanded. "I might have notes."

"Right away, milady," Carling replied, and took off.

Mom looked over her shoulder at me as she pulled Mary and Maxine to the stairs, saying, "First, let's start in Maxine's room. I want your opinion. We're redoing it. There's this lovely yellow wallpaper that we've found."

"Yellow, my dear?" Mary asked while they went up the steps, those words coming out like, *the color of vomit, my dear?* "Everyone knows a bedroom should be *blue*."

They disappeared up the stairs.

Loren turned me into his arms.

Mm.

This felt good.

When I caught his eyes, I said, "Hi."

"We're going to *Le Cirque Magique* for dinner tonight."

Nice.

Our first date.

Instead of shouting *Yippee!* I said, "All right."

"Tell Idina to pack a case. Your mother's home is getting crowded. Tonight, you'll again be staying with me."

Nice!

"Righty ho," I agreed, grinning.

He studied my mouth before he kissed the grin right off it.

I was panting when he lifted his head and shared, "Now, I have some things I need to do. I'll arrive to collect you at seven this eve."

Ummmmmm…

The brazen schemer!

I squinted my eyes at him and held on when it seemed he was going to let me go.

"That kiss was awesome, my lord, but not so fast."

His lips twitched.

"Do these *things* have anything to do with a certain Madam Dupont?" I demanded to know.

"Darling."

I waited.

Apparently, that was all he was going to say.

"Loren," I snapped.

"I won't exert myself. I promise."

"I should hope not, since you also promised you healed fast, and I would hate to feel the need to sleep alone in my own bed to allow you room to do that."

He gathered me back to him and put his lips to mine.

"This is most assuredly incentive to see to my health."

"Indeed," I agreed.

I felt his lips smile against mine, he kissed me again, this time hella more thoroughly, so I was swaying and dazed when he ended it, lifted up, kissed my forehead and murmured, "See you at seven."

And then he was away.

Chapter Nineteen

Associates

Satrine

Scratching him under his chin, I carried Mr. Popplewell purring in my arms into the kitchens at the back of the house.

When I arrived, our cook, Mrs. Soames, looked up and smiled.

"Lady Satrine, how lovely."

I sniffed the air and shared, "I'm accompanying Lord Remington to *Le Cirque Magique* tonight, and it is solely a testament to how wonderful he is that I go and thus sacrifice experiencing whatever it is you're cooking for our dinner."

She blushed.

"Mr. Popplewell tells me he needs chicken," I informed her.

He purred louder.

"Lady Maxine was in here not an hour ago, getting him a bowl of cod," she told me.

Mr. Popplewell hissed.

I looked down at the cat. "You didn't tell me that."

"*Sssssisssy,*" he replied irritably.

"You can wait until dinner," I stated firmly.

He rolled huffily in my arms, leaped out of them, and after shooting me a baleful cat glare, with ginger-ringed tail held high, he waddled out of the kitchens on his white-booted feet.

"That's the fattest cat I've seen in my life," Mrs. Soames noted.

Down the hall, another hiss was heard.

Mr. Popplewell was not fond of being called fat.

I laughed softly and said, "I fear we do him no favors, spoiling him as we do."

"I think a savvy but lost creature who has no home, when he finds one, should have everything he wishes for a spell. Don't you?" Mrs. Soames asked.

I looked into her eyes and answered softly, "Quite right."

She smiled at me.

I got down to the real business for being there.

"Is Carling in his office?"

"He is indeed, madam."

I nodded and moved that way. "Thank you."

Carling's office was more a hidey hole/wine cellar/liquor storage, probably because the door was banded in iron and had a lock. His desk was shoved in amongst the mess, which included barrels and crates full of who knew what. It was likely Dad-not-Dad made him guard all of this, regardless of how stuffy and almost inoperable it made his office.

He was crammed behind said desk, poring over some papers.

"I daresay we can afford it if one of the staff feels the need of a glass of brandy after having a busy day," I said quietly. "We hardly need an ironclad door."

His head shot up right before he shot out of his seat.

"Lady Satrine!"

"Please, do sit," I invited.

He didn't, of course.

"May I come in?" I asked.

"It would be my honor to have your company," he answered.

I really dug this guy.

I came in and made my way with some difficulty to the lone chair in front of his desk.

At long last, I wedged myself between some boxes and found my seat.

"I know my mother has been in here, Carling," I noted as I sat.

He waited until I was down before he sat too. "She has."

"And she hasn't shared you should make it so there's some air that you can breathe while you're in it?"

He cleared his throat and stated, "We're receiving bids to...*alter* some of the belowstairs. And the lady of the house wishes this seen to with all due haste."

I sat still as a statue.

"We're making it into a wine cellar and buttery," he continued.

"I see."

What he meant was, the dungeon Dad-not-Dad had down there for whatever reason he had it was being repurposed.

"It will be in the way during construction. There's nowhere to put all of it until it's done," Carling said quietly. "And I'm used to it, milady. I can wait."

"Of course," I replied. "But could you, perhaps, use my father's study in the meantime?"

Hs expression grew tender, because of my words, as well as what he was about to say.

"Lady Corliss suggested that same thing. You are both most kind, but it simply wouldn't be proper."

One thing Carling exceled at was being proper.

"Very well," I murmured. Then said, "Though, this does segue us rather well."

And surprisingly, it did, thank gods, because I had a plan, but I didn't have a plan on how to broach it.

He appeared confused.

Damn.

As mentioned, I had a plan. It might come to nothing, but considering I had a man to look after, it was worth a shot.

I took that shot.

"Lord Remington shared that my father had access to some rather...*colorful characters*."

Carling's eyes widened.

I hurried on.

"I don't know if word reached your ears, Carling..." I did know. Everything reached his ears. "But my intended had a spot of trouble last night."

"I had heard something of this, milady."

"Well, you see, he's very strong, so you couldn't tell this morning, but he was injured in the fracas. To the point a physician had to attend him last night."

"My goodness," he said with alarm.

"He'll be fine...eventually." I put more weight on the last word than was needed.

"Well, that's good to hear."

"He's supposed to be resting."

Carling said nothing.

"He's not."

Carling stared at me.

"Because he's concerned about this matter, and he is rather a man of action."

"He is that, milady," Carling mumbled.

Yes.

He knew everything.

"And it has me wondering, if…perhaps…some of Father's, erm…*associates* might know something of the foes my betrothed is facing so that, if I were to learn what they know, I can help him—"

I spoke no more as Carling bopped up from his seat, zigged and zagged through the barrels and crates, shoved his head out the door, looked this way and that down the hall, and then, with some effort due to its heaviness, he closed it.

He zigged and zagged back, sat down at his desk and leaned conspiratorially to me.

In turn, I leaned toward him, hopeful at this behavior.

But all he said was, "Milady, it's my honor. Leave this with me."

He sat back and spoke no more.

"Pardon?" I queried.

"I know precisely what to do," he shared.

"And that would be?" I pressed.

"With respect, never you mind. Trust it's in hand. Or it will be."

"I…um, Carling—"

"I know his ways. I can handle this."

"His ways?"

"Indeed."

"Whose ways?"

He leaned forward again, so much farther, he was out of his seat and resting on his forearms on his desk.

"Your sire's," he whispered, and sat back.

"Carling—"

"Don't think again of it."

"Carling!" I snapped.

He shut up.

"You are truly the most wonderful houseman a house could have," I announced.

His face went scarlet.

"And as such, I cannot put you in danger. Not only because I cannot, but also because, if I did, Mother would murder me. Therefore, if you'd advise, I will take care of…whatever I'm doing to take care of things."

Ulk.

Lame finish, Satrine!

"I can't allow that, milady."

"Well, I can't allow you to put your neck on the line either."

He grew quiet.

I did too.

Impasse.

Bloody hell!

Carling broke it.

"We'll work together."

I felt my face beaming.

He grew stern.

"Milady, I won't do this if you don't have a mind that I know what I'm doing…and you don't."

I sat forward on my seat. "Oh, I'll have a mind. I promise."

He studied me.

And then he shared, "When your father would need some information, he'd send the hall boy with a note and the appropriate coin to some urchins in the Quarter. They would see to it that the request in that note was disseminated as it needed to be. We have your father's stationery, though I assume everyone knows his current condition. That matters not. I'll sign the notes in his stead. Anyone will think I'm acting on his behalf."

Excellent!

However…

"Why would my father do this?"

Carling shrugged. "To learn what ships were docking in what ports in what cities and know what they're carrying. To understand what was lost in a warehouse fire in Vasterhague before anyone else heard that word." He took a breath, held my gaze, and continued, "To see to it that a rival took a fall or perhaps drank a hint of poison that might not kill him, but would make him sick, so milord could manipulate his dealings in a manner that was lucrative for himself, and the clients he'd guided to or away from these industries."

In other words, Edgar Dawes was an even *bigger* piece of shit than we already knew he was.

"Right," I whispered.

"We have one issue, milady," Carling said.

"And that is?"

"Lord Remington's guards are still here. And last night, another was added who, if I understood his movements correctly, his brief is to be an extra set of eyes on the alley, the street and the park."

Yep.

There it was.

Carling didn't miss anything.

And yep.

My man liked me a whole lot and went all out to keep me and my family safe.

"It would seem my fiancé has an adversary he's taking seriously, and as such, it would seem our assistance is all the more urgent," I remarked. "Although, I don't know why the guards are a problem."

"Some informants approach the house. It is rare, but it happens. And they will be sure to note your guard, and not approach."

"I see," I mumbled.

"We will share in our missive that we'll set a meeting place, should someone have something they wish to say, and they are not to approach the house."

I smiled. "Grand idea."

"If someone should have something to tell us, you'll need to pay for this, milady," he warned.

"That won't be a problem," I lied, because we were rich as sin, Mom had a ton of money in Ansley's safe, but everything was done on account.

If we had a coffee in a café, they sent word to Carling to pay for it.

If we bought a roll of ribbon to send to Madame Toussaint to add to a gown, same.

And so it went.

I didn't have any money myself.

But I'd figure it out.

And anyway, Mom was always generous with my allowance, even when we didn't have much.

I might not let her in on what was going on, but she'd float me some cash.

No problem.

"Let us go to the study for a piece of stationery, return and write this note, Carling."

His lips curved up and he replied, "Yes, milady. Let's."

Chapter Twenty

Le Cirque Magique

Satrine

A block up from our house, around the corner, and just a block further, there were milliners, dressmakers, jewelers, cobblers, bauble shops, tailors, teahouses and candy stores.

A block down from our house, and three blocks in the other direction, there was a large art museum, cafés, restaurants, bookstores, flower shops and sophisticated drinking establishments.

The streets in between were lined with tall, leafy trees (though now, these leaves were turning to wondrous fall colors) and stately black lampposts.

All the buildings were made of a soft gray that was only perhaps three shades deeper than white. They were clean, and there was something in the stone that made it faintly glitter.

Flowers were as they seemed to be everywhere in my limited experience of this world, placed at a priority. Window boxes abounded. Massive urns burst with blooms in front of houses. Beds were filled in the parks. Hanging baskets fell from lampposts. I even saw a few rooftop gardens that appeared especially verdant.

In between these areas, in a way that reminded me of Savannah, but here it was more prolific, there were parks, some large, like the one opposite our house (and, I'd learned, another one opposite Ansley and Loren's) that took up an entire city block. Some smaller that just offered some greenspace between townhomes.

I loved the area, and Mom, Maxie and I had spent a great deal of time enjoying it.

It was wondrous, as this world seemed wont to be.

But it made me sad that in my old world, the people in power put profit over peace. Building things and selling things and making everything about money, in doing so, covering up all the green.

Make no mistake, even in our area of Newton, one that was clearly clean and upper class, we were in a city and there was hustle and bustle. People going places, striding down the sidewalks. Horses and carriages on the cobbled streets.

But with the trees and the flowers and the green spaces, even with the bustle, there was beauty. There was a sense of serenity. An offer from nature to slow down and witness her abundance and be thankful.

That was my experience in our, perhaps, eight-block radius.

Outside of the ride to the constabulary, I hadn't seen much of the city.

Until I sat next to Loren on the way to *Le Cirque Magique*.

And I learned much of the rest was the same.

Although we rode through districts that were less about townhomes and shops, and more about banks, merchants' offices, brokers, solicitors, physicians and estate agents, and the parks were less plentiful (but they still had them), the trees and streetlamps remained. The buildings still glittered, people strolled the streets, horses and carriages clomped along the cobblestones, and the city seemed alive.

I loved sitting next to Loren.

I loved we were going out on a date.

I loved that, at the end of the date, he was a sure thing.

I loved the gown I was wearing.

I loved that he was holding my hand and that seemed to be a thing with him, which I loved even more.

But I couldn't tear my eyes from the carriage windows so I could drink it all in.

It was a good thing.

For when the hotel in which *Le Cirque Magique* occupied its upper floor, the tallest building in the city, standing at nine stories (all this, Aunt Mary had shared with me, beside herself with glee Loren was taking me to *Le Cirque*, a restaurant in a hotel, both of which were apparently renowned across the Vale), came into view, I gasped.

It reminded me of The Plaza in New York.

Except better.

We stopped at its grand entry, which had three plush, royal blue carpet runners running down the steps to the street from its three ornate double doors, and at once, a footman was there to open our carriage.

He pulled down the steps, and it was Loren who alighted first so he could assist me.

The hotel was called The Heritage.

It was not adorned in gold, but gleaming silver that complemented the glittering gray stone.

It was outlandishly ostentatious.

And I hadn't even walked inside, but I already knew I loved *every inch of it*.

Loren guided me in, and I nearly fainted at the opulence of the lobby.

Black marble floors, veined in silver and blue, blue marble columns veined in black and silver. Enormous dripping crystal chandeliers.

The middle was an atrium domed in stained glass.

It was *staggering*.

"Milord, the private car awaits," a liveried employee murmured to us, and I looked to him, then to Loren, who dipped his chin to the man.

We were led to the side, down a short hall, and the man opened a carved pocket door, where inside, with a magnificently tiled floor, and silver gilded mirrors, there was an elevator.

"Oh my," I whispered.

Loren led me in, our escort came in with us, and at once, he closed the door and pulled a cord.

I felt Loren's lips at my ear.

"The riffraff take the stairs," he whispered on a tease, because no "riffraff" ever came here.

It was just that this elevator was saved for people as important as the Marquess of Remington.

I turned startled eyes to him, it occurring to me for first time since I met him how prominent his title was.

He was.

He winked.

The car lurched, I grabbed on to him, and we started going up.

One could say they didn't have the elevator business quite flowing in that world. It took forever to get to the top.

But I didn't care.

I was holding on to my man and he was taking me on the best date I'd had in my life, I knew that even if it hadn't really started.

We arrived at the top, our guy opened the doors and led us out, but Loren slowed our progress and said something I didn't get.

"Twenty men."

I gazed up at him. "Sorry?"

"The lift. For a smooth ride, they shift around, it's like a dance. I requested they show me how it's done once, and it was remarkable. It takes twenty men to lift us to the top."

Holy cow!

"Men pulled us up here?"

He gazed curiously at me. "How else would that car rise?"

How else indeed.

I shrugged.

He smiled.

He then stopped us at the wide entry to a vast room.

I stood in the middle of the doorway, looking into the room.

And I nearly burst into tears.

Every inch of the ceiling fell with extraordinary crystal chandeliers, one fat white candle burning in each. The walls between the windows had a line of crystal sconces holding three candles. The tables had elaborate crystal candelabrum, the bases of them high so diners could see each other. The smaller tables, the holder had five tapers. The larger, seven candles. Larger than that, there were several holders on the table.

The walls were upholstered in something dark but gossamer. Web-like and subtly glittering.

The tables were covered with pure white tablecloths. The silver and crystal on them picking up the candlelight and sparkling. The plates did too, as they were made of glass edged in silver.

It was dim, the lighting so carefully orchestrated, blow out a single candle, and it would be nearly impossible to see.

And all around there were views of the city.

The black-uniformed waiters, carrying trays of food and drinks, maneuvered the dark space like acrobats.

It *was* a circus.

And it was magical.

I felt Loren divest me of my cloak to give it to a waiting attendant.

And I heard a collective gasp.

My gown, a nude beige silk that was form-fitting to above my knees, then flared out in a circular skirt, but faded to a see-through netting above the bodice, was stitched impeccably with cut-outs of immaculate black lace. The lace floated in lines down the skirt and rounded the hem. It also raised over my breasts and capped my shoulders. And a band of it was stitched at my waist like a belt and my neckline to serve as a necklace.

The back, leading over my ass and down the train, was even better.

My hair was up in a sleek style. I carried a black satin clutch with a rhinestone buckle as a catch. Long black gloves were smoothed up my arms. And I wore no jewelry but large diamond studs at my ears.

And it was good I went for it for my first date with my guy.

Because every eye in the room was on me.

"Well...shite," I breathed.

"You're magnificent," Loren whispered in my ear, tucked my hand in his elbow, and guided me into the room.

Every gaze followed.

We walked behind the maître d' as he took us to a table at the back and to the side that was small, rectangular, had a five-candle candelabra, and two plush, black-velvet chairs on the outside facing the view where the table was set against the window.

And Newton lay before us, twinkling like London while Peter, Wendy and friends flew over it to Neverland.

Loren held out my seat.

I sat.

He joined me and was barely down when two gorgeously etched flutes of champagne were laid in front of us, the bucket with the bottle put on the table, and whoever offered these swept away.

Our backs were to the room, I could still feel the attention even though a hum had struck up.

And I didn't care a whit.

I reached for my glass.

Loren took his.

I turned to him.

He'd dressed for the occasion, apparently, in all black, including boots, shirt and neckcloth.

He looked like a glamorous scoundrel.

Delicious.

I tipped my flute toward him.

"This will be the best, most enjoyable, most memorable evening I'll ever have in my life," I announced.

"Will it?" he asked, sounding amused.

I was not amused.

"It will," I stated, my voice edged with steel.

His attention on me grew acute.

"Satrine," he whispered, his voice rough.

"You may think you're dark," I told him. "And I'm finding you are. Dark like this." I indicated the room with a sweep of my flute. "Edged in gossamer and crystal. Lit with fire. A beautiful cocoon where I feel safe, truly safe, for the first time in my life."

His voice was now thick, and that fire was burning into me from his eyes.

"Sweeting."

I leaned into him and whispered, "So stay dark, my handsome man. I'll take you precisely as you come."

I sat back, clinked my glass against his, and drank.

He didn't drink.

He took my flute after I took my sip and set it beside his own, which was already on the table.

Then he pulled me into his arms, my ass barely still on my seat, my chest plastered to his, and he laid a wet, heavy, scrumptious kiss on me.

He released my mouth but not my body.

I swam up from the kiss.

"I'm falling in love with you," he stated matter-of-factly.

"Good, because the same is happening to me," I replied breathily.

He smiled, a small, happy, *beautiful* smile.

I wasn't sure I gave as good as I got, but I tried.

"Remington, my chap."

We both turned our heads.

At a table a few feet away, a man with a bald pate, bushy white hair at the sides, and even bushier mutton-chop sideburns was smiling at us.

"Here's to your good fortune, sir," he said, raising a glass of red wine our way.

"Yes, hear hear," the woman with him agreed, rising from her seat.

The man followed her as we heard another "hear hear."

And then more.

And more.

Everyone rose and raised their glass to the Marquess of Remington and his bride.

So…freaking…*cool*.

"Is this…uh, *normal?*" I asked under my breath.

"They don't know what I did, but they do know it was offered the highest decoration from the king when I served in his army," he answered low. "And that decoration is rewarded very rarely, so they can assume it was something."

Well then.

Since it *was* something, that most certainly explained it.

I smiled at the room, all on their feet, raising their glasses to my man.

And I did it huge.

"And I believe it's safe to say," he went on in a drawl, "they agree with me that your gown is quite remarkable."

Oh my gods!

He was just...plain...*awesome!*

With that, Loren set me more fully in my seat, took my glass and handed it to me, nabbed his own, and I followed suit as we twisted in our chairs and raised our drinks to the assemblage.

A muted, tasteful cheer broke out.

And we all drank.

Totally.

Best...

Date...

Ever.

Chapter Twenty-One

Days Were Numbered

Satrine

Oh my *gods*.

I needed him to *fuck me*.

"Baby," I gasped.

I was so into it, I could say no more, like, *Slam that gorgeous, big cock of yours IN ME*.

I was in a state.

I was also on my knees in Loren's bed, Loren behind me on his, that big, thick dick of his hard and pressing into my backside. He had one of his hands at my breast, pinching and squeezing my nipple. The other was between my legs, doing things to my clit that honestly were so decadent, they should be illegal.

But no matter how I moved my hips, how desperately I rubbed my ass against his cock, he refused to come inside.

Even with his fingers.

"I think I need you inside," I whimpered.

He growled into my neck.

Oh yes.

But then he said in my ear, "I'm not taking your maidenhead with my fingers."

I grew immobile and blinked at his cobalt damask wallpapered wall.

"What?"

He nipped my ear.

I shivered as he said, "My love, I'll accept your virtue, what's left of it, when I have no more pain. I'm loath to admit I have it, but I do. And I want it all to be about you and me and our coupling when that time comes."

My virtue?

His fingers rolled.

My mind blanked, I moaned, and my head fell back to his shoulder.

Totally freaking should-be-illegal.

"Do you need me to eat you?" he offered into my ear.

At these words, I gasped again, but this time a shudder came after it because I was coming.

He had an arm around my chest, one around my ribs, and he was nuzzling my neck, when it left me.

"Are you all right?" he murmured.

"Yes," I pushed out, and I *so* was.

"I thought you wouldn't stop trembling, and moaning, I was growing alarmed," he teased.

Why was cocky so hot?

"Smug. Bluh," I mumbled.

"Mm," he purred into my skin, and at the sound and feel, my nipples, achingly hard, got harder. "If I can do that with my fingers, I wonder how you'll respond when you have my cock."

Which, of course, brought crashing back to mind the "virtue" situation he'd mentioned before he blanked my mind with an all-encompassing orgasm.

Virtue.

Maidenhead.

Oh hell.

He thought I was a virgin.

Of course he would, considering I'd been secluded in the countryside of Fleuridia since I was six, not allowed any friends or acquaintances until my father came and forced me to fake being my sister.

How could I get laid if that was the case?

Shit.

This begged the question, how did he think I got good at giving blowjobs if I'd never done it before?

Which brought to mind...

"Do you want me to...what I did this morning—?"

I didn't finish because he fell to his back, pulled me down to his side, and used his hand at my jaw to turn my face to him.

Quietly, studying me closely—no doubt, I would find, when he said what he said next, in order to ascertain my reaction, assess if he was pushing too fast, not wishing to take the virgin to a place she was uncomfortable—he shared, "No, my love. I want you to watch me do it. We shall see, but I suspect it will prime you to straddle my mouth."

I whimpered again.

He grinned wickedly and murmured, "That answers that."

Yes, he was being careful with me.

Due to my "virtue."

"Loren—"

He lifted his head, touched his mouth to mine, fell back to the pillows, and ordered, "Watch."

I had no choice.

Because presently, he pulled us both up so he was resting against the headboard, and I couldn't *not* stare at him jacking his big, beautiful dick until he came all over his belly.

Seriously, he was *totally* and *completely* a *sex god.*

He didn't even clean up before he was down again on his back in the bed, and he had to give barely any guidance with his hands before I was swinging a leg over his head in order to ride his face.

And serious to all the gods in two universes, he was good at that.

He left me, drained from two huge orgasms, full of champagne, wine and the best meal I'd ever consumed, in his bed in order to go to his dressing room and clean himself up.

He blew the lamps out on his way back and joined me in bed.

Gathering me close, drowsily, I called, "Loren."

"I have come to the conclusion, my love, that the trials we both faced to be in this bed together were the tribulations we needed to pay to earn what we have right now, and the beauty we will build for our future."

I closed my eyes tight.

But he wasn't done gutting me.

"And as such, I'd do it again, Satrine. All of it. Again and again." He squeezed me tight. Tighter than was comfortable. It was sheer beauty. "If this is where it leads me."

"Be quiet," I begged.

His arms loosened.

"I speak truth," he whispered.

"You're killing me," I mumbled.

"No, darling, finally, we both are living."

Oh my gods.

Yes.

He was killing me.

* * * *

In his rooms, Loren had two window seats.

They faced the park.

And once he was asleep, his breath evening out, his arms not holding me quite so close (but they didn't let go), I gave it time, and then more, to make sure he was out.

Then I slipped away from him, pulled on his dressing gown, and padded to one of those seats.

I curled into it and stared at the park.

I was a lie.

I wasn't a virgin.

I wasn't a count's daughter.

I didn't have a sister.

I didn't know but considering what a big deal it was and how much havoc and heartbreak it caused over centuries in my world, evidence suggested that in some situations, a dude having a bride who was a virgin was a big deal.

I could fake it, of course. Not everyone had an intact hymen when the time came. Shit happened to break it along the way. I could talk my way around that.

But it'd be a lie.

And he'd think, all of our lives together, he was the only one. The only man I sucked. The only body I took.

I'd settled into Satrine. New world, new outlook, new name. And Maxie needed our name.

I'd settled into knowing I didn't come here by choice, but I was staying there because of it.

But this...

This *sucked*.

I jumped when hands fell on me, and then Loren's big body shifted around mine so he could sit behind me, and surrounding me, in the seat.

He'd pulled on his evening breeches, but I could tell his gorgeous chest was bare.

He also pulled me back against that chest.

"Why are you so far away, staring with such pensiveness at the park?" he asked quietly.

Because I just had the best date anyone in my world could even imagine having, and probably most anybody in this world too.

Because Maxine calls you Lorie.

Because you're so respected, you walk into a massive restaurant with your new fiancée, and the entire place stands to toast your future.

Because you laugh at my hats, and Mom's right, you look at me like I keep the world spinning.

Because I can never tell you who I am. I can never tell you stories about growing up. I can't tell you about my friends. I can't tell you the real deal about why Mom is so awesome. I can never tell you all that made me before I came to you.

Because I can never even share how I came to you. I can't tell you about how scary it was. I can't tell you how, if it hadn't been you, this could have gone really fucking badly. So you saved me, my mom, my sister, and you made this a glorious adventure, not a terrifying tragedy.

Because you will never know precisely how deep I'm in it for you, because when myself and the one being I love more than my own life were thrown into the unknown, in the end, you made it so that we were both, in our own ways, blissfully happy.

And because I'm not a virgin, and you might figure that out, and all that will go to shit if you do.

"Dearest," he prompted, wrapping his arms closer around me.

I twisted in them and caught his head in my hands.

He stilled at my movements.

"No matter what, know this, Loren. Know it down to your *fucking bones*," I demanded, my voice ugly, rasping, even scary.

His arms got tighter. "Satrine."

"What I came from, who I am, no matter what, I am who you think I am. I am who you believe me to be. I am that woman. For you."

Something passed his face.

Understanding.

"Sweeting, calm yourself—"

I pressed in at his head. "No. You don't...you'll never get it and...and..."—my voice was breaking—"...and I can't tell you. I'll never be able to tell you. I'll never be able to share it with you. I can't. I just *can't.*"

He pulled me deep into him, and his voice was low and flinty when he said, "You don't need to, Satrine. I don't need that. I have what I need right here."

He was mistaking me, as he would.

And I couldn't correct him.

"You don't get it!" I sobbed. "And you never will."

With a hand behind my head, he shoved my face in his neck. "Hush. Do not let this upset you. It doesn't matter. It's done. Behind you."

"You don't understand," I wailed, pushing deeper into him, pressing my face to his skin.

He turned his head and kissed my hair, one hand stroking my back, his body rocking mine, and urged, "Hush, my love. Hush. You're here. Not there. You're safe."

Oh gods!

He'd never understand!

My body wracked with a sob.

"Hush, my love," he whispered.

It wracked again.

"I wanna tell you, I just can't." I yanked my face out of his neck and stared at his blurry head. "I promise. *I swear*, Loren. I want to tell you *so bad*."

He shoved my face back where it was and stated inflexibly, "I'll not hear talk of this again. I don't need it, Satrine. Do not let it upset you."

And there it was again, all of it, falling into place as if it was meant to.

But *he didn't get it!*

And it was his to have.

But he never would.

I reared in his arms with my emotion, and he held on.

In the end, I cried myself out, and it was so mammoth, I was a ragdoll after it was over.

Never fear, my man was a god and he picked me up and put me to bed.

He held me there too, and muttered irritably, "That man is the foulest in creation, having done this to you. I worried you were handling things too well. You should have let this out sooner, darling."

"Yeah," I mumbled.

"It will come to you, and I hope it will be soon, just how safe you are."

Until Lady Corliss meets a friend she should know well, but she doesn't.

Or Dad-not-Dad makes his defense, and suggests someone go to Fleuridia and find this cottage we were supposed to have been sequestered in and the couple who brought us provisions, and it wasn't there, and they don't exist.

Or a million different threads of the carefully crafted lies Mom and I told started to unravel.

And then, how safe would I be?

We'd have money.

Mom or I would let go of Maxine on our dying breath, so we'd have Maxie.

But there were a million ways to be found out.

And then lose him.

And I couldn't exist in this world without him.

Hell, I couldn't exist in my world without him.

But I knew, down in my soul, somewhere along the way, something was going to get fucked up.

I knew down to my soul…

My days were numbered.

Chapter Twenty-Two

Spoiled

Satrine

"Darling!"

After shouting his endearment at me, the reins were tugged from my gloved fingers so Loren could right the phaeton I was driving.

I noticed this vaguely, seeing as, following the carriage that held Mom, Maxie and Aunt Mary, I'd taken the turn onto an avenue, and I'd seen it.

And *it* being all it was, I lost track of what I was doing with the horses.

"Good Gods, it's amazing," I whispered.

Mom's carriage stopped in front of the block-long building.

Loren guided our phaeton behind it and came to a stop too.

I distractedly noted men wearing smart, blue uniforms loping toward us from a small hut erected on the pavement, as I sensed Loren securing the reins then turning to me.

But mostly, through all this, I sat staring.

"It took five years and was brought painstakingly, section by section, by ship and then by land, and reconstructed here. The stone is so heavy, they could only put one piece aboard one vessel at a time, and there are twenty pieces. It was a scandal throughout the realm, not only the cost of that task of bringing it here, but what the taxpayers of Newton had to pay the Dax of Korwahk simply to have it," he said.

I remained motionless in the carriage, attempting to take in the enormous, exquisitely carved statue of a horse that stood at the front of the long, stately building. He was up on his hind hooves, striking at the air, his mane long and wild, his head proud and fierce, his nostrils flaring, and he had to rise two, maybe even more stories up into the air.

Making him even more magnificent, his hooves looked to be made of real gold, as were his bared teeth, not to mention the tips of his mane and tail, but his eyes could be nothing else but humongous rubies.

There was decorative, but most assuredly tall, stout and dangerous (what with all the spears on top) iron fence surrounding it, as well as a contingent of those men in blue uniform.

My eyes drifted to Loren when he spoke again.

"It's a statue of their horse god, and I'm told it isn't even the most superlative of them. That one, apparently, is on the road that leads to their capital city of Korwahn," Loren went on.

I couldn't imagine a *better* one. That was impossible.

Loren wasn't finished.

"This statue is guarded day and night and thousands of people from all over Hawkvale, Lunwyn and Fleuridia have taken the journey to Newton simply to view it."

"I can see why," I replied. "I've never seen anything so...so...*large*. And so beautifully rendered. And so...so...magnificently *daunting*. I mean, it's incredible, but it's also terrifying, like he was a god at one point, and he's been turned to stone."

And it was a "he." They hadn't left that part out in the rendering.

Loren was smiling. "Most everyone, not Korwahkian, are in concurrence. And the citizens of Newton complain no more, due to the coin spent by visitors in our hotels, shops and restaurants. And now, as you know, Newton's Museum of Cultures has another feather in their cap, beating out all others in the Northlands to show this exhibit of Firenz tribal history. I'm not sure any museum anywhere has ever had an exhibit this large of anything from Triton. It's only recently, due to the Mar-el pirates allowing passage after freeing the seas that made it possible."

This being why we were there.

Multitasking, Loren was giving me a phaeton-driving lesson on the way to see said exhibit.

"Don't think I missed that you nearly took out that unsuspecting milk cart," Aunt Mary snapped.

Loren twisted and I looked down to see her standing by our carriage under her black parasol, something she had open, even if her hat shaded her entire body, and another half a foot in circumference besides. Her ever-present handbag was dangling from her wrist (seriously, she was like the Queen of England, she even brought that thing to the dinner table).

Last, her dour expression was aimed at me.

She adjusted her aim to Loren.

"I told you it was folly, teaching a woman to drive a carriage. Did you listen?" She lifted her handbag in order to snap her fingers irritably, if ineffectually, since her hands were in gloves. "No, you did not."

"I was startled by the horse, Aunt Mary," I told her.

"A pile of stones is hardly startling."

A pile of stones?

I returned my attention to the horse.

The rubies in his eyes had to be bigger than my fist.

I looked back to Aunt Mary, losing a fight with a smile. "Do we need to take you to have your vision examined?"

Her face screwed up and she turned back to Loren. "You spoil my niece."

At the same time he was alighting, Loren was nodding to a blue uniform guy who apparently was there to see to our carriage.

Once to the sidewalk, he lifted his hand to me, I took it, and he helped me down.

Only when he had me tucked to his side, did he turn to Aunt Mary, and completely unperturbed, reply, "Indeed."

I fought melting into a puddle of goo.

Maxie, standing close to Mom who was now beside Aunt Mary, giggled.

I looked to her and winked.

"Just like your father," Mary huffed. "He doted on your mother. She was, fortunately for him, and, I daresay, *us all*, a supremely sensible female, not a woman to have her head turned by such imprudence, may she be held to the bosom of Brigid. Your sister, however, was indulged beyond imagining. You were all very lucky she was so charming and of such a sweet disposition, or it would have been the ruin of her."

After delivering that, she snapped down her parasol, took it by it folds, and shook the handle at me.

She then carried on.

"Mark that, girl," she warned.

"Mary," Mom said softly, before I could say something to tease Aunt Mary.

And the way Mom spoke made me look to her.

When I did, and I saw how she was gazing at Loren, I turned my head up to him.

His jaw was hard, his lips were tight, and my heart lurched.

"My boy," Aunt Mary whispered, sounding contrite.

"It's fine, Mary," Loren said.

"I meant no—"

Loren didn't let her finish. "As I said, it's fine."

Aunt Mary gave big eyes to Mom. Mom stretched her lips down at Aunt Mary.

I struggled to think what to say while standing on a busy sidewalk outside a museum.

"Can we go inside?" Maxine asked excitedly.

"Of course, poppet," Loren murmured.

Maxine broke from Mom, came to Loren's other side, hooked her arm in his, and guided us both toward the museum in a way that seemed, oddly, like she was saving him from Aunt Mary.

Beyond that, although in the last few days there had been a marked change in her—it was evident she was getting used to all of us and her reticence was quickly disappearing—that was in our zone of home and walks to the shops and trips to the park.

We were now out in public, at a large, bustling museum, and although she expressed her desire to come with us, and she was very animated about that, we had all planned to keep a close eye on her to make sure she was good with it.

From the way she charged forth, she was more than good with it.

Which, I had to admit, was a relief, but it was also a surprise.

The place was busy, but of course, there was VIP treatment there too, and Loren availed us all of it.

Therefore, in no time, and with no bothering with the long lines, we were in the thick of the exhibition that included terrifying swords, bows and arrows that were obviously not mass-produced, but they looked far from primitive, and bejeweled daggers. There were also intricately woven rugs, exceptionally crafted silver chalices, extraordinary jewelry, startling mosaics and even an enormous silk tent erected so you could go inside. And the interior was so sumptuously appointed, I was rethinking Loren taking an ambassadorship. Because if that was how they lived in Firenze, I was all in for the adventure.

It took a while, and me fielding a variety of *see to that!* looks from my mother to get Loren to myself, away from the crowd (which, not incidentally, but we were gamely ignoring it, were almost as fascinated with us as they were with the exhibit), as well as away from Mom, Aunt Mary and Maxie.

He and I were standing off to the side when I asked, "Are you all right?"

He didn't seem upset anymore. In fact, his face wore a fond expression (yes, almost to the point of doting) as he watched Maxine's fascination with a painting on the back of a large hide that depicted a mountain range and a huge, beautiful lake.

"Yes, of course, why?" he answered, but he didn't take his gaze from Maxine.

"Nothing," I mumbled.

That earned me his attention.

"Why did you ask?" he pressed.

"Aunt Mary can be..."

He cut me off.

"They lived. People knew them. She's not the only one to speak of them."

He was talking offhandedly, not to mention somewhat tersely, about his mother and sister.

"She didn't mean to sound insulting," I assured. "She gives backhanded compliments like no one I've ever met, because they're completely backhanded, but she actually means them as compliments."

"I'm not angry at your aunt," he stated firmly.

"Okay," I whispered.

His lips twitched. "I do spoil you, though."

"You do not," I returned.

He looked around us, pointing out that it was the middle of the day, and I had learned in finally getting to know my betrothed that he wasn't the idle rich. Although he was considering a future endeavor of serving his king (again) in one manner or another—along with his side pursuits of being a vigilante—he, and his father, had a variety of things they needed to attend to in order to remain wealthy as sin.

I knew this because at dinner (another one we had alone, just two nights ago, outside a delightful brasserie at the edge of a large cobblestone courtyard, surrounded by trees, glass-fronted shops and other eateries—it was no *Le Cirque Magique*, but it was me and Loren alone, so it was its own version of *everything*), he had talked to me about them.

However, I'd glazed over somewhere between his shipping interests, some partnership he had with a rich guy named Apollo up in Lunwyn, and the string of printing presses he and his dad owned across Hawkvale and down into Fleuridia.

In fact, I'd glazed over so badly, I'd only come unglazed when I heard his rich, attractive chuckle before I felt his firm, delicious lips press to mine.

When he'd pulled away, he'd said, "We'll leave it at the fact I have many interests, so there will be a number of soirees you'll need to organize to keep our investors happy, and a number of opportunities to wear wildly becoming gowns as men try to tempt me into investing in their schemes."

"You know, of the last thousand words you've recently said, I only heard 'soirees you'll need to organize' and 'wildly becoming gowns,'" I'd replied.

Which hadn't made him chuckle.

It had made him laugh.

Which had made me happy.

Short story long, when I'd read about this exhibit in the paper, and learned the existence of this museum, and told him we *had to go*, he'd rearranged his schedule in order to escort us here.

In truth, he gave into my merest whim, as evidenced by the fact we'd walked by a shop after our dinner two nights ago, I'd seen a hat pin in the window that I'd said in a throwaway manner, "That's pretty," and it was delivered to our house the next morning.

So, yes.

Totally spoiled.

Something he'd been doing since I lost it in his bedroom after *Le Cirque Magique*.

Or maybe this was just Loren. From what Aunt Mary said outside, and every indication I'd had since I'd met them both, the Copeland men tended to indulge the women in their lives.

But I couldn't get past thinking that he was trying to help me make up for lost time, secluded in Fleuridia, away from Maxie and even Aunt Mary.

All this on my mind, I blurted, "I'm going to find my way."

His brows slid together. "Pardon?"

"I don't know what I'm going to do, outside earning the reputation of the best hostess in all the Northlands, entirely so your investors will understand how clever you are for marrying such a prize as me," I joked.

He grinned.

I moved closer to him and went on quietly, "But I'll find my way, Loren. You don't have to look after me. You don't have to worry about me. About any of us."

As I was speaking, he'd slid his arm around me, but he pulled me closer when he replied, "It's good Mary is here. I fear your mother being away so long, she, as well as you, will need a guiding hand in society." He sent a small smile down to me. "I'm uncertain Lady Longdon murders a party, but I've no doubt she can set you on the path to figure out how you intend to do it."

My insides froze.

Murders a party.

I'd told him I murdered a party.

And I did.

I mean, my friends were probably lamenting the demise of my yearly Halloween bash as much as the demise they thought became of me.

But Loren thought I'd said that to him in the stables all those weeks ago in order to play the game my father had forced me to play.

When, for once, I'd been telling him the truth.

"Satrine?" he called.

I focused on him and repeated, "I'll find my way."

He was studying me closely, his arm warm around my waist, his gaze affectionate at the same time troubled, because he no doubt thought I'd had a bad moment, remembering my plight.

I pressed my gloved hands into his chest. "I promise."

"I believe you, sweeting," he said gently.

"Though, feel free to continue spoiling me," I teased, hoping it didn't sound forced.

"So you admit it."

I shrugged.

And there came that rich, attractive, chuckle before he did what he was quickly becoming expert in doing: angled his head to avoid my enormous hat so he could touch his lips to mine.

When he lifted away, he didn't go far.

So I went for it. "And if you ever want to talk about them…"

I let that hang.

I found it concerning he only nodded before he straightened completely from me.

But I let it go.

Because I was going to need him to let things go, a lot of them, practically every real thing about me.

The least I could do was return the favor on occasion.

"Does this mean you're going to give up on forcing me to teach you how to drive yourself around?" he asked, and I was getting to know him, so I was more than sensing he wasn't entirely joking.

"It isn't that hard," I returned.

"You're rubbish at it," he stated bluntly.

I was not wrong. He hadn't been joking.

And he was not wrong.

Who knew it was harder than heck driving a carriage through busy streets filled with other carriages, carts, horses, and people crossing (the concept of jaywalking clearly had not been introduced in this world, and although, on the busier streets, there were constables directing crossways, there was nary a stop sign to be found), but also errant dogs, cats and sometimes pigs and chickens?

Horses turned left and right and went faster and slower, depending on what you told them to do. And they weren't real big on running into anything, so they took their own evasive maneuvers.

But a lot of the time, it got hairy.

"I'll get the hang of it."

"Perhaps, if you stop gazing around like you're touring instead of paying attention to where you're going," he suggested.

He was not wrong about that either.

"There are a number of distractions," I pointed out.

"Indeed. This is why women don't drive. Too easily distracted. They see a hat they like in a window, they'd drive into the window next to it because they can't stop looking at it. And then they'd argue it's the hat's fault."

"Oh. My. *Gods*," I whispered irately. "Did you just say that?"

He smiled down at me, hugely, his warm brown eyes dancing, and his arm still around me tightened as his head dipped.

"You are very easy to tease, my Satrine," he whispered.

"You are very lucky you're so gorgeous, my Loren," I retorted.

And there came an even bigger smile.

"I would like to see a lake like that."

We both turned toward Maxine's voice to see she'd come close.

"And mountains," she went on.

Not missing a beat, Loren replied, "Then we shall make plans to show you as many lakes and mountains as can be found, Maxie."

Maxine beamed.

Mm-hmm.

Totally.

Loren Copeland spoiled the women in his life.

Outlandishly.

But I wasn't going to breathe another word about it.

Ever.

Because it was him.

And as were all things Loren, it was beautiful.

* * * *

Loren

He felt her lips as Satrine trailed them up his chest and into his neck before she rested her weight against him.

Loren barely accepted her warmth when he rolled so he was on her.

He was not fully recovered from the ministrations of her mouth, but although he very much liked her soft curves resting on him, he preferred resting his body on those curves.

"How's your wound?" she whispered into his ear.

He grinned and lifted his head.

"Better," he told her.

"Mm…" she hummed.

Still grinning, he touched his mouth to hers, and not moving away, he said, "Soon, my darling."

Her expression shifted and he felt her hand gentle over the bandage at his wound. A bandage she demanded to change morning and prior to bed, so his clothes nor the sheets would aggravate the stitches.

Therefore, he assured, "Very soon, sweeting. There's hardly any pain anymore."

That was not precisely the truth. There was pain, which was why he had not taken their bedplay forward to consummation.

But it *was* getting better, and further, he didn't want her worrying about it.

He got his wish. Her gaze cleared and focused on his.

"Okay, honey," she replied.

"Are you sated for tonight?" he asked.

"Yes," she answered.

"Are you sure?" he teased. "It usually takes three or more before you seem replete, and tonight I only gave you two."

Her eyes rolled to his headboard, and she mumbled. "Ugh. Smug."

Loren laughed.

Her eyes came back to him, and she watched as if enthralled.

It was safe to say his betrothed found his humor of far more interest even than a gilded statue of a Korwahkian god.

Loren gazed at her, her golden hair all over his pillow, her expression now content and serene, her lips bruised from his kisses and gorging on his cock.

So enamored was he in looking at her, he started when her hand came to his face, her thumb sweeping his cheek.

"What are you thinking?" she asked softly.

"That you're beautiful," he told her.

Her expression melted to one of such exquisiteness, if she hadn't already undone him, it would be his undoing.

"You make it worth it," she whispered.

"What?"

"All of it. All that happened, all that's to come. All I lost and never will have again. You make it worth it, and it may seem crazy, but you do it in a way I know you always will."

Fucking hell.

He groaned before he took her mouth.

They embraced for some time before he felt her satiety shift to somnolence. Only then did he move to extinguish the lamps, then tuck her close to him, his body curved into the back of hers under the covers.

He endeavored to time it well, when her sleepiness sapped her craftiness, before he asked after something he'd seen that afternoon when they'd arrived home from the museum.

"What does Carling touching the side of his nose, and you returning that gesture, mean?"

Her relaxed body grew tight in his arms.

He grinned into her hair.

She was appalling at subterfuge.

Carling was worse.

Both, however, were to Loren's favor.

"Nothing," she lied.

"Whatever it is you two are cooking up, my dearest heart, take note that I'd prefer to know beforehand, should I need to wade in and rescue you."

"I don't know what you're talking about," she lied again.

"It is my father's birthday in but weeks, and I have not missed how you've grown fond of him." He gave her a squeeze. "He is a man who has much, so he doesn't need more, except he does very much enjoy the company of people he cares about."

"Right," she whispered.

"So you don't have to murder a party for him. However, if you plan one as a surprise, I can assist with that."

Her voice sounded curiously strangled when she responded, "I'll bear that in mind."

Loren pulled her even closer, burying his face in her hair, "I daresay, he already has his present for this year, three of them, and they all have blonde hair."

"Stop being wonderful," she warned.

He shifted to kiss her shoulder.

And when he settled back, he said, "I'll try."

She was silent long moments, and he thought she was asleep.

He was proved wrong when she murmured drowsily into the dark, "Liar."

He was indeed.

One last time before sleep claimed him, Loren smiled into her hair.

Chapter Twenty-Three

Three Kings

Loren

As Loren approached, the sergeant at the doors, and the four other soldiers besides, saluted smartly before he moved, opened one of the double doors, and Loren strode into the room.

The Royal Suite at The Heritage took up an entire floor.

And it looked like the sitting room of the suite took half it.

"I'm now seeing why you refused to stay with Father and me," Loren drawled as Tor, standing at one of several arrangements of sofas, turned his gaze in Loren's direction.

Cora jumped from one of the settees and moved directly to Loren.

"Lore, you devil, you're getting married?"

He shifted his attention to his king and lifted his eyebrow.

"I left it as a surprise," Tor explained. "My queen has less patience than I do with my nobles making arses of themselves. She didn't want to come. She arrived and received a reward. Now, she's pleased she's here."

As he explained this, Cora made it to him, and he fell into a deep bow, knowing what response that would get.

"Oh my God, stop it," she complained.

But he was struck.

He'd heard that before.

Oh my God.

Singular.

He'd heard his queen say it.

And in the beginning when he met her, he'd heard it from Satrine.

Something vague but strange started to plague his stomach.

He ignored it as he bent to kiss Cora's cheek, and when he was done, Tor was there.

He didn't bother with the bow, teasing or not. He just shook his hand.

And gave his attention to the other people in the room.

Two, he knew, and he did another quick bow to the blonde, but took the hand of the dark giant who stood at her side, and he shook it.

"Dax Lahn," he greeted. "Dahksana Circe," he said to the Dax's queen.

"Good to see you again, Loren," Circe said.

"You're well?" Lahn asked.

He nodded.

"You've made a long journey," he noted, and they had. All the way up from their kingdom of Korwahk in the Southlands. A journey that took at least three months.

"My Circe misses her friend," Lahn explained, pulling his wife close.

Lahn likely missed his friend too.

Loren smiled, finally understanding these matches that came in a variety of ways, and proved not only enduring, but unshakeable (Lahn and Circe's the most unusual), and it wasn't love that forged them.

Yet it absolutely was.

He turned to the last two people in the room.

"I'm not sure you've met," Tor said, as Loren took in the tall, straight, handsome man who, at one glance, he knew was like Loren, a soldier, and the dark, striking beauty with him. "This is King True of Wodell, and his queen, Farah."

Loren bowed.

"We know who you are," the king from across the Green Sea stated. "And what you've accomplished. I am a brother, sir," he confirmed what Loren had surmised. "Do not bow."

Loren straightened, his gaze moving to Tor briefly, he got a nod, then he looked back to True.

"It's still an honor to meet"—he took in Farah with his gaze—"two of the warriors who defeated the Beast."

"Wish we knew all it would take was pushing the monster—" Lahn began.

He stopped when Circe turned and slapped his arm, hissing, "Lahn, there was no 'all it would take' in that heartbreaking situation."

A string of words came from Lahn, calm, gentle, sounding like song, and since Loren didn't speak Korwahkian, he had no idea what the king was saying.

But it made his queen appear less cross.

Tor caught his attention, asking, "And where is your future bride? We're keen to meet her."

"This is an excellent question," Loren replied testily.

Tor's eyebrows went up.

It was nearly a fortnight after her fit in his arms in his rooms.

Not including the fit, obviously, it had been the finest two weeks of his life, and this was quite a claim, considering his father gave him a wonderful childhood, regardless of what they two had lost.

Openness, honesty, sharing, outings with her family, meals together just them alone, and Satrine in his bed at night suited them both.

Magnificently.

They were not inseparable. He had things to do. And she had a wedding to put the finishing touches on.

Also, she and her mother had to make plans for travel to Dalwin for said wedding, a wedding after which Satrine would be with him wherever they landed, so she had to be prepared for it.

She was further embroiled with her mother and Mary in some renovations they were seeing to in the cellar, not to mention restyling Corliss, Maxine *and* Mary's rooms (Mary had decided to stay indefinitely, which, considering she was nosy, meddling and a widow who lived alone, but now had family she cared deeply for that she could order about, was not a surprise).

And last, Satrine had begun a strangely intent, but not surprising project of learning the history and anything else she could devour about the Vale, the Northlands, indeed all the lands. As such, she often had her nose in a book, and she read the newspaper front to back every morning.

In other words, his bride was even more busy than he.

That said, when she was with him, she was *with him*. It seemed she'd made it her mission to cause him to laugh often, urge him to share every nuance of his life (or those he could share), and she had a particular skill in making him climax as hard as he could orgasm.

This was unsurprising too, considering her vow to see to him, never to leave him, never to let him lose his hold on all things good.

She was that, top to toe to bones to soul.

Good.

As such, he had completed the journey to falling in love with her.

It was now simply a matter, day by day, of finding ways to love her more, an endeavor that was far from a struggle.

His only concern was, of late, he'd noted Satrine seemed to be getting anxious. She tried to hide it, but this anxiety was such, she couldn't.

This, he knew, was due to her father's upcoming trial, and regrettably, all Loren could do in the face of that was be steady for her and her mother, until it was over, which fortunately would be soon.

But he, too, had saved Tor and Cora's imminent arrival as a treat for her, even if she knew they were coming, as her father's trial was the day after tomorrow.

However, when he went to collect her to give her the surprise, she was not there, and it seemed no one knew where she was.

Corliss did not appear concerned about this and shared, "As you know, Lorie, she wanders. When you're not around, she likes to read in the park. And she knows Carling is partial to that fudge from the candy store, so when he runs out, she always heads off to get a new supply. And right now, I think he's out."

One of the many pleasing things about his wife-to-be was that she was a busy woman who had many pursuits.

And he suspected, even more strongly now, that she was up to something in regards to his father's birthday, for she had very poorly maneuvered Maxie asking everyone at the table after their favorite pies three nights before when they all shared dinner.

This being something they'd need to know so his father would have his preferred birthday pie.

The problem with this was that Loren had been commanded to meet his king and queen, and bring her with him, and he couldn't wait for her nor did he have the time to look for her, so now he was there...without her.

"You know her story," he said low to Tor.

There was a change in the mood of the room, and with it, Loren knew everyone in it knew her story.

Then again, if they all attended the trial, they'd learn it, and considering the story, it was better they were forewarned.

"She's finally free and she tends to go about enjoying that to the fullest," he explained.

"I think I'm going to like her," Cora decreed.

"I know you will," Loren told her. "She's the most likeable woman

I've ever met."

Cora's eyes lit and her mouth curled up.

"Is she, indeed?" she murmured delightedly.

"She is," he answered firmly.

Cora gave eyes to Circe, then Farah.

But Loren looked to Lahn. "It's good to see you," then to True, "and meet you." He returned his focus to Tor. "But may I ask why they're here?"

"All is well," Tor assured calmly. "Just visits. We haven't seen True and Farah in some time and it was Lahn and Circe's turn to come up."

"And Hayden and Leighton and Devon?" he asked after the realm's two princes and princess.

"Hayden's regiment is stationed on the northeast coast. He'll be granted leave to attend your wedding. Devon is at school, but will be leaving soon, also to journey in order to attend your wedding. And Leighton is undoubtedly testing the efficacy of pennyrium as he beds the maids in Karsvall while training with Apollo in the House of Ulfr's seat. I'm afraid he's too far away to return in time for your wedding."

"I wish I could refute this about Leighton, but sadly, I've birthed a rake," Cora grumbled. "That said, he's half Tor's, so it really comes as no surprise."

Everyone laughed, except Tor, who looked at the ceiling.

Loren laughed as well.

However, he did being reminded about pennyrium, wondering if Corliss had already taken care of that for Satrine.

The time was nigh for them finally to consummate their relationship. The stitches were probably not ready to be cut out for a couple of days, but the pain was all but gone.

And he could be creative, but his fiancée's libido rivaled his own. As splendid as his creativity was, and her response to it, it now carried a vein of frustration.

It was time to give them both what they desired.

Loren looked forward with great relish to them having a family.

But in the now, he looked forward to practicing, copiously, making that family.

She needed to be taking pennyrium, which would guard against pregnancy, until they decided they were ready.

He'd be certain to make sure all was well with that and made a mental note to do it tonight.

"Hopefully, she'll be found before dinner. We look forward to meeting her," Circe put in.

"That is my hope as well, Your Majesty," he replied, just as the door opened.

They all turned to it.

Marlow strode in, only two feet, and he stopped.

"Tor," he said. Then, "Cora, would that I had found you first. I would have made you far happier than this tall, dark lout."

Cora giggled.

Tor let out an audible sigh but said nothing, as he knew well this was Marlow's way.

"Royals all," he greeted casually, then his gaze hit Loren. "I'm afraid I must steal you."

"Marlow, come in and meet the king of Wodell and his queen," Tor bid.

"My most fervent wish," Marlow replied to them. "But I'm afraid a game is afoot and at this moment, Lore's fiancée, her houseman, and one of their grooms, who is large, but I fear that's all he has going for him, are meeting with some ruffians in an alley not too far from here. And I'm afraid they're going to need rescue."

Fury seized his head while something else took hold of his heart.

"*What?*" Loren barked, striding toward his friend.

"Search me," Marlow replied. "They thought they were being clever, and that they'd lost their guard. They did not and he sent word to me. Further word shares this might be about a certain madam. In short, we must be away."

Loren had a strong suspicion Satrine and Carling touching the sides of their noses had not been about birthdays.

However, as necessity demanded, they'd added that machination along the way.

Loren was at the door with Marlow when he pivoted to bow to those who occupied the room, and nearly ran into Tor.

"Tor, what the—?" he started.

"I think, since Lahn and True followed me, we're all feeling the need for some adventure."

"Of course they are," Farah remarked.

"Horses, sergeant," Tor ordered.

The guard at the door started sprinting.

"A certain madam?" Tor asked as they marched to the stairs. "The one involved in that extortion business you shut down?"

By the gods.

How had he forgotten?

Satrine had said, "We need to defuse her."

We.

"I may not have mentioned my affianced is spirited," he said by way of reply.

Lahn emitted an amused, approving grunt.

They all ignored the attention they received as they jogged past patrons and staff at the hotel.

Their horses were waiting for them at the front doors.

They swung up and followed Marlow's lead.

But Loren came abreast of him.

"You deal with the others, I'll be seeing to Satrine."

Marlow grinned, then bent over his horse, dug his heels in, and expertly navigated his galloping mount through the busy streets.

Loren did the same.

And three kings behind them did the same.

Chapter Twenty-Four

Marquess of Badass

Loren

"I can't even with you!" his beloved snapped, rounding on him and slamming her hands on her hips. "You nearly rode right over Carling!"

"My dearest love—"

"And the minute you and your...your..." She twirled and took in Lahn, her head tilting far back to do so. She staggered away a step and muttered, "Whoa, you're huge."

Lahn slowly smiled.

"*Whoa*," she repeated, this time breathily, not tearing her eyes off the warrior king.

"Satrine," Loren bit out.

She focused on him and remembered her snit, not allowing a moment to lapse before taking up where she left off.

"Your merry band of hot guys, they scattered. And they had something to tell us about that awful Dupont woman."

He opened his mouth.

And said not a word.

"Did we get the chance to hear what they had to say?" she demanded. "*Noooooo*. Galloping in comes the Marquess of Badass..."

Cora and Circe gasped.

Satrine ranted on.

"...picking me up *while you kept riding*, and I was treated to the indignity of racing through the streets of the fine city of Newton with my belly in a pommel and my arse in the air!"

"Are you finished?" he asked.

"No," she bit off, and carried on, "Then, behaving like a savage from a savage land, you *drag* me through The Heritage, where *but two weeks ago*, all the patrons of *Le Cirque* applauded our betrothal, but as you noted at the time, and I too feel safe in saying, some of them were applauding my *amazing gown*."

"I only saw the end of it, but that was very 'savage from a savage land,' and I should know," Circe mumbled.

Farah and Cora laughed softly.

"*Now* are you finished?" Loren pushed.

"Do I need to say more?" she pushed back.

"Allow me to introduce you to King Noctorno, the ruler of our realm. His lovely queen, Cora, the Gracious. The King of Korwhak, Dax Lahn and his Dahksana, Circe. And from across the Green Sea, King True and Queen Farah of Wodell."

He indicated them each in turn while, woodenly, Satrine shifted, taking them all in.

The color had rushed from her face as he spoke, but then it rushed right back. And when it did, there was quite a bit more of it.

"Am I...supposed to curtsy?" she asked out of the corner of my mouth.

"It *is* customary," he answered.

"Don't you dare," Cora ordered. "Loren knows we don't stand on ceremony, at least not in private quarters. I'm afraid my king demands I be 'Your Majesty' in company, but now, I'm Cora, and I'm *very* pleased to meet you."

Cora had come forward, she took Satrine's hand, and Satrine remained dumbstruck as she touched cheeks with her.

Circe and Farah followed suit.

And Loren found it odd, regardless of her indecorous behavior, the way Cora and Circe continued to regard her even after they stepped away.

"I'm sorry. So sorry. I had no idea," Satrine muttered. "Sir. My lord. Your grace. Your magnificence. Uh...my king." She bent her head to Tor.

"By the gods, I like her for you, my man," Tor decreed.

Her head snapped up.

"It was the 'your magnificence,' I'm pretty sure," Cora murmured under her breath to the other women.

They again laughed.

"Allow us to continue our conversation elsewhere," Loren requested.

"Please don't," Lahn drawled. "It's been some time since I've seen a woman spit such fire." He turned his eyes to his wife, they gentled, and he said, "I spoil you."

"He does do that," Circe agreed.

More laughter from the women.

"I would…maybe I would…like a hole to open up and swallow me," Satrine remarked, just as the door to the suite opened.

Marlow sauntered in, fist in the collar of one of the cretins that, as he'd ridden upon them, Loren had seen meeting with Satrine, Carling and Beacher in that alley.

The most filthy, fetid one.

Carling and Beacher followed him, Carling fretting, Beacher staring in shock at the king.

They both went into deep bows, with Carling adding, "Your Majesty."

"Rise," Tor ordered.

They did and Carling instantly looked to Satrine.

"I'm fine, Carling," she said gently.

He relaxed.

"Carling, Satrine's houseman, and Beacher, one of her grooms," Loren introduced. "That one"—his lip curled as he stared at the man who Marlow had forced to his knees—"I don't know."

The man moved his wide-open mouth, but not his stunned eyes from Tor, as he mumbled, "Buttersnatch, my king."

"An informant of her father's, milord," Beacher added.

At this detail, spots formed before his eyes, he waited until they dissipated, then, very slowly, he turned to the love of his life.

"Okay, I see you're mad," she said swiftly.

"Mad?"

"Angry."

"I know what mad means in this instance, darling. Though the word does not do justice to what I'm feeling right now. However, the other definition of it is what *you* are for being in the presence of one of your father's delinquents."

She kept speaking swiftly. "Right, we had a plan—"

"Who is 'we' in this scenario?" he demanded.

"I'm omitting names to protect the innocent," she returned.

"Like the two innocents in this room with us who are on your staff? Both, I'm relatively certain, men so devoted to you, they'd throw themselves in front of runaway carriages in order to save you?" he inquired.

"I would do that, Your Majesty, with pride," Carling announced, addressing Tor, his back ramrod straight. "She's the finest lady in the realm, outside her mother. Er...present company excluded, my other Majesty," he finished with his eyes on Cora.

Loren wasn't sure, but he thought he heard Farah actually snort with amusement.

True was looking at his boots but not hiding his smile.

Lahn and Tor were grinning widely.

Cora and Circe appeared about ready to collapse in laughter.

Loren didn't find anything funny.

He crossed his arms and invited his bride, "Let's hear this plan, my dearest love. Me and the rulers of three great realms are agog with interest."

Her eyes narrowed.

"Have I shared yet I'm not a fan of sarcasm?" she asked.

"Not yet," he answered.

"I'm not a fan of sarcasm."

Right then.

Right.

He was done.

"*Are you out of your mind?*" he roared.

"Honey—"

"In an alley in the fucking Quarter with the likes of that?" He pointed a finger at Buttersnatch.

"He's not 'that,' he's a man, Lore."

Loren turned to Marlow. "Did you search him?"

Marlow reached behind his back and came around, tossing a straight razor onto the floor a few feet in front of Satrine.

"Oh dear," she mumbled, staring down at it.

Loren decided it was time she discovered what *he'd* been learning about Winnow Dupont.

"She's ordered kills on all of us. By all of us I mean you, me, my father and your mother," he informed her.

Eyes huge, she looked from the razor to him.

"And you're attempting to shirk your guard and meet in an alley with someone who undoubtedly would not mind collecting one of those bounties," he stated.

"I didn't know about the bounty part," she said.

He scowled at her.

Then he tipped his head back and scowled at the ceiling.

"How much do you feel like continuing breathing after all this is done?" Marlow asked.

Loren turned to his friend to see he was addressing Buttersnatch.

"A lot, milord," Buttersnatch answered the floor.

"How does she get word out, all the way from Lincstone?" Marlow demanded.

Buttersnatch kept his knees but twisted to look up at Marlow.

"I usually—"

"If you think you're getting paid, you piece of shite, think again. You can talk in front of your king, or you can talk somewhere else. That being where I take you and you'll tell me what I want to know just so I'll finish it, put you out of your misery and make you *stop* breathing," Marlow promised.

Buttersnatch swallowed.

"Talk," Marlow whispered ominously.

"It ain't 'er," Buttersnatch said.

"Explain," Marlow ordered.

"The madam. It ain't 'er. 'E wants it thought it's 'er. But she's scared as piss." He turned to Cora and the queens. "Sorry, miladies." Back to Marlow. "'E's scared the knickers off 'er, 'e 'as. She don't want no more trouble from 'im." He then jerked his head to Loren.

"And so these kill orders came from…?" Marlow demanded.

"From 'is lordship. Derryman."

A charge shot through the room, this coming from Satrine.

"My father ordered my mother killed?" she asked.

Buttersnatch turned to her and nodded. "And you. And your lord. And 'is da."

"Darling," Loren said quietly as Satrine, unsurprisingly appearing struck, stared at the man on his knees.

"He ordered my mother and me killed," she pressed.

"Yes, milady," Buttersnatch confirmed.

"He brought us here, used and imprisoned us, we had to learn to fend for ourselves," she stated.

"Tor," Loren heard Cora whisper.

"I know, my love. Later," Tor whispered back.

"And now he wants us dead, taking with us the two men who made us safe here. Made us a family," Satrine finished.

Buttersnatch watched her closely, then nodded.

She turned to Loren. "Can you take me home, honey?"

He looked to his king.

Tor nodded.

Satrine looked to Tor and Cora. "It's been my honor, but—"

Cora cut her off. "Go, we'll see you later."

Loren went to Satrine, took her hand and curled it around his elbow.

He didn't break stride as he led her out of the room, when he asked Marlow, "You'll continue hunting?"

"Middy and Holt arrive this eve. The job will be done by the end of the week."

It was Wednesday, so that seemed about right.

Loren nodded.

Then he set about getting his bride home.

* * * *

Tor

They were all lounging on the couches.

They had wine.

Their company had all just left.

And Cora started it, eyes to the dahksahna.

"She's from our world."

Lahn grunted, his gaze also on Circe.

"Does Loren know, or doesn't he?" Circe asked.

"He doesn't," Tor answered. "He's one of the few Cora and I have trusted with this information about her. We have contingencies, just in case someone nefarious discovers it and causes problems. Further, he, and Marlow, by the way, as well as the rest of their squad, are fully briefed should anything happen to me, and a challenge was made regarding Hayden's ascendency. They're the only ones I trust to keep my family safe. And they're the only ones with the skills to assist Hayden to keep, or if it's taken, regain his throne. If Lore did know, he would have told us where she was from, and he would have likely brought her to us sooner and not in the manner we met her."

"She said, 'He brought us here, used and imprisoned us, we had to learn to fend for ourselves,'" Cora reminded them, and then turned to her husband. "And we know this man, her father, is not a good man. Not by any stretch of the imagination. I can understand why she wouldn't tell Loren, it's fantastical, and we all know it's very difficult to believe. She plays a good game, but regardless, she isn't hiding it very well, so my guess, she doesn't have anyone assisting her in this world. I'm stunned Lore hasn't figured it out."

"He holds deep love for her. The depth of that kind of love is blinding," Lahn remarked knowingly.

"Baby," Circe murmured, those syllables dripping with feeling, and Lahn rewarded her with a look filled with shared memories and tenderness.

But Cora nodded and returned her attention to her husband. "In short, something is not right, Tor."

He executed his own nod and looked to Lahn. "We need to get word to Valentine."

Lahn lifted his chin and replied, "We need the Green One."

Chapter Twenty-Five

Frustration

Loren

Thursday, Late Afternoon

Loren was frustrated because he'd been summoned by his king when he was needed by his bride.

After she'd holed herself in her father's study with her mother for a long conversation, they'd had a quiet evening, and when they were abed, it was the first night they hadn't explored each other.

He sensed her mood, therefore, he simply held her the very long period of time it took her to fall asleep.

The next day, he understood her preoccupation, only after he demanded she share it.

She did just that.

"You are you," she said. "You must be free to be you. Do the things that make you feel right inside. Therefore, the Madam Duponts of this world need to be dealt with. And the Satrines and Corlisses need to be helped, though, never again in that exact way," she'd attempted a weak joke.

As weak as it was, he still smiled at her.

"But those are risks you accept, situations you control, things *you* decide to do," she carried on. "Father has brought danger to you, and that was *not* yours to decide. And I can't…I can't…well, I find I can't abide it."

"It will be dealt with by the end of the week," he stated, instilling his words with the determination he knew Marlow would be utilizing to see that statement made true.

"I know. I don't doubt your skills. I just don't…" She sighed. And then she gave it to him. "How evil can one man be?"

That was when he took her in his arms.

"He keeps surprising me. All my life, he just keeps surprising me," she mumbled against his chest. "And obviously not in good ways."

"He will be dealt with soon as well, my love," he reminded her.

"Yes," she replied, but he could tell she remained despondent.

Loren did not remember much of his mother. But he held vague memories of bright smiles and gentle touches and the sound of much laughter shared with her husband.

However, he remembered everything about the rearing he received from his father.

So he had no foothold to understanding what she was feeling.

Which meant his only recourse was to return the favor she was extending to him.

Hold her close and keep her firmly tethered to the belief that there was good in this world, and he was giving it to her.

In the midst of this, he'd received his summons from his king and had to leave her.

It was a summons from a king, he could not say no.

It also expressly asked he come alone.

As such, he was frustrated.

That frustration dissipated when he arrived at their suite to see True, Farah, Cora and Circe were not there, but a redheaded woman wearing an attractive, but very strange garment was with his king and the ruler of Korwahk.

She studied him, thoroughly, and then smiled a small smile that was both spectacular and terrifying.

"Lore, we need you to sit down," Tor said quietly.

"Satrine is—" he began.

"Please sit down," Tor said, still quietly, but now firmly.

It was then, Loren took full note of the look on his king's face.

And he sat down.

Chapter Twenty-Six

Everything Turned Good

Satrine

Friday Morning

Idina tucked a curl more firmly into the fluffy chignon she'd crafted at the nape of my neck. It had escaped after she'd dressed me.

But with that curl tucked away, I was now ready to face the day.

And I was petrified.

It was a natural build up to the terror I'd been experiencing more and more each day as Dad-not-Dad's trial got closer.

It was also more.

A ton more.

I had spent the last weeks preparing for the biggest project I'd ever present.

A presentation that would last the rest of my life.

I'd read snippets to long passages of everything I could get my hands on, history, fiction, poetry, to give me a greater sense of this world I lived in. I'd also made a catalogue of which of those to return to when I had time for more study.

I read the papers from masthead to obituaries to understand what the people of this world found important. Although I skimmed the articles simply to get a sense of the news, I turned my focus to the things I hoped really mattered in the day to day. I picked apart the advertisements. I taught myself the scoring for the games. That being, after I taught myself what the games actually were.

I especially combed the society pages and memorized names, titles, who was married to whom, and any tidbit I could consume to assist Mom and me not to put our foot in it when the time came, we met people she was supposed to know.

But now, I'd done what I'd done with our darling Carling and Beacher and lost it in front of kings and queens, and in doing so, I didn't guard my words (I mean, I'd called him a badass, *in front of kings and queens*).

And although Loren had been his usual wonderful after it, his king had then summoned him, and I hadn't seen him since.

He'd sent a note, as was his way, even if things had gone south, he wouldn't neglect me.

No, he'd say it straight to my face.

The note shared that the king had something he needed Loren to assist with, and he had to do that. But he assured me he'd be there that morning at nine with his father to collect me and Mom (and Aunt Mary, who had decreed she was coming with) to go to the magistrate's court where King Noctorno would be hearing, and deciding, Dad-not-Dad's case.

It was the first night in precisely thirteen days I'd slept in my bed at Mom's house, alone.

With the way he treated me, loving and romantic and attentive, I couldn't believe Loren left me alone the day before…well, what was going to happen today.

So…

Yup.

I was petrified.

"You don't need to worry," Idina said.

I came into the room and looked at her through the mirror, seeing her hand on my shoulder, and having been so deep in my thoughts, I hadn't felt her touch.

"You must live your life." She gave me a small smile. "And you'll be away with your new husband soon."

What was she—?

"And your mother must live hers as well," she went on. "I know you both make it so one of you is in the house with her at all times. But she is used to us too, and she cares for us. We will be here for Lady Maxine."

Oh.

She was speaking of something Mom and I did, indeed, do for Maxie.

"I'll take her to the park with her paints and easel. She'll be lost in her pictures. She won't know you're gone," she shared.

I felt tears sting my eyes.

"You're...you're incredibly lovely, Idina. So much so, I'm sorry I haven't mentioned it until now."

"One doesn't have to say such things amongst family," she said shyly.

I lifted my hand to hers at my shoulder, covering it to share my agreement (about the family part, that was), and we heard a knock on the door.

I tensed.

Loren was here.

It was time to go.

Gods.

"Come in!" I called as Idina and I broke the contact of our hands and turned toward the door.

It opened, and in came Maxine.

Right, I had to get myself together. Maxine could not sense me freaking out. It might make her freak out.

I had to be calm.

I smiled brightly at her. "Hello, my beautiful sister."

She tipped her head to the side and glided to us, her lovely rose-colored gown made of layers of diaphanous chiffon floating around her.

"Hello, my beautiful sister," she repeated.

"Idina is going to take you to the park to paint today," I shared.

She turned her eyes to Idina and used them to smile.

Then she asked, "Can I talk to Sattie?"

Idina started, but I focused more acutely on Maxine, because we'd had many alone times, but we'd never had a discussion.

"Milady, their lordships will be here—" Idina began gently to refuse her.

"I wish to talk to Sattie," Maxine declared.

Oh boy.

I wasn't sure I'd heard Maxie declare anything.

Idina and I exchanged a look.

"It's all right," I said to her. "We won't be long."

Idina nodded.

"Don't forget your gloves and hat," she bid as she left the room.

She closed the door behind her.

I watched Maxine lean her tush against my dressing table, pick up an intricately shaped bottle, open the stopper and smell what was inside.

"Maxie," I called quietly.

She lifted her eyes to me.

My eyes to me.

"You're who I'm supposed to be."

My heart squeezed and I froze.

"Momma is not my momma," she continued.

Oh gods, oh gods, oh gods.

"But she's my momma."

"Maxie—"

"You're Maxie too."

I reached out and touched her knee. "Honey."

She put the bottle down, picked up my hand, and placed hers beside it, examining it, and I knew, seeing they were exactly the same.

"Thank you for bringing Momma back. And giving me a sister." Her eyes came to mine. "And Annie and Lorie and Mr. Popplewell. Also Auntie Mary. She didn't come see me very often, and then she stopped seeing me at all. Papa didn't like her visiting me. He didn't like anything about me."

Gods.

My beautiful, broken sister.

Not only broken by what happened on that horse, but how he'd treated her after.

Seriously, the asshole Edgar Dawes of this world beat out the deadbeat Edgar Dawes of my world by a mile.

"Maybe not, but you do know we all love you," I told her fiercely. "You know we all love everything about you."

She laced her fingers in mine and pressed our hands gently back and forth.

"I know."

"You're sure?" I pushed.

She kept doing the hand thing, which was sweet, and sad, because it was a childlike thing to do.

"I *know*, Sattie," she stressed.

"And I know it's confusing, but Momma and me were brought here for you."

Her brows drew down. "It's not confusing. Love is not confusing. People think I don't know things. But I know the way Papa was, that was confusing. You and Momma, you aren't confusing. Not at all."

My smile at that was again bright, but this time genuine.

"I'm glad you know that."

She held my gaze, and suddenly, her lower lip trembled. "You'll make it so Lorie will make it so he won't come back, won't you?"

Mental note: Maxine absorbed a lot of shit that went on around her. And that was okay, that was good.

But we had to see to her along the way as she did it.

"We'll make that happen," I whispered.

"Lorie took us out of the bad room."

"Yes." I was still whispering.

"Momma was strong, but we stayed down there a long time, and she was getting scared. I could tell she was getting scared, even if she tried hard not to let me see. He made her stop being scared."

"Yes, he did."

"He said you sent him."

My voice was throaty when I said, "I did, baby."

"And then everything turned good."

"I hope so."

She jumped and I jumped, but her jump was to throw her arms around me.

"Love you, sissy," she said into my ear.

Then she let me go and darted from the room.

That was enlightening, frightening…

And beautiful.

I sucked in a ton of air (in other words, I took a gigantic sniff so I wouldn't burst into tears) and blew it out.

"Okay, all right, okay…" I chanted.

Idina's head popped around the door.

"Their lordships are here," she announced.

I nodded.

Her head disappeared.

"Okay, all right, okay…" I chanted again.

I went to the bed, took up my gloves and hat, and deep breathed my way to the hall, through the hall and down a half a flight of stairs.

I'd pulled it together by the time they could see me.

And I knew something was wrong even before I made it anywhere near him.

I greeted Ansley first, saw Mom studying me curiously, but mostly, I was all about Loren.

He had his chin tipped down and his gaze was moving all over my face like he'd never seen me before.

Also, it was important to note, he didn't touch me.

"Everything okay?" I asked, my words sounding feeble, strangled.

His beautiful, lushly lashed brown eyes came to mine.

And I found it alarming in the extreme that he didn't answer my question.

No.

Instead, he offered his arm in a formal manner.

And stated simply…

"We must be away."

Chapter Twenty-Seven

The King's Leisure

Satrine

As mentioned, I studied the newspapers from back to front every day.

So it wasn't a surprise when we arrived at the magistrate's court that there were throngs of people there.

It was such because this was the trial of the century, and not simply because King Noctorno was gracing this fair city to adjudicate it, and his queen had accompanied him.

But because a member of the aristocracy was standing to defend his crimes, and the Newton paper (which, it had to be said, had a liberal bent), was in fits of glee about it.

Thus, when we arrived, there were people lining the pavements.

A lot of them.

There was also a massive police presence, in the form of actual police, but also men in smart, navy-blue uniforms that had a half-cape in admiral blue flipped over one shoulder (seriously, if I wasn't so out of it, I would have noted how totally cool these uniforms were and how Loren probably looked super-hot wearing one). They wore admiral blue berets with short, sharp feathers stuck in. Sabers at their belts.

And held long, silver spears in their hands.

Spears!

It had to be the royal guard that lined the sidewalk from building to curb to keep the people back in order that we could get in.

And one could say, a spear was a good incentive to stay back.

However, all of this just added weight to already weighty

proceedings.

As such, things were primed for people to lose their minds, something they did with shouts and cheers, when our carriage doors opened—Mom, Ansley and Aunt Mary's in front, Loren's and mine behind—and Ansley and Loren alighted.

And it felt alarmingly like things would careen out of control when Mom and I appeared.

Because the crowd…went…*wild*.

Fortunately, Madame Toussaint had outdone herself.

Mom was in a mulberry-colored confection with some shades of mauve and heather in the feathers of her hat.

I was wearing a complementary color of a warm, wintery pink with creamy accents.

Aunt Mary, as was her usual, was wearing all black.

I clutched Loren's elbow, and he moved us swiftly, careful not to be too swift so we wouldn't trod on Mom's train.

I was officially totally freaked out.

And as such, was making moves by rote.

Sure, the shrieking and shouts of, "The countess lives! Long live the countess!" and "You can't keep a good lady down!" were flipping my shit so much it didn't occur to me these shouts were positive.

Mostly, it was because Loren had been silent and remote the entire ride there, and my heart was hammering in my chest so badly, I felt I had to have a care not to exert myself so it wouldn't explode.

I vaguely noticed Maitland and the two, tall, gorgeous dudes standing with him at the top of the steps, one gorgeous dude having black hair, the other having dark blond.

And I vaguely heard the clamor mute when we were inside, and the doors were closed behind us.

I also vaguely felt Loren stop us and say formally, "Satrine, I wish to introduce you to two more of my brothers. Ridley Middleton, the Earl of Hartley. And Ford Holton, the Duke of Bloodworth."

"How do you do," I said stiffly.

They murmured in return, and I sensed Marlow startle at my reply, but I was watching Mom disappear into a room at the same time fighting back a smothering sense of dread.

"Sattie, love, it'll be all right," I heard Marlow murmur comfortingly.

I lifted my gaze to him, noting then that my fiancé hadn't said anything to comfort me, not that first word.

And, like a robot, I nodded.

That was when Marlow began to look less startled, a hella lot more worried and a hella lot more than that…pissed.

His attention jerked to Loren when he spoke.

"Let's get in," Loren said curtly.

It didn't escape me his two friends were watching me with acute interest.

But I was ready to move on, face whatever there was to face in that court, and then face whatever was wrong with Loren, which was clearly something he thought was wrong with me.

I mean, it wasn't a shocker he'd finally figured it out.

Figured out I wasn't right.

What was a shocker was that it took this long.

But as ever, if there was music to face, I'd face it.

I'd die in my bed in my room at Mom's house, or wherever we might be spending the night that night. I'd then learn how to exist without truly existing tomorrow.

Such were these thoughts, I noticed only distantly that the magistrate's court looked more like a throne room, but with seats set in rows for an audience.

Or maybe it was set up that way for King Noctorno, who was on a dais sitting in a large, elaborate chair, Queen Cora next to him, seated in an equally elaborate chair. Adding to this pomp and circumstance, the other kings and queens were off to the side, lounging in their own extravagant chairs.

Though, with them was a striking woman with red hair, alabaster skin, and an emerald-green outfit and hat that rivaled (but didn't beat) Mom's and my own.

Loren led me to where Mom was standing at the front row of chairs. Ansley was at her side. Mary at her other side. Loren's friends moved to gather around us.

It struck me then that the packed room was not packed only with rich people. There seemed a mix of grand to not-so-grand to normal outfits declaring a mix of economic statuses.

Apparently in King Noctorno's realm, the aristocracy not only didn't carry on blithely thinking they had the run of the country. When they did something wrong, they also weren't judged privately, in the company of people they thought were their peers.

They were judged publicly in the company of all their peers.

Loren's squeeze of my elbow reminded me to curtsy, which I did, beside him as he executed a courtly bow.

And it was then, the din from outside rose again, this time with jeers and boos.

Dad-not-Dad was arriving.

My throat closed in panic, my gaze found Mom's, she was as pale as I felt, and it all began.

It felt like a whirlwind. Like I was seeing it through a flurry of snow, what was happening playing out in the center of a snow globe I'd shaken like crazy.

Edgar came in, dressed to the nines, but with a guard on either side, and some tall, slender man accompanying him.

They came to stand in front of the king and queen, just off to the side, and another man joined them to the other side. He was the opposition.

They didn't have tables or papers or anything.

Edgar was going to stand trial.

Literally.

Fortunately, we didn't have to stand while watching it.

We were told to sit. We sat.

Some guy in a uniform came forward and cried out a bunch of stuff that eventually hit me was the litany of charges against Edgar, the only one of which penetrating my haze was "conspiring the attempted murder of four citizens of the realm and suspicion of murder of anonymous by burning!"

I fully came into the room when the uniform guy demanded, "Now, sir, tell the king how you plead!"

And Dad-not-Dad bellowed, "*Innocent!*"

Aunt Mary, sitting between Mom and me (this wasn't what I'd want, but she'd horned in), reached out and took both our hands in both of hers and held them together in her lap (okay, so maybe it was good Aunt Mary being right there).

It was then Dad-not-Dad boomed, "*This is utter rubbish!*"

The slender guy at his side got closer with some urgency, but Edgar stepped away from him and addressed Noctorno. "This is a disgrace."

"My lord, see to your client," the king rumbled to the slender guy.

He tried to do that, but Edgar sidestepped him again.

"I am a peer of your realm, sir," he said to the king.

"Every person in this room is a peer of my realm," Noctorno replied.

Well then.

There you go.

Dad seethed, "That's frankly *outrageous!*"

"I suggest you collect yourself," the king advised.

Dad-not-Dad swung a pointed finger our way and shouted, "They aren't even of this—"

I got tense.

I felt Mom's hand jump.

I also felt Loren get tense beside me.

And Edgar started choking.

As in, a fit of coughing that was deep and guttural and hurt just to hear. It did this to me, and I didn't like the guy.

"Get him water," the queen bid softly.

Someone rushed to Edgar with a glass of water, but he lashed out, the tumbler went flying, water splashing all over the marble floor, the glass shattering, and he'd gotten himself together enough to state, "I will be heard! And they are *liars! Swindlers! Frauds!* They do not even come from this—"

He started choking again, worse than before.

But something struck me when he did it this time.

Because...

Oh my gods.

Was this...?

I sat forward and looked toward Mom.

She sat forward and looked toward me.

We turned back to Edgar when he tried to force out, "They are from a—"

Gasps all around, including from me, when a bubble of blood bloomed from his mouth.

"My word," Aunt Mary murmured in horror.

"Call a physician," the king bid.

But Dad-not-Dad was now opening and closing his mouth, no blood coming forth, however his eyes were bugging out.

I wondered if he was choking, but he stood still, calm(ish), and it hit me that he was moving his mouth like he was trying to speak.

However, no words were coming out.

Holy *shit.*

Right, one thing was absolutely and undeniably certain.

I was never bringing that curse down on Mom and me. No way. No how.

I wasn't going to do it before.

But...*yikes.*

Another man approached Edgar. Dad-not-Dad allowed the man to examine him, even clutched on to him, still appearing like he was trying to talk.

In the end, the guy turned to Noctorno and reported, "Elevated pulse, but that is all, Your Majesty. The coughing brought the blood, I believe. But outside the curious fact he doesn't seem to be able to speak, I can find nothing wrong with him."

"Thank you, and thus, we will proceed," Noctorno decreed.

Proceed?

After Dad-not-Dad coughed up blood and was struck mute?

"What?" I whispered.

"Do you wish to speak in your client's defense?" the king asked the man who came in with Edgar.

"I'm sorry, my king, but he didn't allow me to know what defense he wished to use. He wouldn't speak of it, only asked me to accompany him to advise should things look like they were not to go his way."

Noctorno nodded and declared, "Foolhardy and pompous, which is no surprise. It matters not, as we have eye-witness statements, and a mountain of evidence, this was always a matter of being a ceremonial proceeding. As such, you'll hear my judgment, Mr. Dawes."

Mr. Dawes?

Edgar didn't miss the address, I knew, because he went statue-still, attention riveted on the king.

Noctorno didn't waste any time.

"You are found guilty of all counts, and as such, I strip you of your title," Noctorno proclaimed.

Dad-not-Dad sputtered nonverbally.

The room went wired.

"It remains held by Lady Corliss Dawes, Countess of Derryman, until her death. It then will be held with her daughter, Satrine, to be transferred down her line," Noctorno went on.

Edgar kept sputtering, his face getting red, not with the effort to speak, but fury.

"I strip you of all your lands, holdings and assets. By my decree, these will be transferred into the name of the Countess of Derryman and inherited down her line. I do this, save the amount it will cost to procure a cottage of no more than three rooms in a region near our northern borders."

At that part, Aunt Mary chuckled low and whispered, "Edgar hates the north." Pause then, "And northerners." Pause and further, "And the cold." Pause and last, "And Lunwynians, and the north is rife with diversity."

"Plus, a small stipend for you to be clothed, fed and kept warm," the king continued. "Not to mention, a two hundred and fifty thousand pound fine paid to my treasury. You will be secluded in this cottage for twenty years, or until your death, after, of course, you serve a seven-year sentence at my leisure."

Since Edgar was Dad, I knew he was fifty-three. That meant he'd be out at sixty. Which wasn't old, but I had a feeling the king's "leisure" wouldn't be leisurely for Edgar, so he probably would not come out nearly as robust as when he went in.

"If word should be heard, or actions taken, that you have connived to cause harm to any citizen of my realm or any other, for purposes of vengeance, or any purpose at all," Noctorno carried on, "you will stand another trial. And if found guilty, your sentence will mean you shall be hung by your neck until dead."

Holy crap!

Dad-not-Dad stopped sputtering, moving, and lost all color in his face.

"That's all," Noctorno said to uniform guy. "He can start seeing to that now. And clear the room."

People started moving. The place was an excited hum.

But Noctorno finished speaking, looked right to Loren and nodded.

So I didn't twitch even a muscle.

As constables and the king's guard started shifting people out, Mom asked, "Should we…leave? I mean, is that it?"

"We're to stay, Corliss," Ansley said.

At that comment, I looked to Loren.

He was not holding my hand. He was not asking me if I was okay. He wasn't appearing like he had any reaction to all that had just gone down. He wasn't even looking at me.

His gaze was aimed at the redhead that was sitting with the other king and queens.

My skin felt cold.

So cold, my mind blanked at the extremes of it.

"Satrine."

I stared at my lap and my hand covered in a cream, kid leather glove sitting in it.

That hand not held in Loren's.

"*Satrine.*"

Did he know?

Did he just suspect?

Or did the king tell him I was mad and a harridan besides, and he wasn't having his decorated soldier marry such a strange, foul woman?

Mom and Mary both squeezed my hand.

"*Satrine!*" Mom snapped.

I turned to her.

But I said nothing because the king spoke, his deep voice echoing in a now mostly empty room.

"Are you quite all right, madam?" he called.

Stiltedly, I turned my head to where he was looking.

And saw, sitting alone at the far back, the witch who had brought us to this world.

And it was then my heart didn't explode.

It rent in two.

Because it was then I knew.

That Loren knew.

Everything.

Chapter Twenty-Eight

Away

Satrine

"Valentine, bring her before me."

I didn't move or speak, and not only because I couldn't believe what I was seeing.

That being, her feet drifting in the air, the rest of her immobile, the witch at the back was lifted from her seat and she floated...

Literally *floated*...

Until she came to a swaying halt in front of the king.

"I assume you know why we detained you," he remarked.

"Your Majesty—" she said in a trembling voice.

"I believe I made myself clear on this subject," Noctorno noted.

"My king—"

"Regardless that he needed to learn when to be silent, it is illegal to place curses in this realm, or any realm in the Northlands or Southlands," Noctorno shared. "I sense, as you took pains to hide your powers, you're quite aware of that fact."

She decided not to try to speak this time.

"And it's a high crime to amass magic without permission from the crown," he went on. "But more, you aren't even registered as magical."

When Noctorno finished speaking, and didn't start again, she decided to give it another go.

"I—"

"We found Sjofn ice diamonds," he cut her off. "Firenzian rubies. Lunwynian furs. Dellish wool. And a good deal of coin. You've become quite rich, selling curses and spells."

"My magic is almost depleted, laying down that curse," she informed him.

"Laying down *those curses and* bringing forth women from the other world."

Mom made a quiet noise.

Slowly, my eyes closed, and I felt my shoulders slump.

Yes, Loren knew.

He knew I was what Dad-not-Dad said I was.

A swindler.

A fraud.

A liar.

"What's he on about?" Aunt Mary whispered.

No one answered her.

"I came from nothing. I have a talent. It is not fair that magic is regulated," the witch asserted.

"She has a point," the redhead noted in a droll, silky voice.

The king shook his head with exasperation but kept his attention on the woman floating in front of him.

And his voice was quiet, and even mildly forlorn, when he said, "You know the punishment for this."

"My king!" she cried, which meant she knew, and it was less fun than being at the king's leisure.

"I wouldn't have denied you," he informed her. "I have denied no witch who has come forward. If her intentions were pure and good, she was granted my leave. We have many witches who have greatly grown in their craft since we defeated Minerva and her connivers. I've even sent some talented youngsters to Lunwyn to study with Lavinia."

"I...did not know that," the witch replied wretchedly.

"Because you didn't submit your application," he returned. "And because public sentiment will need much healing in its regard of witches before these women feel safe and comfortable to practice again openly. And, I will note, something that doesn't assist in this matter is witches who practice *like you*."

She grew silent again.

"You've given me no choice," he stated. "And it disappointments me, because it's clear you have a gift, and it has been a gift squandered."

He waited.

She said nothing.

He turned to the redhead. "Is she bound?"

"She is," the redhead replied.

"Is her curse broken?" he continued.

"On the women, yes. On that man, no."

On the women?

Mom and I weren't cursed anymore?

Noctorno sighed. "Release him from the curse."

The woman in green rolled her eyes, kept them rolled, lifted her fingers and snapped.

"There. That odious man can speak again. Happy?" she asked insolently.

Who was this woman?

The king didn't answer her.

He looked somewhere else and murmured, "You can take her now."

Two women, well-dressed, eyes focused on the witch, came forward, and it was then I glanced around the room to see no guard, no person, no one but the king's retinue, our group, the witch, and those two women.

One lifted a hand and the witch who brought us to that world drifted toward her.

They didn't use the main doors to leave.

They went out a door in the back.

It was over.

I watched, feeling weird. Hollow and listless and spent and numb besides.

So it was slowly that I realized when Noctorno spoke again, he was doing it to Mom and me.

"You are no longer under her curse. You are also no longer imprisoned in this world." He lifted a hand in the direction of the redhead. "Valentine will spirit you home. And I will allow, if it is your wish, the other you"—he was looking at me—"to return with you." His regard went to Mom. "Say your goodbyes, if that's your wish. Valentine will be ready first thing tomorrow to take you home."

He stood and turned to help his queen to her feet.

When he did, Loren, Ansley, Mary, Marlow and Loren's friends stood too.

So Mom and I did as well.

"Will someone tell me what in blazes is going on?" Aunt Mary demanded.

I didn't pay attention to Mary.

I turned directly to Loren.

"Honey—" I said urgently.

He looked down his nose at me.

"I'll be at your father's house at eight tonight. We'll say our good-byes then."

I made a noise like a king's guard speared me through my stomach, which was what I felt Loren had just done to me.

"Brother," Marlow bit off.

"I'm away," Loren bit back.

And then he was just that.

Away.

From me.

Chapter Twenty-Nine

Shadowland

Loren

To his surprise, as he was shrugging on his evening coat, it was Lahn who came to him.

Loren said nothing as the large man slipped silently into his dressing room and went directly to the window, where he looked out.

"I am always amazed by all the green."

Loren righted his lapels and made no reply.

Korwahk was very hot.

And very brown.

Thus, no reply was necessary.

Lahn didn't look at him when he went on, "He does not come because he's angry with you. When Cora was torn from him, he had no control."

Only then did Lahn turn his attention to Loren.

"When I lost my Circe, it was my doing."

This was interesting, of course.

Loren didn't wish to hear it, however.

"Have you been there?" he asked instead.

Lahn shook his head.

"You should go," Loren stated shortly. "It's most illuminating."

"Circe has told me much. It sounds hideous."

Loren thought about the turn around Satrine's...

No, *Maxine's* world that Valentine had treated him to the night before.

And Lahn was right, even if he'd never experienced it.

It was hideous.

"She was cursed if she told you," Lahn reminded him. "And you saw today how that would have come about."

"In all we've recently learned, that didn't escape me," Loren returned.

"It is a marvel she did so well in this world."

"Maxine is cunning."

"Clever," Lahn corrected.

She was both, and he admired her for it.

"We'll agree to disagree."

Lahn shook his head and shared, "I will warn you, Valentine is not happy with you. And she is not a woman to cross, especially when she is one of the only beings on two worlds who can get the woman you love back. If you let her go, she could be lost to you. Forever."

It felt like his neck was gripped in a vise.

To alleviate the pain, Loren let out a breath.

And then he said, "I appreciate your counsel—"

"Circe was carrying our twins when she spirited herself from me. While she was gone, every day waking was a new death that she was not at my side," Lahn told him. And with impeccable timing, he changed course. "She isn't going to die like them."

Loren felt his innards twist.

"You don't have to shield yourself from your father's fate," Lahn continued. "That fate has been played. Yours is your own."

He held the king's eyes.

And he told him the truth.

"I bring death."

Lahn shook his head. "You have killed for your country. The loss of your mother and sister were the whim of the gods. It is not the same thing."

Loren turned his gaze out the window.

Lahn started to the door, saying, "You can remain in this shadowland for the whole of your life, it is your choice." He stopped at the door. "But you know shadows are just a play of the light. No matter what you do, you will have to live, experience loss, pain, disappointment. There is no way to protect yourself from it." Lahn lifted a hand and stabbed a long finger his way. "But it is up to *you* if you experience love and laughter." He dropped his hand and finished, "The man I saw sparring with her was alive. Alive in a life filled with fire and challenge and amusement and love. This man is a shell. Remain a shell or let her banish your shadows. It is your choice. And you make that choice now. She could not wait for you to come to her. She is downstairs."

And with that, he disappeared out the door.

Loren stared at the empty doorway, thinking of the heartrending despair Satrine…no Maxine had poured into his neck whilst they were in his window seat in the next room, undone because she could never tell him who she was and how she came to him.

This took him to thoughts of how she was brought to his world, not of her choice. A world so different from her own, she could never have imagined it in her wildest dreams. Yet she found a way to navigate it even having been ripped from all she knew. Her mother imprisoned. Her father forcing her to woo and win and sleep with a man…

He could think no further on that, for it had, since he'd learned all of this, frequently occurred to him a number of disastrous scenarios of what might have befallen her if it was not *he* she was set to woo.

And then there was confronting the image of herself.

Her twin.

Valentine had shown Loren the him of the other world.

It had shaken him.

What shook him more was Valentine telling him something he knew.

"He is not to find his other half. She isn't his to have. He'll never know why. But mark this, my stubborn soldier, he'll feel her loss. He won't know what's missing, but he'll feel it in every breath until the last he takes in his life."

Rattled, Loren had watched himself drinking an ale in a pub with the twins of Marlow and Middy, Holt and Croft around him, all while they talked, and jested and intermittently glanced at a strange box with moving images on it.

"Unless she comes home and misses you and finds that the other you lives close. Then she'll discover the truth. The you of this world is not you, but he *is* rather amazing," the green witch had finished.

That hadn't rattled him.

It infuriated him.

And it did then.

Spurring him to move, stalking out of the dressing room, through his room, into the hall and down the stairs.

He found her in the parlor.

She, too, was at a window, staring at the park.

"Sa…Maxine," he gritted.

She turned to him.

And Loren knew when she did, he'd already lost her.

He felt the bleakness that seemed always looming begin to overtake him.

The words had not been said, but he knew he loved her, and she loved him. So, before she left him and returned to her home, she was owed the understanding of why he was aloof and removed on a day of spectacle and fear. A day he forced her to face at his side, but without his love and care.

"I talked Father into getting her that puppy, she wanted one so badly."

Her lovely faced blanked.

Yes, he had lost her.

He persevered, nevertheless.

"It took years for him to convince me it wasn't my doing that pup went into the creek and Columbia went after him. I still don't quite believe it. As Father does not quite believe that it wasn't his fault Mother was lost. He'd made her pregnant, of course, and her recovery from having Columbia was slow. She did not regain her strength as quickly as she had after me. Though, as Father tells it, there was no convincing her. She carried on with all the things she'd done before as if she was just as robust, which only served to further weaken her. Another mark on Father's soul, according to him, for he allowed her to do it."

"Women aren't fond of being 'allowed' or 'disallowed' to do things," she said quietly.

"Indeed," he returned brusquely. "As, from Father's stories of her, I deduce Mother would have also contended. It was her choice. But I bid you convince Father of that."

"An effort doomed to fail, I'm sure," she muttered.

"Yes," he agreed. He then shared, "Last night, I went to your world."

Her eye grew enormous.

The bleakness encroached further.

By the gods, he would miss her.

"I did not like it. It was grimy and loud. Everyone seems to be in a hurry, like the place they're going will vanish in but seconds, or what they're doing is more important than the deeds of those around them. That last reminds me of your father of this world, except it was most everyone who behaved in this manner. People don't meet each other's eyes. They don't nod hello. They are too busy rushing. They are too consumed with thinking of themselves."

"That about describes it," she said.

"And it looked like Korwahk, but there was all this false green that seemed out of place. Unnatural. When what was supposed to be there would have been so much better."

"I live in Phoenix, it's a desert."

"It doesn't look like a desert."

"Man on my world fiddles. They want things as they want them and find ways, or invent them, to make that so."

"I sense this is foolhardy."

"It is," she murmured.

"I saw the other me," he announced.

Again with the big eyes, but accompanying them this time, her body started.

"And Marlow, Middy, Holt and Croft. When you return, I would ask you not to seek him out. This other me. It would destroy me, knowing you are with him. But then, it would that if you were with anyone. And you will find someone. And it is no longer my place to make demands."

"Was it ever?"

"You're right," he conceded. "It was not."

"I didn't like lying to you," she said.

"That was abundantly clear, though I didn't understand until recently the true reasons behind your emotion."

"I wouldn't have...I mean, it was going to be a last resort, you know, playing you. Making you have feelings for me. Marrying you and having your child. I needed to get Mom safe, but I hoped to do that and not involve you at all."

"You are safe now and set finally to go home."

"We're not going home."

Loren stilled in all manners that word could describe. His body. His heart in his chest. His blood in his veins. His ability to think.

Except one thought.

They weren't going home?

"It's too different there. Maxine couldn't hack it. She's happy now. We don't want to rock that boat," she explained.

Loren had also lost the ability to speak, thus he remained silent.

"Mom likes being Lady Corliss too. We're hoping the woman in green might take us back for a quick trip, so people we love don't think anything bad happened to us. But then we want to come right back.

Maxine was okay with us being gone today, but I don't think us being gone more than a day or two would be good for her. Maybe a little later, when we've been around for a while. But not now."

"You wish to remain?" he pushed out.

She shrugged. "However it came about, no matter how wild and terrifying, Mom and I talked about it a while ago. It might sound crazy, but we figure we're meant to be here. We'd decided to stay then. And obviously, there was no way I was leaving you."

He felt something weighing on his chest, the weight was mighty, crushing him.

"I promised I wouldn't do that and so"—she held her hands out to the sides—"I'm not."

"Maxine," he forced out.

"Satrine," she corrected gently.

"You are not that," he whispered.

She nodded. "Maxine knows I'm her, and she's me. Don't ask me to explain. I just think she's in there, somewhere, deep in her head. We don't give her enough credit. But I'm Satrine here, and not only because I think it will help with any confusion."

"You didn't come here to end things with me." He stated it, but it was a question.

"I came here thinking you were going to end things with me, and ready to beg you not to exit Maxine's life. I came here ready, no matter how much it would kill me, to promise I would absent myself when you visited. You saved her from that situation in the cellar, and until today, I didn't realize how deeply she experienced that and depends on you to keep her safe. I probably should have, but I didn't. So it would harm her, I think, if you—"

"Cease speaking, darling."

The instant he called her "darling," her eyes filled with tears.

"I love you to my soul. It's like you're a part of me. I'm scared as fuck of losing you," he whispered.

Her face grew tender. "I can't tell the future, honey, but right now, I'm right here."

"Come to me," he ordered.

"Meet in the middle?" she offered.

"Fuck yes," he replied.

They didn't meet in the middle.

They collided there.

She was Satrine, so she went for a kiss.

Instead, Loren swept her up in his arms and began to exit the room.

"What are you doing?" she demanded.

"Taking you to bed."

She clearly didn't mind that, but asked, "Can we kiss first?"

"Not if you don't want to consummate our love on the parlor floor."

"I don't want that, but Loren, we—"

He looked down at her as he took the steps, two at a time.

"You've had others." He grinned at her. "I am the beneficiary of your experience, as you are of mine."

Her astonished eyes on his mouth, she asked, "You're not angry?"

"Why would I be?"

"Dudes like virgins."

"Dudes?"

"Men."

They'd made his room, and he kicked the door closed behind them.

He then took her to his bed and tossed her on it.

He watched her bounce.

And then he stated the obvious. "I like *you*."

She stared up at him.

Then she said, marvel in her voice, "I get to be me with you."

He tipped his head to the side. "Weren't you always?"

"Yes, but you get me."

Her language was much changed, the oddness far more pronounced.

So he "got her" and he loved what he got, because now she could be herself to the fullest.

And he was on the receiving end of that.

"I get to tell you everything. Everything about me," she continued.

"Yes, you do, and I relish those future chats. Now, may I ravish you?"

She grinned a grin he felt throughout his body.

And she replied, "Absolutely."

* * * *

Satrine

I held him with everything I had, limbs and eyes and heart, as he slid his beautiful, thick cock inside me slowly.

So very slowly.

Until I took all of him.

Gods, I knew he'd fit perfectly.

Having him, *finally*, my lips parted, this movement happening against his mouth because he was right there.

Right there.

"The best thing I've ever done in my life was try to save some horses from the rain."

"The best thing I've ever done in mine was try to stop you."

"I don't know how to ride a horse," I admitted.

His beautiful eyes right there, so close, widened in shock, before they hooded when he started moving inside me.

Oh yes.

Perfect.

"How about I ride something first, and then we'll worry about you," he murmured.

"I'm totally down with that."

I knew he understood my lingo, even though he didn't, with the way his head ticked.

But he didn't miss a stroke.

"You know I love you," I remarked.

"Not nearly as much as I do you."

"Totally more."

"Impossible."

Gods, this guy was *da bomb*.

"This is gonna be fun," I decided.

"Is it not already?"

It *so* was.

"Oh yeah," I breathed. "Totally."

His eyes smiled.

His hips moved faster.

And my sex-god, future-husband, vigilante, badass hot guy from a parallel universe kissed me.

And all was well in my world in a way that I knew, with Loren at my side, no matter what was thrown at me...

In the end, it always would be.

Chapter Thirty

Gossamer in the Darkness

Satrine

Hawkvale
Dalwin Castle
Cottishwell Region

"If you're nice to Valentine, she'll bring you peanut butter," the Winter Princes of Lunwyn, Sjofn Drakkar, known to those close to her (which I now was) as Finnie, said. "And marshmallow fluff."

"Nice to her and give her diamonds."

"Or emeralds."

"Or pearls, rubies, sapphires or gold, she isn't picky."

They all laughed.

"They all" encompassed Cora, Circe and Maddie, otherwise known as Lady Ulfr, the wife of the head of the most powerful House in Lunwyn. Her husband, incidentally, being the dude with the kickass name of Apollo. The man Loren had mentioned those weeks ago he was partnered with in some business ventures.

I mean, there was pretty much no better name than Loren Copeland (in my opinion). That name screamed badass, vigilante rock star (again, in my opinion).

But "Apollo Ulfr" was pretty danged cool too.

And Finnie's hubster's name was Frey Drakkar.

That rocked as well.

What rocked more was that the dude commanded elves and…

Wait for it.

Dragons!

There were a couple of those beasts up on the craggy cliffs just north of the castle *right now*. The first time I saw them, I kid you not, I nearly passed out. They were mammoth, scaly, scary AF.

And insanely *awesome*.

As a gift from Frey and Finnie, they were going to do something after the wedding and I...could not...*wait*.

Update: Cora, the Gracious was from my world. Dahksahna Circe was too. As were the Winter Princess and the Lady of the House of Ulfr.

Yep.

All of them.

Although that seemed rather a coincidence, as far as they knew, we were the only ones. And Valentine kept an eye on these things. It had just been so long since anyone had traveled between worlds, she wasn't paying as close attention as she used to, and Mom and I slid under the radar.

"She'll also bring you letters from people you love," Circe said, regaining my attention.

"Yeah, those are the best," Cora noted softly.

I bet they were.

However...

"Will Valentine bring people to visit, if you pay her, of course?" I asked.

"Yes," Circe answered. "Dad has come several times to be here for important things for the kids."

"And my mom and dad have been here too, not loads, but our babies know their grandparents from both worlds," Cora said, but then she warned, "We have to be really careful though. My this-world parents are around too, and we have to handle it so no one who shouldn't sees them both together. Things could get a little freaky if people were to figure it out."

"And dangerous," Circe put in. "The other me lives in New Orleans. She's hitched to the other Lahn. They've never visited because she never wants to return, but also because all hell could break loose." She grinned. "I mean one Lahn is enough for *any* world."

We all laughed because she told no lies with that. Her guy was *a lot*, and fortunately it was all good.

But...yeah.

Loren had cautioned me about that before he told me I wasn't the only one from my world living in this one.

It had been another Loose Lips Convo where he went on for a while even though I got it.

Queens and princesses and wives of powerful Houses were from a parallel universe. If that got out, considering how magic was looked at in this world, and just how crazy it was on the whole, shizzle could get real and quick.

"Do you go home?" I queried.

Update Number Two: Mom and I had gone back.

Our trip was okay, but fast, and mostly sad. Furthermore, if Valentine wasn't with us and she didn't do some of her mojo, I'm not sure we would have been able to convince folks we hadn't lost our collective minds.

But in the end, it was good-bye, and not an I've Decided to Be a Beach Bum in Thailand Good-bye where we were far away, but they could send emails and do Facetime and had an opportunity to visit us and get some authentic tom yum goong in the process.

It was a serious *good-bye*.

And those always sucked.

The women glanced at each other like they were trying to decide who was going to deliver the bad news.

It fell to Finnie, who I'd found out had been there the longest.

"First, it *is* really important that no one learn about that world," she said carefully. "So going back and forth, us there or people we love here, isn't the smartest thing to do. For any of us. Second, Loren might feel differently, but we've all been separated from our guys in one way or another. So, although they could come with, a total and complete absence like that, of one but especially both of us, could be noticed. It's been decided amongst us that it's better not to court that danger. It also must be said that it takes an extreme amount of magic to travel between worlds. Valentine is powerful. She goes back and forth like it's nothing to her, but it is. She doesn't have a neverending reserve of power. And she does take payment, but really, even if she hides it, she has the kindest heart you could know, and one of the fiercest. In the end, no diamond is worth the magic she expends to bring us something from home. It's a sacrifice for her. One she makes because she cares for us and looks after us. So please, be aware of that."

She paused there, probably because all that was important, and she needed me to acknowledge it, so I nodded to her.

Then she continued.

"And last, our men know what we've given up for them. Our worlds and everything we know, which is a really big deal. It hurts them to think we pine for it, when we don't. I love my friends." She smiled. "I love fluffernutter sandwiches. But I love Frey more than anything on two worlds. And I can't say I don't experience nostalgia every once in a while, but there's nowhere I'd rather be than here, with him."

"Yeah," I whispered with feeling.

"It's up to you, of course," Cora chimed in. "We just ask that you be very, very careful."

"Kingdoms depend on it," Circe added.

"And think of Valentine," Finnie concluded.

"Yeah," I repeated.

There was a knock on the door.

"Yes?" I called.

Idina stuck in her head. "It's time to get ready, Lady Satrine."

My heart jumped with happiness.

"I'll be right there," I told her.

She shot me a huge smile and ducked out, closing the door.

I looked to Finnie. "Please tell me they breathe fire."

She shot me a huge smile too. "Oh yes. They breathe fire."

"Awesome," I whispered.

Circe shifted forward, lifting up her coupé glass (obviously, since it was my wedding day, and I was sitting around, gabbing with my gals, we were drinking champagne).

"To savages in savage lands," she toasted.

Cora sat forward and raised her glass. "To men on horseback."

Maddie did the same and offered, "To breeches and boots."

Finnie mirrored her friends and said, "To love that spans worlds."

It was my turn.

My glass high, I offered, "To gossamer in the darkness."

Joyous, knowing smiles before we all clinked.

And then we all drank.

* * * *

"Idina," I called when I made it to my rooms after leaving the women.

Well, not my rooms.

My rooms were *our* rooms.

It was just that, I'd asked one thing of my world from Loren for our wedding, and that was that he wouldn't see me until our garland was wound around our arms before we walked to the altar at the temple.

So last night after dinner, I left him and slept in these rooms, which Idina had set up to be Get Ready Central, and he went to ours.

He had not liked it, like *really*, and that was sweet.

But he was Loren.

I'd been right those many weeks ago, he couldn't deny me anything.

So he gave me what I asked.

"Idina?" I called again when she didn't answer.

And she again didn't answer.

She, and Mom, and obviously Mary, were self-appointed Wedding Planners Extraordinaire. Therefore, she was probably off doing something wedding related.

But she'd be back because my hair had to be done, and no way would she fall down on that job.

Mary, by the by, had been filled in about everything, and to say she was shocked was an understatement. But in the end, Edgar being a dick times two, and this spanning entire worlds, wasn't surprising to her. She had adored Corliss and was glad to have a version of her, even if she couldn't have the real thing. And she regarded me as a bonus.

Plus, she was an extreme patriot and would do nothing to endanger the kingdom, so she'd vowed in her inimitably dramatic way to keep her mouth shut.

And obviously Ansley knew, because Tor and Loren let him in on it, and his fealty to crown and country was even stronger than Mary's. But more, his son was in love with a parallel universe chick, and in his way, he was too.

In other words, we were good on that score.

FYI, Ansley requested us to delay the wedding another two months, because, after the goings-on at the magistrate's court, Mom and I got super-famous and super-popular, and Ansley and Loren already were. This meant Ansley was getting some pressure to make this a grander, more political affair, and as such, since it took forever to get anywhere in this place (they didn't even have *trains*), we needed to give time for the invitations to go out, and more time for people to show up.

Loren wasn't a fan.

But, shades of that aforementioned fealty, I could tell Ansley struggled with not doing what was requested by his king for his country, and it had to be said, just to be polite, so I talked my man around.

I could wait. I had him. And I knew he wasn't going anywhere.

I moved to the window and looked out.

It was now nearly winter, and we were in Dalwin Castle, which was situated on the northeastern cliffs of Hawkvale. Loren told me we were parallel to Bellebryn, which was at the same latitude, just on the western coast.

I probably didn't have to say, castles were *da bomb-diggity-bomb-bomb*. Talk about fairytale.

It had turrets and banners and moats, the whole shebang.

It was *everything*.

Adding to the ambiance, it was chilly and crisp here. I'd always been a fall and winter girl (I lived in Phoenix, so fall and winter were *the best*), and Loren told me Hawkvale didn't have the fierce winters that Lunwyn did. Sometimes there were only dustings of snow in the northern regions, but in the central and southern ones, the temperature changed only slightly.

So I thought it was perfect the seat of his House was here, where it got cold(ish), and I could wear long sweater gowns that clung to my body and made my man hot and hungry (so sometimes, I didn't wear those gowns very long before he took them off).

I stared at the Riven Sea that, miles and miles east, led to The Mystics, and as such, reminded myself how beautiful this place was, with its glittery, gray rock cliffs and that blue, blue ocean that was so clean and clear, it was a blue we didn't even have in my old world.

I also saw Frey's galleon, The Finnie, anchored out there.

And the Premier of Fleuridia's ship, which was smaller than The Finnie, and strange to me, because I'd never seen anything like it. The only way to describe it was sleek and chic and *rad*.

There were a few other ships anchored, because our guest list had gone from around seventy-five, which was what could fit in Dalwin's private temple, to over five hundred, which was what fit in the temple in Castledge, the large-town-almost-city just down the coast.

This was my life, this magical world filled with glitter and castles and galleons, kings and queens and dukes, flowers and hats and blue, blue seas.

In a couple of hours, I was going to be a Marchioness.

I was going to miss my friend Holly, and the Aunt Mary I knew all my life, and tons of other people and things.

But I smiled at the vista before me knowing the girls were right.

I was about to become Satrine Copeland, Marchioness of Remington, the future Duchess of Dalton.

Far more importantly, I was officially about to become Loren's.

This world was his.

And there was nowhere else I'd rather be.

* * * *

Loren

"It's fucking ridiculous," Loren muttered.

"Calm down, man," Croft ordered, but his voice was filled with amusement.

Loren seared him with a look.

Which, of course, made Croft burst with laughter.

And his other brothers besides.

"What reason could there possibly be to separate a man from his woman on the eve of their wedding?" Loren went on grumbling. "They're madder in her world than they seemed when I visited, and they seemed unhinged when I was there."

"It's as if he thinks she'll flee," Middy said to Holt.

"I would flee, laying my eyes on this bloke," Holt replied. "He's a foul-tempered bastard. No one would think he's imminently to marry one of the greatest beauties in our land."

Loren's brow went up and he asked dangerously, "One of?"

"Right, *the* greatest beauty," Holt muttered, his lips quirking.

"Fucking hell," Marlow whispered.

Loren turned to Marlow.

He then turned in the direction Marlow was gazing, which was out the windows.

And there she was, his father assisting as she alighted from the carriage.

Her gown was mostly white, an odd choice, but on Satrine, it was incredibly fetching. The long-sleeved top was netting stitched with the finest embroidery which made it seem like her very skin shimmered and was adorned with flowers. The skirts fell in full, gathered sheets of tule, with an underskirt in dark gray that gave it depth and made it interesting.

And on her head was a wide, graceful hat, a large rosette at the front, the brim lined and double-edged, dropping cheekily over one eye, but it was much longer in the back, dipping down like a veil. It was the most graceful, stylish hat Loren had ever seen.

Her lips were bright red.

And the wedding garland she carried draped across both palms was rife with velvety black roses that looked as if they were snipped after a rain, and there were tufts sitting amongst the blooms of something Loren didn't know what it was, but it was webby and delicate and shimmering and ethereal.

At sight of it, he felt his chest seize.

She carried *him*, or how she thought of him, in their garland in her hands.

On this thought, his throat closed, something happening at his eyes, and there were cuffs on his arm and slaps on his back as his brothers left him to take their places lining the aisle opposite Cora, Circe, Idina and Maxie. The line of honor they would stride through to the altar, where Corliss and Ansley would await them and stand with them as they were wed.

The only reason he tore his gaze from her was when he felt a slight pain in his shoulder at how hard he was being gripped.

He shifted his attention to Marlow, who was gazing at him with feeling and meaning.

And his tone was gruff when he said low, "I forgot how to dream, until now, witnessing one come true for you."

"Brother," Loren whispered.

"Glad as fuck she makes you happy, gladder still you're letting her."

Then with a squeeze, his friend disappeared.

And she walked in.

They locked eyes.

It was not lost on him that his father, her mother and her sister, who had arrived with her, all came to him and touched him in different ways, murmuring their greetings and well wishes before they rushed to take their places in the temple.

But it was only Satrine he paid any real attention.

As their family faded away, she finally came to him.

"Hey," she whispered.

Loren gazed down at her and said nothing.

"We need to wind this around our arms and get this show on the road," she prompted when he didn't speak or move.

"This is lovely," he whispered.

Her expression grew soft, but her eyes, as they had been from the moment she entered the atrium, shined bright with the depth of her love for him.

A bright so bright, it drove deep into his soul.

He allowed that to settle before he lifted a hand, pulled that remarkable hat off her head, and sent it flying.

She cried out in surprise.

"But it has to go," he finished.

She stared up at him for but a brief moment.

And then his soul exploded with radiance as his bride filled the vestibule with laughter.

* * * *

He had his hands full of her ass and his gaze full of her beauty, bouncing as it was on his cock.

He lifted up to sitting, and then he had her arms around his shoulders and her lips on his.

"Baby," she breathed.

He pulled her off his shaft.

"Loren!" she snapped.

"Knees," he ordered. "Offer yourself to me."

They were in the shadows, but he didn't miss her eyes catch fire.

Then, facing the head of the bed that sat along a bank of arched windows that had a view to the now-stormy sea, she positioned her exquisiteness before him, offering her ass and her cunt.

Loren took it, his fingers curling into that glorious flesh, his cock pounding into her sleek wet.

He raised a hand to his mouth, sucked in his thumb, then returned it to her ass, slipping his thumb into her hole.

She reared back into his cock, emitting a soft whimper of pleasure, as he knew she would.

She loved him inside her, any way she could take him.

"Fuck me, sweeting," he growled.

She did, he watched, stroking her hole, and when he knew from the clutching of her pussy that she was close, he pulled out.

"Honey," she begged.

He turned her to her back, covered her, and entered her again.

He laced their fingers on one hand, wound his others in her riot of curls, and she circled him with her legs.

The look on her face, the feel of her sheath, the sounds she was making, the intermingled smell of their bodies, he was going to lose control.

And he always wanted her to climax first, of course, but tonight, he wanted them to climax together.

He shifted a hand between their bodies, moving it down to her clit.

He touched her.

She whispered, *"Husband,"* as she climaxed under him, around him, for him.

And at that word, Loren lost it, and he went with her.

The room exploded in light as the dragons outside their windows blazed fire through the air above the Riven.

And the stone of their room turned incandescent all around them with the flash.

But it was only her for him, and him for her in their wedding bed as Satrine accepted his seed, and he accepted her love, and in her ear, he whispered, *"Wife."*

* * * *

Buttersnatch

Hawkvale
Newton
Oxblood Region

Some weeks later…

They'd cornered him.

He squatted like a rat and stared into the fog, breathing heavily.

It didn't take long before they formed through the dark and mist, still mounted on their powerful steeds.

Six of them.

Six tall, handsome commanding men, staring down their noble noses at him cowered in an alley.

They were led by the king.

Buttersnatch stared in shock up at the mighty Noctorno, knowing it was his end and feeling a strange sense of pride he would meet it at the edge of a royal blade.

"Fancy serving your king?" his monarch asked.

Buttersnatch blinked into the fog.

Another, stranger sense of pride stole through him, and he was surprised at how strong it was.

This meant he straightened from his squat.

Only to bend forward and bow.

Epilogue

Let's See about You

Loren

They rode up to the back of the house.

It did not bode well to see his wife standing in the open doorway, Carling lurking at her shoulder, her arms crossed on her chest, her lovely face set to, as they put it in her world, really seriously pissed off.

He grinned.

She caught it and looked even angrier.

"Carling! Break out the whisky," Marlow ordered.

"Do that first, milord, or call a physician?" Carling asked in return.

"Physician," Middy scoffed through a broken lip.

"We had a deal, you and me," Satrine called to her husband.

They reined in, and his four brothers were much swifter in dismounting than he.

Corliss's stable boy rushed forward to grab the reins.

Loren took his time sauntering to his wife, who barely moved as his friends slid by her into the house, Croft being the last and sending him a "best of luck" expression.

Carling followed them.

Loren stopped in front of her.

"I'm not *sure* what you find *amusing!*" They heard Mary say loudly and imperiously from inside. "My niece was in *a state*. There's nothing amusing about a lady in *a state*. No, you there, also grab a bottle of brandy. We're out in the parlor, and I'm parched."

They waited, and when no more could be heard from the house, she started it.

"I wasn't in a state."

"I've no doubt."

And he didn't. It would take a lot more than their activities that night to shake his Satrine.

"You're bleeding," she told him something he knew.

"Tonight was supposed to be reconnaissance. We weren't expecting action," he explained.

"*I promise, dearest heart, I will do my utmost to keep myself safe. I vow, love of my life, that I will keep you apprised of everything.*"

He tried but failed to stop his grin as she pretended to talk in his deep voice.

Thus, she slapped his arm. "Loren! You didn't tell me a thing about tonight. And when we decided that you would tell Tor that you and the boys would resurrect Tor's program that was the brainchild of Tor and *your dad*, the deal was that you would keep me in the know about *everything.*"

He pulled her stiff, vaguely resisting body into his arms.

"Darling, you were at the theater with Maxie, Mary and your mother."

"Did you temporarily lose use of your hand? You couldn't write a note?"

"There wasn't time."

"Your mouth seems to be working just fine. You couldn't brief Carling?"

"Again, there wasn't time."

"You're going with us to the theater every time we're in Newton," she threatened.

"Please, gods, no," he teased. "My transgression wasn't that bad."

She tipped her face to the stars.

"Honestly, my love," he said in all seriousness, and her gaze returned to him. "There wasn't time."

She put her hands to his chest and started fiddling with his collar. "It's very annoying, people doing stupid things that hurt other people, requiring you to go out and stop them from doing those stupid things. Especially when you don't tell me you're going out to be all hardass and kicking ass to stop them."

"It is indeed very annoying," he murmured, pulling her closer and feeling his lips twitching.

She narrowed her eyes. "If you think you're gonna get yourself some, mister, you're very right. Because you rock in bed. And because we've been married all of six weeks, and I'm still feeling honeymoon vibes. But I'm also still holding a grudge."

"Will you stop complaining so I can kiss you?" he requested.

"No. You're going to clean the blood from your nose and your penance tonight is that there will be no kissing. In fact, you can't touch me at all. You have to lie there, arms over your head, while I take care of business."

His cock jumped and a growl rumbled from his throat.

She melted into him trying to pretend she wasn't melting into him.

"I warn you, my lovely wife, this is not much of a penance."

"You don't get it. The penance is, the offer is rescinded if you don't get your arse inside, safe, and out of the cold in...*oof!*"

Loren made note that was one way to quiet her pretty mouth.

He then set about leaving his brothers to whisky, brandy and Mary, who right then, he knew from experience, was going about wringing every last detail of their night's adventure from his friends, and he carried his wife to bed to finish his penance.

Something he achieved.

Valiantly.

And elatedly.

* * * *

Ed

At About the Same Time
In Phoenix...

The green mist formed in the corner.

A woman formed of the mist.

She was a knockout.

And he was totally buying more coke from that guy.

Still, he said, "What the fuck?"

"Your daughter married," she announced.

"Hunh?" he asked.

"And your ex is the second wealthiest woman in the land."

Okay, either that shit was laced with some serious other shit or maybe he should just lay off...well, everything for a while.

He shook his head like it'd clear her away, but it didn't.

Instead, she kept talking whack.

"It is very good that the leaders of this world don't believe in magic. They can't put restrictions on it."

"Okay, baby, if you're gonna be a fantasy that sticks around, how 'bout sucking my dick while you do it?" he suggested.

She smiled a cat's smile.

And said, "As such, I curse you, Edgar Bradford Dawes. I curse every woman who might have meaning to you, to spurn you. I curse everything you touch to turn to dust, figuratively, of course. I curse everything you desire, to be elusive. I curse you to living the rest of your life chasing dreams, and falling short. I curse you to misery, Edgar. Unrelenting."

She took a step forward.

And Ed felt his balls shrivel up.

"And when you die, Edgar, you will remember your beautiful daughter and the woman you used to love who you threw away, both you used and sent into peril. Maxine was beaten, Edgar, pressed to whore herself not of her volition, and Corliss was imprisoned and starved."

He felt his throat close.

"That guy said that they'd—" he pushed through it.

"He is you, thus, *he lied.*"

She lifted a hand and opened her fist. A puff of what looked like green chalk dust formed out of it and made its way to him.

"You are cursed," she whispered as she began to fade away.

The dust grew as it got closer, and Edgar scrambled up, falling over the back of his chair to try to escape it, but it enveloped him all the same.

In the end, he'd spend decades trying to escape it, doing everything he could, going insane in the effort.

But just as she promised he would, he always failed.

* * * *

Two Hours Later
In another room in the Derryman house in Newton...

The green mist formed in the corner.

And the witch formed of the mist.

She wore clothing from her world.

Her heels were high.

Even so, she walked to the bed on silent cat's feet.

She gazed down on the sleeping woman, her glorious leonine hair unbound and all over the pillow.

"Finally, a challenge," she whispered.

She took in a breath.

And then Valentine Rousseau stated, "Now, Lady Maxine, let's see about you."

The End

* * * *

Also from 1001 Dark Nights and Kristen Ashley, discover After the Climb, Chasing Serenity, Taking the Leap, Wild Wind, Dream Bites Cookbook, Wild Fire, Quiet Man, Rough Ride, and Rock Chick Reawakening.

Sign up for the 1001 Dark Nights Newsletter
and be entered to win a Tiffany Key necklace.

There's a contest every month!

Go to www.1001DarkNights.com to subscribe.

As a bonus, all subscribers can download
FIVE FREE exclusive books!

Discover 1001 Dark Nights Collection Nine

DRAGON UNBOUND by Donna Grant
A Dragon Kings Novella

NOTHING BUT INK by Carrie Ann Ryan
A Montgomery Ink: Fort Collins Novella

THE MASTERMIND by Dylan Allen
A Rivers Wilde Novella

JUST ONE WISH by Carly Phillips
A Kingston Family Novella

BEHIND CLOSED DOORS by Skye Warren
A Rochester Novella

GOSSAMER IN THE DARKNESS by Kristen Ashley
A Fantasyland Novella

THE CLOSE-UP by Kennedy Ryan
A Hollywood Renaissance Novella

DELIGHTED by Lexi Blake
A Masters and Mercenaries Novella

THE GRAVESIDE BAR AND GRILL by Darynda Jones
A Charley Davidson Novella

THE ANTI-FAN AND THE IDOL by Rachel Van Dyken
A My Summer In Seoul Novella

A VAMPIRE'S KISS by Rebecca Zanetti
A Dark Protectors/Rebels Novella

CHARMED BY YOU by J. Kenner
A Stark Security Novella

HIDE AND SEEK by Laura Kaye
A Blasphemy Novella

DESCEND TO DARKNESS by Heather Graham
A Krewe of Hunters Novella

BOND OF PASSION by Larissa Ione
A Demonica Novella

JUST WHAT I NEEDED by Kylie Scott
A Stage Dive Novella

Also from Blue Box Press

THE BAIT by C.W. Gortner and M.J. Rose

THE FASHION ORPHANS by Randy Susan Meyers and M.J. Rose

TAKING THE LEAP by Kristen Ashley
A River Rain Novel

SAPPHIRE SUNSET by Christopher Rice writing C. Travis Rice
A Sapphire Cove Novel

THE WAR OF TWO QUEENS by Jennifer L. Armentrout
A Blood and Ash Novel

THE MURDERS AT FLEAT HOUSE BY Lucinda Riley

THE HEIST by C.W. Gortner and M.J. Rose

Discover More Kristen Ashley

After the Climb: A River Rain Novel, Book 1
By Kristen Ashley

They were the Three Amigos: Duncan Holloway, Imogen Swan and Corey Szabo. Two young boys with difficult lives at home banding together with a cool girl who didn't mind mucking through the mud on their hikes.

They grew up to be Duncan Holloway, activist, CEO and face of the popular River Rain outdoor stores, Imogen Swan, award-winning actress and America's sweetheart, and Corey Szabo, ruthless tech billionaire.

Rich and very famous, they would learn the devastating knowledge of how the selfish acts of one would affect all their lives.

And the lives of those they loved.

Start the River Rain series with After the Climb, the story of Duncan and Imogen navigating their way back to each other, decades after a fierce betrayal.

And introduce yourself to their families, who will have their stories told when River Rain continues.

* * * *

Chasing Serenity: A River Rain Novel, Book 2
By Kristen Ashley

From a very young age, Chloe Pierce was trained to look after the ones she loved.

And she was trained by the best.

But when the man who looked after her was no longer there, Chloe is cast adrift—just as the very foundation of her life crumbled to pieces.

Then she runs into tall, lanky, unpretentious Judge Oakley, her exact opposite. She shops. He hikes. She drinks pink ladies. He drinks beer. She's a city girl. He's a mountain guy.

Obviously, this means they have a blowout fight upon meeting. Their second encounter doesn't go a lot better.

Judge is loving the challenge. Chloe is everything he doesn't want in a woman, but he can't stop finding ways to spend time with her. He knows she's dealing with loss and change.

He just doesn't know how deep that goes. Or how ingrained it is for Chloe to care for those who have a place in her heart, how hard it will be to trust anyone to look after her…

And how much harder it is when it's his turn.

* * * *

Taking the Leap: A River Rain Novel, Book 3
By Kristen Ashley

Alexandra Sharp has been crushing on her co-worker, John "Rix" Hendrix for years. He's her perfect man, she knows it.

She's just not his perfect woman, and she knows that too.

Then Rix gives Alex a hint that maybe there's a spark between them that, if she takes the leap, she might be able to fan into a flame This leads to a crash and burn, and that's all shy Alex needs to catch the hint never to take the risk again.

However, with undeniable timing, Rix's ex, who broke his heart, and Alex's family, who spent her lifetime breaking hers, rear their heads, gearing up to offer more drama. With the help of some matchmaking friends, Rix and Alex decide to face the onslaught together…

As a fake couple.

* * * *

Wild Wind: A Chaos Novella
By Kristen Ashley

When he was sixteen years old, Jagger Black laid eyes on the girl who was his. At a cemetery. During her mother's funeral.

For years, their lives cross, they feel the pull of their connection, but then they go their separate ways.

But when Jagger sees that girl chasing someone down the street, he doesn't think twice before he wades right in. And when he gets a full-on dose of the woman she's become, he knows he finally has to decide if he's all in or if it's time to cut her loose.

She's ready to be cut loose.

But Jagger is all in.

* * * *

Dream Bites Cookbook: Cooking with the Commandos
Short Stories by Kristen Ashley
Recipes by Suzanne M. Johnson

From *New York Times* bestseller Kristen Ashley and *USA Today* bestseller Suzanne M. Johnson…

See what's cooking!
You're invited to Denver and into the kitchens of Hawk Delgado's commandos: Daniel "Mag" Magnusson, Boone Sadler, Axl Pantera and Augustus "Auggie" Hero as they share with you some of the goodness they whip up for their women.

Not only will you get to spend time with the commandos, the Dream Team makes an appearance with their men, and there are a number of special guest stars. It doesn't end there, you'll also find some bonus recipes from a surprise source who doesn't like to be left out.

So strap in for a trip to Denver, a few short stories, some reminiscing and a lot of great food.

(Half of the proceeds of this cookbook go to the Rock Chick Nation Charities)

Welcome to Dream Bites, Cooking with the Commandos!

* * * *

Wild Fire: A Chaos Novella
By Kristen Ashley

"You know you can't keep a good brother down."

The Chaos Motorcycle Club has won its war. But not every brother rode into the sunset with his woman on the back of his bike.

Chaos returns with the story of Dutch Black, a man whose father was the moral compass of the Club, until he was murdered. And the man who raised Dutch protected the Club at all costs. That combination is the man Dutch is intent on becoming.

It's also the man that Dutch is going to go all out to give to his woman.

* * * *

Quiet Man: A Dream Man Novella
By Kristen Ashley

Charlotte "Lottie" McAlister is in the zone. She's ready to take on the next chapter of her life, and since she doesn't have a man, she'll do what she's done all along. She'll take care of business on her own. Even if that business means starting a family.

The problem is, Lottie has a stalker. The really bad kind. The kind that means she needs a bodyguard.

Enter Mo Morrison.

Enormous. Scary.

Quiet.

Mo doesn't say much, and Lottie's used to getting attention. And she wants Mo's attention. Badly.

But Mo has a strict rule. If he's guarding your body, that's all he's doing with it.

However, the longer Mo has to keep Lottie safe, the faster he falls for the beautiful blonde who has it so together, she might even be able to tackle the demons he's got in his head that just won't die.

But in the end, Lottie and Mo don't only have to find some way to keep hands off until the threat is over, they have to negotiate the overprotective Hot Bunch, Lottie's crazy stepdad, Tex, Mo's crew of frat-boy commandos, not to mention his nutty sisters.

All before Lottie finally gets her Dream Man.

And Mo can lay claim to his Dream Girl.

* * * *

Rough Ride: A Chaos Novella
By Kristen Ashley

Rosalie Holloway put it all on the line for the Chaos Motorcycle Club.

Informing to Chaos on their rival club—her man's club, Bounty—Rosalie knows the stakes. And she pays them when her man, who she was hoping to scare straight, finds out she's betrayed him and he delivers her to his brothers to mete out their form of justice.

But really, Rosie has long been denying that, as she drifted away from her Bounty, she's been falling in love with Everett "Snapper" Kavanagh, a Chaos brother. Snap is the biker-boy-next door with the snowy blue eyes, quiet confidence and sweet disposition who was supposed to keep her safe...and fell down on that job.

For Snapper, it's always been Rosalie, from the first time he saw her at the Chaos Compound. He's just been waiting for a clear shot. But he didn't want to get it after his Rosie was left bleeding, beat down and broken by Bounty on a cement warehouse floor.

With Rosalie a casualty of an ongoing war, Snapper has to guide her to trust him, take a shot with him, build a them...

And fold his woman firmly in the family that is Chaos.

* * * *

Rock Chick Reawakening: A Rock Chick Novella
By Kristen Ashley

From *New York Times* bestselling author, Kristen Ashley, comes the long-awaited story of Daisy and Marcus, *Rock Chick Reawakening*. A prequel to Kristen's *Rock Chick* series, *Rock Chick Reawakening* shares the tale of the devastating event that nearly broke Daisy, an event that set Marcus Sloane—one of Denver's most respected businessmen and one of the Denver underground's most feared crime bosses—into finally making his move to win the heart of the woman who stole his.

Wildest Dreams

Fantasyland Series Book 1
By Kristen Ashley
Now Available

Seoafin "Finnie" Wilde was taught by her parents that every breath was a treasure and to seek every adventure she could find. And she learns this lesson the hard way when they perish in a plane crash. But she never forgets and when she discovers there is a parallel universe where every person has a twin, she finds a witch who can send her there so she can have the adventure of a lifetime.

But upon arrival in the Winter Wonderland of Lunwyn, she realizes she's been played by her twin and finds herself walking down the aisle to be wed to The Drakkar.

Thrown into inauspicious circumstances, with years of practice, Finnie bests the challenges and digs into her adventure. But as Frey Drakkar discovers the woman who is his new wife is not Princess Sjofn, a woman he dislikes but instead, his Finnie, a free-spirit with a thirst for venture just like him, without her knowledge he orders his new bride bound to his frozen world, everlasting.

But at the same time Frey plunges Finnie into a web of political intrigue that includes assassination plots, poison, magic, mystery and... dragons.

* * * *

"Finnie!" Claudia snapped and I looked back at my friend.

"I get it sweetheart. You think I'm nuts."

"You *are* nuts if you..." she leaned forward again, her eyes darting with more than a little obvious distrust at Valentine before coming back to me, "think you're going to a *parallel universe*."

"I can assure you," Valentine put in smoothly, "she *will*."

I looked at Valentine. Her hair was a dark, shining auburn, real as far as I could tell. Her skin was alabaster. Her body was long and very thin. Her descent, she declared, was pure Creole. In other words, *her* people were there before *our* people were there (her people being the Europeans and when she explained this to us during our first meeting with her a couple of days ago, after, of course, corresponding with her for months to set up this gig, it was *she* who added the emphasis). She had a kickass place in the French Quarter. She had major class from her perfectly coiffed head to her killer Jimmy Choo clad toes. She reeked of money even more than *me*, and I was loaded.

And, incidentally, she was, I'd learned from a variety of reliable sources, an extremely powerful witch.

"Okay," Claudia stated. "Say you do this. Say you send Finnie there—"

"Her name is, Seoafin," Valentine cut in haughtily, her green eyes sliding elegantly to me. "That is far more chic then…" her lips turned down and one nostril quivered delicately, "*Finnie.*"

The nostril quiver, I thought, was a good touch.

"Well *I*, and all her friends who know her and love her and don't want to see her get gouged by someone like *you*, call her *Finnie*," Claudia returned.

Valentine forced her gaze to Claudia (and made it obvious she did so) and she said one word. The ice dripping from it underlining a meaning the word did not exactly have but could not be missed.

"*Indeed.*" Then she looked back at me and her face warmed, *slightly*. "Sjofn is the Goddess of Love. And love," her eyelids suddenly fluttered dreamily. "*Love*," she breathed then she focused on me with a strange intensity that made me—even *me*—squirm a little. "Love is *everything*."

About Kristen Ashley

Kristen Ashley is the *New York Times* bestselling author of over eighty romance novels including the *Rock Chick, Colorado Mountain, Dream Man, Chaos, Unfinished Heroes, The 'Burg, Magdalene, Fantasyland, The Three, Ghost and Reincarnation, Moonlight and Motor Oil, Dream Team* and *Honey* series along with several standalone novels. She's a hybrid author, publishing titles both independently and traditionally, her books have been translated in fourteen languages and she's sold over five million books.

Kristen's novel, *Law Man*, won the *RT Book Reviews* Reviewer's Choice Award for best Romantic Suspense. Her independently published title *Hold On* was nominated for *RT Book Reviews* best Independent Contemporary Romance and her traditionally published title *Breathe* was nominated for best Contemporary Romance. Kristen's titles *Motorcycle Man, The Will, Ride Steady* (which won the Reader's Choice award from *Romance Reviews*) and *The Hookup* all made the final rounds for Goodreads Choice Awards in the Romance category.

Kristen, born in Gary and raised in Brownsburg, Indiana, was a fourth-generation graduate of Purdue University. Since, she has lived in Denver, the West Country of England, and now she resides in Phoenix. She worked as a charity executive for eighteen years prior to beginning her independent publishing career. She currently writes full-time.

Although romance is her genre, the prevailing themes running through all of Kristen's novels are friendship, family and a strong sisterhood. To this end, and as a way to thank her readers for their support, Kristen has created the Rock Chick Nation, a series of programs that are designed to give back to her readers and promote a strong female community.

The mission of the Rock Chick Nation is to live your best life, be true to your true self, recognize your beauty and take your sister's back whether they're friends and family or if they're thousands of miles away and you don't know who they are. The programs of the RC Nation include: Rock Chick Rendezvous, weekends Kristen organizes full of parties and get-togethers to bring the sisterhood together; Rock Chick Recharges, evenings Kristen arranges for women who have been nominated to receive a special night; and Rock Chick Rewards, an ongoing program that raises funds for nonprofit women's organizations

Kristen's readers nominate. Kristen's Rock Chick Rewards have donated hundreds of thousands of dollars to charity and this number continues to rise.

You can read more about Kristen, her titles and the Rock Chick Nation at KristenAshley.net.

Discover 1001 Dark Nights

On behalf of 1001 Dark Nights,

Liz Berry, M.J. Rose, and Jillian Stein would like to thank ~

Steve Berry
Doug Scofield
Benjamin Stein
Kim Guidroz
Social Butterfly PR
Ashley Wells
Asha Hossain
Chris Graham
Chelle Olson
Kasi Alexander
Jessica Saunders
Dylan Stockton
Richard Blake
and Simon Lipskar

Made in the USA
Las Vegas, NV
11 April 2022